To Peggy

Best Wishes

Rochelle Gadany

March 20, 2010

Destiny and Desire

Rochelle Gadany

AuthorHouse™
1663 Liberty Drive, Suite 200
Bloomington, IN 47403
www.authorhouse.com
Phone: 1-800-839-8640

© *2010 Rochelle Gadany. All rights reserved.*

No part of this book may be reproduced, stored in a retrieval system, or transmitted by any means without the written permission of the author.

First published by AuthorHouse   1/14/2010

ISBN: 978-1-4343-6295-7 (e)
ISBN: 978-1-4343-6342-8 (sc)

Library of Congress Control Number: 2008900220

Printed in the United States of America
Bloomington, Indiana

This book is printed on acid-free paper.

Chapter 1

LONDON, MAY 1814

Christa Devereax paused as she entered the dimly lit room, then walked slowly to where Shane Coulter stood near the fireplace. There was a chill in the evening air, but she was flushed. She smoothed her sweaty palms down the folds of her gown and lifted her chin. She could do this. The thought of going home to her father's plantation, La Fleur was all the motivation she needed.

Shane wondered why Christa wanted to see him alone, and how she could be even more beautiful then he remembered. Christa was anxious as she approached him because she didn't know how to start. " Won't you sit down, Captain Coulter " she began, then waited until he lowered his large frame onto the expensive green and rose sofa and made himself comfortable. She cleared her throat and began again. " I read the message that you sent my uncle this morning. That's how I knew you'd be here tonight. As you can tell there's a party going on. I told James to wait fifteen minutes before informing my uncle of your arrival. I wanted to talk to you first. You probably know why I wanted to see you. Please take me home."

Before he could answer, she rushed on. "I'll pay you."

He frowned, "I don't want your money."

" Then what? I've heard it said that everyone has a price.

What's yours, Captain?"

Resisting the urge to take her in his arms and giving her a demonstration, he sucked in some air and let it out slowly. Was she offering herself to him or was he mistaking her words?

Miss Devereax, I don't think you understand. There's a war on," he said slowly, as if explaining to a child.

"I know and I'm an American, Captain. I don't belong here, if there's to be any more fighting, I want to be home with my family."

She sat on the edge of the sofa and told him, seriously, "There's another reason I want to leave now. My uncle is pressuring me to marry soon."

"I want to choose my own husband, I want to live my own life. If I make a mistake, then so be it, but at least it will be *my* mistake. I know my father would let me choose for myself," she tipped her head to the side and smiled. "He might try to talk me out of it, but the final decision would be mine."

"Miss Devereax, our country is at war. The British are blockading our harbors and we've had some heavy losses. Cargos are rotting on the wharfs because we can't ship them anywhere. The Royal Navy has succeeded in closing our trade with foreign ports. I am a privateer, and once in a while we manage to get a ship through, but most are destroyed or captured. It's very *dangerous* for me to be here."

"There are those in this country who sympathize with our cause and your uncle is one of them. I have cargo to trade and then I'll be leaving. Besides I know your father and I won't be responsible for putting you in danger," he explained, patiently.

Seeing her chances slipping away Christa decided to try a different tact. Getting to her feet, she asked, "May I get you some wine?"

"That would be nice, thank you."

Shane couldn't take his eyes off her as she walked gracefully over to a small table beside the fireplace.

He noticed the soft rustling sound her gown made as she poured him a drink. The gown itself was very modest, but the way the bodice was molded over her breast left nothing to the imagination.

She took a seat at the far end of the sofa, and a sip of her own wine, then asked, "Well, how is Angela?"

"Angela?" Shane repeated his eyebrows coming together in puzzlement. Then he realized she must mean Angela Stanton, that is Angela Sabastian since her marriage a few years ago. "Fine, I guess. I haven't seen her in some time," he shrugged, thinking, the poor girl must be starved for news from home.

"Oh, yes, of course," Christa answered, thinking he was referring to his voyage.

"I didn't think you were friends," he probed.

"We aren't, I was just trying to be polite," Christa said, her heart pounding as she realized he was going to make it easy for her. He had been away from his wife long enough to take comfort in the arms of another women, but was she prepared to be that other women? She wanted to go home, but how much was she willing to pay?

She decided to try again, and smiling what she hoped was her best smile, she moved closer to him. Her voice was soft and husky as she laid her hand on his arm, and asked, "May I call you Shane?"

"Yes, of course, if I may call you Christa." He smiled, put down his drink and covered her hand with his own.

She hesitated, then plunged on. "Do you remember when we met in New Orleans? I thought there was a bond between us that night."

"Yes, you're even more beautiful now then you were then," he murmured, looking her straight in the eyes.

Christa almost forgot what she was going to say next she was so flustered by his nearness. He reached out and touched a strand of hair that hung down on her shoulder. He wanted to take out the pins that held it up in the back. He wanted to play with the silky mass.

"Your hair is lovely. You should always wear it lose," he smiled. It felt good to touch her again. He could see the tops of her creamy breast above the square cut neckline of her gown. She was like a flame and he was getting hot. She forced herself to move back. She couldn't think straight when he was so close.

She smiled then tried again. "When I,...well when I didn't see you again I thought I must have been mistaken."

"I was planning to come calling, but some business took me to Washington," Shane explained as he continued to play with the silken strands of her hair. Then when I returned you had already left for England. I was very disappointed," he said, his eyes resting on her mouth.

Lowering her long lashes and leaning forward so he could see her cleavage, Christa asked sweetly. "Were you?" So disappointed that you married Angela Stanton, she thought bitterly.

Shane knew that she was deliberately using her wiles on him and he had been without a women too long to withstand anymore of her seductive behavior.

"Oh, hell," he said to no one in particular, as his restraint crumbled and he pulled her into his arms. "You talk to much," he breathed, just before his mouth covered hers.

Christa was rocked by the force of her own reaction to him as she felt a surge of joy bubble up from somewhere deep inside her heart. A shock wave vibrated through her body and she clung to him. A rush of desire so strong that it frightened her, washed over her as the kiss deepened and Shane moved his lips sensuously on hers.

There was only the sound of the music from across the hall and an occasional crackling from the fire.

She let herself be pushed back down onto the sofa cushions. He was kissing her neck, with little hot kisses that left a trail of burning flesh behind, but reality suddenly hit her as she felt his hand cover her breast.

Her eyes flew open and she knew she couldn't do this, in spite of the passionate flame that burned between them, he was still a married man. "Stop, please stop." She meant to shout, but the words came out in a hoarse whisper.

Shane's sexual passions were totally aroused. He was lost in the feel and the smell of her, but when she started to hit and push at him, he realized that she didn't want him to go any further. Their eyes locked. They stared angrily at each other, breathing hard.

Still thinking he was married, Christa was angry with herself for wanting him and Shane was angry with her for tempting him into losing his self control.

"How dare you," Christa shrieked and slapped his face, jumping to her feet shakily, as soon as he sat up.

Shane sat where he was for a moment. The fire of his passion was gone, but another kind of fire was taking it's place. Robbing his stinging cheek, he rose to his feet and replied coldly, "I just wanted to see how far you'd go to get your way."

"If you were a gentlemen, you'd take me home," Christa shouted, "Please, Christa, keep your voice down, you'll rouse the whole house," Shane cautioned

"I don't care you insufferable dolt," she cried.

"I'm sorry, I can't take you with me," Shane told her stiffly and turned towards the door. He hated to leave her so upset but he couldn't put her in danger. He stopped with his hand on the knob as something crashed against the oak panel right next to his ear.

Turning back to see what was happening, he saw Christa reaching for another vase. Moving quickly he grabbed her arm before she could hurl this one at him too. He succeeded in stopping her but found himself in even more trouble. His left hand was holding Christa's right wrists, and he was so close to her that he could smell her fragrant hair and feel her body heat.

Christa forgot everything except that he was touching her and then his other hand went around her waist. She let go of the vase as he drew her trembling body to him. He held her captive with his searching eyes until he saw her blazing fury turn to surrender. Then his eyes left hers and dropped to her lips and she knew he was going to kiss her again.

Now her anger turned to fear, not of him, but of herself because she wanted him to kiss her again. Oh dam you, Shane Coulter. Why now, when it's too late for us, she thought, before his mouth drove all coherent thought from her. He smelled of cologne and tobacco and his mouth was firm and warm and sweet.

She was acutely aware of the raw masculinity of his hard muscled body pressing against her own softness. Fire flared in her veins and she was never more aware of her own passions. The kiss was everything she knew it would be and more.

He finally took his mouth away and turned his head aside, still holding her close. They were gasping for air and Christa's head lay against his hard chest.

He kissed her temple and then his lips slipped down to her cheek, but it was too late as her memory came back stronger with each breath she took.

"Please take your hands off me, Captain Coulter," she ordered and something in the coldness of her voice made him release her.

"Have you no loyalty to your wife?" Christa asked indignantly.

"Wife?" Shane repeated, puzzled again. "Miss Devereax, you have been misinformed. I have no wife."

Shane knew that Christa's surrender had been to get him to reconsider and take her with him, and it was working. He was very tempted to take her as he looked at her passion flushed face, her beautiful eyes pleading with him.

No. No, if he took her with him it would only double the danger because he would never be able to stay away from her and he couldn't take her to his bed without marrying her first, could he? Why hadn't he pursued her when she was in New Orleans like he had intended? Well, how did he know she was going to get stuck in England for two years.

Shane had known Charles Devereax for years and he knew Charles had a pretty young daughter but she was ten years younger than he was and they hadn't met, partly because of traveling in different social circles. While Shane was traveling in the west and gambling and womanizing, Christa was still a child. He recalled that after her mother's death Charles had sent her to a girls school in Richmond for a few years.

When they had finally met at a party in New Orleans, he had stood up with her for a dance and was dazzled by her beauty. The party was a farewell for her uncle William Devereax and his family, who were returning home to England after a long visit in the United States.

It had taken a few minutes for Christa to comprehend what Shane had just said. "Did you just say you have no wife."

"That's right, what made you think I was married?" Shane's sensuous mouth curved into a grin and amusement lit his eyes.

"I don't understand before I left New Orleans, it was common knowledge that you were all but betrothed to Angela Stanton. Then after I arrived here I received a letter from home telling me that Angela had married. I guess I just assumed that she had married you," Christa explained, as hope blossomed in her heart.

"Oh, I see," he laughed, and Christa laughed too, but for another reason. Lifting his broad shoulders in a shrug he went on.

"Well, it's a long story. I never proposed and I'm sure there was a lot of gossip. Angela married Dominic Sabastian, a very rich man."

"Yes, I believe I met him once," she acknowledged. She was so happy she wanted to throw herself into his arms again, but she restrained herself and decided to let him go for now. She had to be alone and do some thinking.

Offering her hand, she smiled brightly and said in her most cordial tone, "Captain Coulter, please except my apology. No hard feelings? You can't blame a girl for trying now can you?" Perhaps we'll meet again under more favorable circumstances."

Women, Shane thought, as he pecked her hand, just when you think you have them all figured out they do something to unravel the whole fabric. First, she was happy to see him and then she was angry and now she was happy again.

No wonder she was so upset, she must have been horrified at herself for her wanton response to his kisses, thinking that he was a married man.

They stood there looking at each other, neither one wanting to say good-by but knowing they would have to soon.

Shane finally broke the awkward silence. "Christa, I can't take you with me. You're safe here and when things are settled I'll come for you, I promise."

She wondered how he could go and leave her here after the way he had just kissed her.

They were so absorbed that it startled them when the library door opened and William Devereax appeared. Smiling, he held out his hand to Shane. "I see you've already renewed your acquaintance with my niece."

"What's this, a broken vase?"

"I was showing it to Captain Coulter. I'm afraid I dropped it. How careless of me," Christa lied.

"I see" William said, although he didn't really. "Come sit Captain." He took the overstuffed chair opposite the sofa where Shane and Christa returned to their previous places.

"I'm glad you made it through my boy. Have any trouble?"

"No, we managed to out run the ship that did spot us. I have letters from Charles." As he spoke Shane pulled two envelopes from an inside pocket of his coat. He handed one to Christa and the other to William.

Christa scanned the letter in her hand. It was much the same as the last one she had received over a year ago. Her father told her that most of the fighting was along the Canadian border, and that she was safe where she was for now.

The letter only added to her resentment of the war. She knew Britain had the right to impress Englishmen any time she needed more sailors and sometimes they weren't to fussy about nationality.

Also the British resented the audacious Americans for aiding Napoleon, but why couldn't she go home and wait? Why must she stay in England and pretend everything was all right. In London the social life was going on as if nothing was wrong but she had noticed more and more of the young men were in uniform.

In his letter Charles mentioned the blockade and told her of several American ships that had been lost trying to make it through, and in the end he asked her to stay in England until the war was settled one way or another.

The mention of staying in London spurred Christa into action bolder then she normally would have taken.

"Uncle William," she started but as she got his attention she almost faltered. Some times he could be very intimidating. She swallowed the lump in her throat and went on. "Please, let me go home with Captain Coulter," she blurted. She expected him to be a little angry but she hoped he would give his consent anyway.

William Devereax pushed himself out of his plush chair and came to his feet. He took a deep breath and let it out slowly. Ignoring Christa, he spoke to Shane. 'I apologize, Captain Coulter, it seems my niece has tired of my hospitality and without my knowledge wrote a letter to her father some time ago, asking him to come for her. Of course, he's asked her to wait until things are more settled."

Shane felt uneasy but thought he should say something. "Miss Devereax, I'm afraid I must agree with your uncle." He wished he hadn't been looking directly at her when he saw the cold fury in her eyes as she heard his words.

William folded his letter neatly, then spoke seriously to Shane. "Captain Coulter, I'm sure you are aware that Napoleon has abdicated and Louis the XV111 is King of France."

"Yes so I've heard."

"And you know what that means?"

"No doubt the British forces will turn their attention fully on the United States now. Perhaps they'll try to invade at Mobil or New Orleans," Shane observed, turning his attention reluctantly from Christa to William.

"Well, I for one have no quarrel with you Americans. I'll be glad when this blasted war is over and things get back to normal. I'd like a little time to compose an answer to this letter, Captain. When are you leaving?"

Christa turned when she heard this question because she wanted to know the answer herself. They waited expectantly for Shane to speak.

"With the morning tide the day after tomorrow. I have some things I have to take care of. I have to deliver some more letters and check with my first mate, Adam Michaels, who's seeing to the trading of our cargo and hoping to fine a boy to help in the galley. But it's not that important we've made do so far.

The idea just came to her as she thought about the ship and she knew when Shane Coulter left London she would be with him.

"Captain Coulter, we're having a party. Would you care to join us?" William asked. Shane hesitated, "What if someone ask about me?"

"Not to worry, I am in the shipping business. I'll just tell the truth that you're a trader from Jamaica."

A few minutes later Shane was dancing with Christa. He knew he shouldn't have stayed this long, but he wanted this last dance with her. It was going to be a long trip home. At least now he would have these moments to remember.

While Shane was thinking this was the end, Christa was thinking this was a new beginning.

William watched them waltzing by and wondered if he'd made a mistake. Maybe he should let her go home. It would be the solution this problem of trying to marry her off. She had found fault with every young man of the ton.

This one's too stuffy, that one's too wild. Another drinks too much. As if that was anything for a woman to worry about. As long as a man had money and a good name, what more did a woman want? Now widowed Robert Wolf was taking an interest in her, and she was keeping him at bay too long. Speak of the devil. Robert Wolf was making his way towards William and he didn't look happy.

When she reached her room, Christa closed the door and leaned against it, closing her eyes. What a day this had been. So much had happened all at once. She felt drained as she walked over to her dressing table and looked in the mirror.

Her maid Mary, looked up from turning down the bed. " Miss Christa, is anything wrong? Is there something I can do for you? "

"Christa had grown very fond of the plump middle aged woman these last two years. If she missed anyone after she left, it would be Mary.

"Yes," Christa sighed, "will you help me get out of this gown? I'm very tired and I want to go to bed."

Mary frowned as she began undoing the hooks at Christa's back. "I never seen you quit a party so early before."

"I'm afraid Uncle William is going to except a marriage proposal for me from Robert Wolf, " Christa explained.

" Oh, my dear, I'm so sorry. I know how you feel about that man. "

Christa let the dress slip like a soft golden cloud down to the floor, then changed into a long white night gown. As Mary brushed her vibrant auburn hair, she started to think about her plan.

The first thing she would need was some boys clothing. They would be upset when they discovered she was gone, so she would have to write a letter of explanation. Once the ship was out to sea it wouldn't matter anymore.

" Mary, you have a son about fifteen years old, don't you? "

" Yes, Miss Christa."

"I need a favor from you. You must promise me you won't tell anyone else what I'm about to do. I don't have much money, but I do have some jewelry. You can have your pick, but I have to keep some of it, because I won't be able to take very many things with me. "

" Are you goin' some place Miss Christa, " Mary whispered, looking around as if someone might be listening.

Chapter 2

"Well, what's yer name boy?" Harry Patch, wanted to know. "Ya look pretty scrawny to me. Can you lift a pail of water? Well no matter. At yer age you'll fill out fast enough."

"Ah, I, ah," Christa stammered.

"Don't mumble boy. Speak up now. Ain't scared are ya?"

"It's Raymond," Christa blurted. Raymond Christy, sir."

She knew she couldn't keep this up for long. Just till they were out in the middle of the ocean then she didn't care. Shane would be angry but she didn't think he'd throw her over board. He'll get over it, she told herself.

She took a deep breath and looked around her at the tall mast and the men who were scampering up into the rigging high above. As the sun began to climb up the horizon, a breeze filled the sails and they were moving and the farther out away from land they got the wind picked up and the ship began an age old dance with the sea.

They were standing at the starboard rail, watching the land slip away from them, when she saw Shane standing with another man on the forecastle.

"Come with me boy, I'll show you what you're to do and we'll find a place for you to sleep. I guess you can take the bunk Frankie used to use in the Captain's cabin. Frankie used to be a skinny little feller like you and by God in no time he shot up almost as tall as the Captain his self." Harry chuckled, patting Christa on the top of her head.

Careful you fool don't knock my hat off and show my hair, she thought, but smiled joining Harry Patch in his little anecdote.

Harry led the way down the stairs and a passageway and stopped in front of a door. "This here's the Captain's cabin. He's up at the wheel with his first mate Adam Michaels," Harry explained, as he opened the door and stepped inside.

The room was larger than she had expected, because the *Falcon* was a merchant ship and not built for carrying passengers.

"Just throw yer bag over in that corner. It'll be all right. Captain knows about you. Mr. Devereax sent word by his man that brought a packet of letters."

Harry took her to the galley, where he introduced her to a couple of other crewmen. A big, dark, sinister looking man called Turk and another wild eyed, nervous little man named Jack. He showed her where the food was stored and what the cupboards held. He explained that she would help to serve meals and do clean-up work. "Don't worry you'll catch on soon enough, I reckon."

Christa never had to do any kitchen work and she was grateful when Harry patiently showed her how to do the simple task of doing dishes.

When he had prepared a tray for Shane, he ordered her to deliver it to the Captain. "Sometimes he takes his meal in his cabin, when he has to chart a course or something."

It was still early morning and Christa hadn't slept much the night before. She had lain awake afraid she might over sleep and miss this opportunity. For the first time she wondered if she had done the right thing.

As she lifted the tray she lifted her chin and taking a deep breath, straightened her shoulders. The next problem would be to keep

Shane from getting a good look at her. Balancing the tray as best she could she knocked lightly on the door.

"Come in," came Shane's deep resonate voice, and she struggled with the panic that overcame her. Closing her eyes for a moment she shakily opened the door.

Shane Coulter sat at his desk, his dark head bowed over the charts spread out in front of him. "Ah, my breakfast at last," he said, looking up. "Just in time to keep me from starving to death."

Christa hesitated and kept her head down.

"Bring it over here boy. I'm starved, but I won't eat you," Shane laughed.

She quickly sat the tray in front of him and turned just as quickly to the door.

She had never worked so hard in her life, as a matter of fact, she had never worked at all but she did like learning how to do things and was proud of herself.

At lunch time Shane took his meal in the mess hall with his first mate, Adam Michaels, and some of his other officers. They paid her no heed as they discussed the possibility of encountering a British ship, and how they would handle such an event.

The evening meal was much the same as the breakfast one had been, only Adam Michaels had been in Shane's cabin, again they had paid little attention to the new cook's helper. The *Falcon* heaved and dove and then lurched ahead on it's homeward voyage. Christa ached all over and her hands were sore as she entered Shane Coulter's cabin her chores done for the night. In the dim light of the whale oil lamp she found her worn tapestry traveling bag.

She wasn't able to bring much with her: only two gowns, one set of underclothing, two pair of slippers that matched the gowns, her paisley shawl and a nightgown. She dug deep and found her brush and hand mirror, then laid them aside and checked to see if her few coins and jewelry were still there. They were. She had hoped to have a room of her own, even if it was the size of a closet.

It never entered her mind that she would be sharing sleeping quarters, let alone sharing them with Shane himself. She hoped he would be too tired too take any interest in her tonight.

She only had to keep this masquerade up for another day, then it wouldn't matter anymore they wouldn't turn back after that.

His men seemed to like and respect Shane. Harry Patch had said, "If you're right with the Capt'n he'll be right with you, but look out if you cross him. He's a real mean fighter. He's part Indian ya know, and he knows how to use a knife. A few years back, him and Adam went out west explorin' with Lewis and Clark, you'll see what I mean by the time we get to New Orleans.

You look whipped boy. Ain't used to so much work are ya? Well, you'll get used to it in no time t'all."

Harry was a medium sized man of about forty years old and Christa liked him because of the patience he had shown when she didn't know how to do the simplest of task.

After the meals were served he fixed heaping platters and poured two mugs of coffee for them. There was a proper place for everything in the galley Christa soon learned.

She picked up her mirror, maybe it was just as well that she couldn't see herself very well in this dim light she thought, as she pulled the tie that held her hair under the concealment of the boys coat she wore. She brushed her long auburn hair and tied it back into a queue, and put the mirror away. She yawned and stretched.

She was so tired, and she hated wearing this rough heavy frock coat, but at least it was warm.

She had forgotten how cold it could get at sea when the sun goes down. The worn leather shoes hurt her feet too. She was used to the light slippers that were in fashion for ladies now.

Finally she lay down on the small bunk in the corner with her clothes on and covered herself with the wool blanket. She closed her eyes at last, and imagined Shane looking at her mouth again the way he did just before he kissed her in London.

Shane Coulter smiled to himself as he stood at the wheel and tried to hold it steady. There was a stiff wind tonight and if it didn't blow them off course, they would make good time getting to Jamaica.

What am I going to do about Christa he wondered. He recognized her the moment she came aboard dressed as a boy. She was so utterly feminine that it would take more then the cut of her clothes to make herself look like a male.

He talked to Harry Patch and asked him to keep her out of harms way but should he go on letting her think she was getting away with it or should he do something to force her out in the open.

He might as well confess, to himself at least, he was glad she had the spunk to do it, because he wanted her here with him in his world. He didn't know why. She was beautiful, yes, but he knew a lot of beautiful women. Why was she any different?

It was time for Adam to take the wheel, Shane thought. He was tired, but would he be able to sleep knowing Christa was only a few feet away? And what about later when the truth was finally known? Would it appear that he was in on the plan or that it was his idea all along. He should have thought about that before they left England he chided himself. Christa probably hadn't given a thought to her reputation at all. She would be ruined, if it got out. A beautiful young woman aboard a ship full of unrelated men, with no other woman to be a chaperon.

He had avoided marriage so far, but he wasn't totally against it.

She was the marrying kind and he could do worse. It was just that he had plans and those plans didn't include a wife.

He was deeply involve with the war and he wanted to go to Texas for a look see after it was over. Well, he was an honorable man and he would do the honorable thing. He stretched and yawned. Having made his decision he headed for his cabin as soon as Adam came to relieve him.

Opening the door softly, he immediately saw her on the bunk in the corner. She appeared to be sleeping soundly. He would wait until morning to confront her. Now that the decision was made maybe he could sleep after all. Sitting on the edge of the bed, he pulled off his boots, then lay back leaving his clothes on and ran his hands through his thick, dark hair and yawned.

When he closed his eyes he saw Christa's lovely face the way she looked the other night in London when he kissed her sweet honey lips.

Shane was awake before dawn. The storm he expected had fizzled out during the night, so they should be on course, and as he put on his boots, he noted that Christa was still sleeping soundly. He decided to tell Adam about Christa, he was his best friend as well as first mate.

Standing over the bunk he gazed at his sleeping beauty. She was turned on her side facing him, and the glow of the dim lamplight danced in her hair. Her long dark brown lashes fanned out on her cheeks, making him want to touch her.

He noticed her queue had come lose from its tie and a long curl had fallen across her chest. The soiled white shirt she wore was open at the neck and he fought the urge to pick her up and carry her to his bed.

Instead he granted himself the pleasure of lightly touching her hair. It felt cool and soft. Careful, he warned himself, drawing his hand back as if it had been burned.

Desire stirred in his blood and again he marveled, and wondered why? He picked up his jacket and ran his hand though his own hair then went to find Adam.

Shane handed Adam a cup of Harry's strong coffee, and they stood at the wheel watching the glorious sunrise. Since they first met at Princeton, they had been closer than brothers.

Adam was from a very prominent Tennessee family and Shane was a frequent guest. Adam was almost as tall and about the same build. Both had a love for horses and ships and adventure. It was that love of adventure that had led them to volunteer to go with the Lewis and Clark expedition.

After their return from the west they took a ship to Europe, where they visited Shane's Grandfather, who died with Shane holding his withered hand.

On the return voyage, the ship they were on was stopped and they were impressed by the Royal Navy. Rather than fighting their captivity they decided to learn how to handle the ship, and after about a year, Shane and Adam, with the aid of Harry Patch, had lead the rest of the crew in a mutiny.

They put the British officers and those of the others who wished off on a small island near Bermuda. That ship was now the *Falcon*.

By the time they returned to Tennessee, Shane found his father, Stephen, had died and his stepmother remarried. He left his inheritance, Oakmeadows plantation, in the capable hands of an overseer and moved back to New Orleans, where he had many friends, among them Charles Devereax and Jean Lafitte.

Of course, Adam and Harry went with him, just to see what would happen next.

After a few minutes of trying to find the words Adam spoke first. "All right Shane just spit it out, I know there's something on your mind. What is it?"

Shane smiled at his friend then asked, "Have you noticed our new cook's helper?"

Adam's friendly blue eyes grew attentive and a smile curved the corners of his mouth at Shane's question. "I was wondering when you were going to tell me about it. Not like you to sneak a woman aboard. I must admit I was a bit surprised. Who is she?"

"Christa Devereax. And it was her idea," Shane added defensively.

"Charles Devereax's daughter?" Adam wondered.

"She wanted me to take her home. When I said no, I guess she decided to sneak aboard. I really believed that she would be safer in England, and so did Charles. That's what he told her in the letter."

"So, why didn't you stop her from coming with us."

"Exactly. That's what I've been asking myself and I really don't know except that I'm attracted to her. So far I've made three mistakes with her. The first one was telling her no when she asked me to take her home."

"And the second?" Adam inquired.

Shane looked Adam straight in the eye and laughed out loud. "I kissed her, of course."

Adam laughed too. "Of course, what else does one do with a beautiful woman?" After a minute, he prodded, "and the third mistake?"

"I underestimated her" Shane confessed.

"Knowing you she must be special," Adam teased and when the humor left him, he reassured, "We can protect her from the British, Shane."

"Yes, but who's going to protect her from me?" Shane asked. "I would rather not be forced into something so permanent, but I may have to marry her."

"To protect her good name?"

"Partly, but mainly to protect myself from Charles' wrath if he thinks I've taken advantage of his daughter. I'll move in with you, and we'll let her take my cabin, at least it will give her some privacy. I'm going to go talk to her now, I don't think she's thought about the consequences of her actions."

Christa, had awakened and was relieved to find she was alone.

She made her way to the galley where Harry had things all ready well under way. When the time came to take Shane's breakfast tray, she lifted it slowly, taking her time. Her mouth watered at the sight and smell of the simple meal of biscuits and honey with slices of apples and cheese. It was time to reveal her identity. The sooner she got it over with the sooner she could eat.

She had always had servants to do these things. No wonder most of them are so unhappy with their lot in life, she thought. She hated having red, raw hands and broken fingernails and a backache.

Knocking softly, her fears mounted when the door swung open, and she was confronted by Shane's large muscular body. He stood aside to let her in and she sat the tray on the table that he used as a desk.

When she turned around she found she was looking right into the ruffled front of Shane's white shirt. She tried to turn aside but he put out a hand and caught her shoulder. Holding her firmly with one hand he lifted her chin with the other one.

"All right, you caught me," she snapped at him defiantly crossing her arms, and trying to pull away from him, "but I'm here now and you can't very well throw me over the side. I had good reasons to do it."

"The question my dear, isn't why you did it. The question is why I let you," Shane laughed releasing her shoulder.

Her expression changed from self-righteous defiance to angry realization. "You mean, that you've known it was me all along?" she asked, shoving his hand away from her face.

"Are you saying that you knew who I was all along and still you let me make a fool out of myself. You let me work in the galley like a slave?" Her voice was getting higher and louder with each word and fire was shooting from her eyes.

Shane was very amused by the whole incident, until now. He had seen that look before and knew she was searching for something to throw.

"Now, Christa, let's just talk calmly about this," he said, putting up a hand as if to stop her. By now she had picked up a water pitcher from the night stand by the bed. Shane grabbed her arm again just as he had the other night in London. She dropped the pitcher as their eyes met and he wrapped his other arm around her narrow waist.

"Let me kiss you, Christa, let me love you," he whispered hoarsely, drawing her closer.

"Shane," she breathed, lifting her arms to circle his strong neck, giving herself over to his flaming desire that was melting her token resistance. His lips were warm and firm and a thrill of passion like a bolt of lightning flashed down her spine.

She felt weak with desire, but also from lack of air, and she clung to Shane to keep from falling. When he finally ended the kiss, they were gasping for air. Shane kissed her cheek and then nibbled her ear lobe and she couldn't think of anything to say as a matter of fact, she couldn't think of any thing at all.

He found her queue and untied it and spread out her silky tresses.

He kissed her again and this time his lips pressed harder, and she curled her fingers in the soft hair at the back of his neck, delighting in the feel of his powerful body pressing against her.

Some how he had slipped off her coat and was now unbuttoning her high necked shirt. Putting his hand to her throat he dipped his head and kissed the pulse throbbing there, and the fire of his passion ignited her own like dry tinder. Drunk with wanting her, he tore at the remaining buttons in his way.

When her shirt fell open, Christa gasped in surprise at the touch of his hand and then his warm moist mouth on her full firm breast.

Somewhere in the back of her mind a little voice was telling her she should make him stop, but it was silenced by the pounding of her heart when he kissed her again.

Just as he was about to carry her to his bed, there was an excited knocking at the door. "Captain, Captain, there's a ship on the horizon," a husky male voice shouted, "You're needed on deck."

Chapter 3

Setting Christa on her feet, Shane took a deep breath and closed his eyes cursing the British and adding another reason to his list. He kissed her one last time and then reluctantly released her. "Did you bring any other clothes with you?" he asked.

"Yes, a few gowns," she answered, pulling her shirt together, as embarrassment washed over her.

"Put one on, I like you better as a woman." He winked, opened the door, then turned back. "Duty calls, but we'll talk some more later, and by the way, Miss Devereax, you are now relieved of your duties in the galley."

After he was gone, Christa sat on the big bed and took a deep breath. Well, what an eventful morning. At least she could get out of these clothes now and Shane wasn't too angry. She smiled remembering his burning kisses. When she noticed that Shane had forgotten breakfast, she picked up his cup and drank a sip of his still warm coffee.

An hour later, she was feeling refreshed and much better but was getting restless, so she straightened up the cabin, putting things away and hanging things up.

She decided to leave the maps and charts where they were on the desk. She knew her father always had a fit when anyone attempted to straighten his desk, and thought it was a universal masculine trait.

She had read most of the books that lined the shelf built into the wall opposite the bed, and the sun was out now so she decided to get some fresh air. Adjusting her large paisley shawl over the long sleeved blue gown, she left the cabin.

On deck the bright spring sunshine warmed her spirit as well as her body. She breathed deeply and smiled. At last she was going home and Shane Coulter wasn't married. Contented, she stood at the rail and watched the waves.

A short time later clouds covered the sun and a cold wind made her shiver. Everyone seemed very busy and no one spoke to her, so after awhile she went down to Shane's cabin.

Harry brought her a tray with lunch, and when she explained the reasons for her masquerade, he was very sympathetic.

"Did Shane..., I mean did the Captain say something to the crew about me? I couldn't help notice that no one seemed to be surprised at seeing me as I really am today when I was up on deck."

"Yup, sure did. Told em' we had us a woman passenger and they better behave themselves or they'd have to answer to him. Said no one was to bother ya."

Shane avoided Christa the rest of the day, but instructed Harry Patch to look after her. He needed time to think, and that seemed impossible when he was near her.

The ship that was sighted disappeared, but there was no telling when another one might take it's place.

The *Falcon* was heavily armed and the crew was experienced in battle, but still he would rather not fight. The *Falcon* was fast and had out run the few British ships they had encountered.

In spite of her willing response to his kisses, Shane was glad now that they had been interrupted because he was sure Christa was still a virgin.

Should he offer marriage and hope for the best? No. At least not yet. He decided he would try to restrain the physical side of their relationship for the time being and if he was still interested in her after they got home he could court her then.

Christa read for most of the afternoon and wondered why Shane was avoiding her after his ardent advances earlier.

She couldn't believe the wanton way she had acted with him. She actually let him fondle her bare breast and now as she remembered her face flushed a deep red.

What must he think of her? Would he expect to pick up where they left off? Could she just let him take her so easily? What if he offered to marry her? Did she want a marriage based on lust alone?

Finally, after she had been pacing and contemplating her next move, there was a knock on the door and she knew it must be him because of the way her heart pounded.

"May I come in?" Shane's tone was polite, when she opened the door. "I've asked Harry to serve us supper in a little while, but first I think we should talk," he told her seriously.

"Yes," Christa agreed. She sat on the edge of the bed and waited while he took the chair from behind his desk and seated himself in front of her.

She was so feminine and lovely in her blue gown that he wanted to haul her up on the bed and ravish her. Instead he fought to keep his voice steady. "You do realize that you have compromised us both by coming aboard this ship without a proper female companion," he told her.

He spoke softly, but she knew she was being taken to task. She hung her head and looked at her hands folded in her lap. "I didn't think that far ahead."

"My Uncle William was going to accept a proposal for my hand in marriage from a man I despised after you left the other night. I decided I would rather take my chances with you. What ever happens, won't be any worse than it would have been if I had stayed in London."

"Just because he's one of the richest men in England I was supposed to be thrilled that he wanted me. Well, I wasn't, so do your worst Captain."

Finishing her defense, she looked up and saw sympathy instead of reproach in those big brown eyes.

Shane reached out and took her hand in his. "I'm sorry, Christa, I just don't understand why you couldn't put him off or just refuse."

"No, that's because you're a man, and men can come and go as they please." Snatching back her hand she got to her feet then walked to the window at the bow and looked out.

The sinking sun hung suspended just above the horizon spreading a beautiful rose and gold glow over the silvery waves.

Christa was so absorbed in trying to compose herself that until Shane opened the door she didn't know Harry was there with their meal.

"I've asked my first mate to join us," Shane explained as Harry arranged the plates and food after putting a board in the center of the table to make it larger.

Christa knew she should be pleased they wouldn't be alone, but she was rather disappointed.

"We'll eat in here tonight, but after this we'll take our meals in the mess hall," he told her, and the savage in him fought with the gentleman. The savage wanted to grab Christa and make love to her and dam anyone who tried to stop him. The gentleman won this time, but Shane knew this wasn't going to be easy. He wanted to give the relationship a chance to grow and then maybe he would talk to Charles.

At least that's what the gentleman in him wanted.

"Thanks Harry, that'll be all for now," he said, as Adam Michaels arrived. Harry gave Christa a wink and a nod and left.

When Shane introduced Christa to his best friend, he felt a pang of jealousy at the way they seemed to take to each other right away, but then everyone liked Adam. He was very friendly as long as you didn't give him any reason to dislike you.

Christa had been mixing with the cream of London society for almost two years and could probably talk to anyone about anything.

When Christa couldn't suppress a yawn Shane decided to call it an evening. So things settled into a routine. Shane and Adam and some of the other men made a place of some packing crates and fixed a canopy so Christa could sit on deck and read for part of the day without getting burned.

The voyage from London had been uneventful except for some stormy weather the second week out.

Christa was a good sailor most of the time but she had gotten seasick and she hated being sick. She was terrified when the ship rose up and then slammed back down as if being thrown by the hand of Neptune himself.

Now they were in warmer waters and she was beginning to relax and enjoy the trip. The sun shown brightly during the day and at night she sometimes thought she could reach out and touch the stars.

Late one afternoon, the third week out she was standing at the rail when she saw some dolphins playfully swimming beside them. They were jumping up out of the water and diving back in quickly. Christa laughed happily feeling free and thought how much fun it was to go places and do things.

After watching for a long time she realized the sun was sinking lower on the horizon. It would be time for the evening meal soon so she went below.

Shane had been keeping his distance, and she wondered if he had lost interest in her, but then she would look up from her reading and catch him watching her.

She took most of her meals in the galley with Harry Patch except at dinner when she dined with Shane and Adam and some of the other officers of the ship. She was never alone with Shane for very long.

Christa noticed from the first that Shane had a very democratic attitude. He treated every man the same, no matter if he was rich like William Devereax or some one much lower on the economic scale like the cook Harry Patch. She liked his attitude very much and knew that his crew did too, but when he gave an order, he expected it to be obeyed and it was, because they respected him.

Shane had been jovial and friendly at first. After the meal they would have some wine and play cards or other games and Shane and

Adam would relax and talk about their many adventures together, from fighting Indians to exploring the wilderness, and even liking the same women.

Sometimes they talked about her father Charles, whom they seemed to like and respect, and Christa discovered she loved the sound of Shane's laughter. It made her feel safe and happy.

Late one night she lay awake for a long time listening to the noises of the ship as it creaked and heaved. She decided as she listened to the snapping of the canvas that she would confront Shane and ask him why he was avoiding her.

Perhaps he had some other woman waiting for him and would be embarrassed if it got out that she was on his ship.

Or maybe he was embarrassed by his own actions towards her. One way or the other she had to know how he felt about her. Was she being foolish? Should she just let it go?

She heard footsteps and as they passed her door she knew it was Shane coming off his watch. Being one of those people who always wanted to know where they stood, she decided to talk to him, or she wouldn't get any sleep at all.

She got up and put her large shawl over her nightgown. There was no use getting dressed because she wouldn't stay long.

Taking the candle that was by her bed she slipped into the companion way. She knew Shane was sharing Adam's small cabin and soon found the door. Her heart pounded and she almost turned back, but then forced herself to knock lightly.

Shane had just poured himself another drink and when he heard the knock thought it might be Harry or one of the men. "Come," he called.

He had taken off his shirt and boots and was reclining in a half sitting position on his bed. Holding his glass in one hand, his other arm was folded up behind his head. "What the hell," he couldn't believe what he saw.

Christa Devereax stepped into his cabin as innocent as a babe, like a fly landing on the spider's web.

She held a candle and put it down on the table.

"What the hell are you doing in here in the middle of the night. Don't you have any sense at all. Get out now, before it's too late, you little fool," he warned angrily.

Christa was stunned by his attack. His rejection was like a physical blow and with a little cry of frustration she grabbed up her candle and fled back to her cabin. Well, at lest she knew what he thought of her now. He thought she was a fool. What she thought was his attraction to her was nothing more than lust. He wanted to bed her but didn't want to face the consequences if it were found out.

Regretting his harsh words, Shane jumped to his feet and it was all he could do to keep from going after her and keeping her with him for the rest of the voyage. *The rest of the voyage?* They should be sighting land tomorrow.

How could he explain to her how he wanted her. How it was driving him crazy trying to stay away from her and in her innocents she didn't know the effect she was having on him.

He was beginning to think marriage was the answer, she was beautiful, but hardly the kind of woman he wanted to marry. He had hoped to marry someone who would pick up on a moments notice and follow him anywhere, Texas or even California.

Christa Devereax probably couldn't wash her hair without the help of a maid. About the only useful thing she knew was riding a horse. She couldn't skin a rabbit, let alone cook one. She had been pampered and petted all her life. And could she, would she ever be able to leave Plantation life behind.

Land was sighted the next morning and soon there was Jamaica raising up out of the ocean like a jewel in the sun.

Richard Fontaine had once told her that he had a sister living here Christa remembered as she stood at the rail. Funny, she didn't think about Richard much any more. He had told her of the valuable crops grown and sold in Jamaica, and of the many large and beautiful plantations.

Shane was at the wheel as Christa watched the island get closer, and when Adam Michaels came up beside her she was glad to see his friendly face.

"It's breathtaking," she said reverently. "The waters so clear and the air smells so clean and fresh, but it's an English port isn't it? We shouldn't be here, should we? After all we are at war with England." She put her hand up to shield her eyes from the sun and waited for him to speak.

"You can go anywhere if you have the right flags and papers. Of course, we couldn't stand too much scrutiny," Adam explained.

Christa was excited about going ashore. Life on a ship was so confining. She couldn't wait to go for a walk and take a bath in a tub and wash her hair.

The *Falcon* slipped into the natural harbor at Kingston on a balmy afternoon in the middle of May. They were flying a British flag so they probably wouldn't be searched by the authorities.

When it was time to go ashore, Shane came up behind Christa, then took her hand and helped her into one of the long boats.

"Adam is going to take care of some business, he'll join us later for dinner at the hotel," he explained, as he took a seat beside her.

She didn't know what to say to him. She was still hurt from the way he had called her a fool, so she just nodded in agreement. When a large wave finally hurled them onto the beach some of the crew jumped out and pulled the boat up farther on the dry sand.

Christa was very aware of her appearance. She had pulled her long thick hair into a queue, but in spite of trying to be careful the skin on her face and neck was turning pink.

She was wearing the same blue gown and wished it wasn't so wrinkled, but it would have to do for now. She was thinking about getting some new clothes when Shane spoke to her.

"Here let me help you out of the boat," he suggested stretching out his arms to her after jumping lightly over the side himself. He lifted her and held her close then looked into the turquoise depths of her eyes as if he was searching for the answer to some unasked question.

Finding none, he sat her down slowly on the sandy beach.

As they walked across the hot sand, Christa marveled at the lush beauty around her. She felt like a little girl again as she stopped to pick a large red hibiscus and Shane had to prod her to move on.

Soon they came to the main street, with a potpourri of eclectic buildings scattered around. There were a few white walled mansions up on the hill and a large adobe church down a little side street.

Now they were passing through a make shift market place. There were carts and stalls with an assortment of exotic things for sale. As they passed by the venders hawked their wares.

"You'd better stay close to me Christa. Here take my arm," Shane advised her when some rough looking sailors staggered out of the café and eyed her hungrily. "When we get to the hotel I'll inquire about getting you some new clothes and…," Shane was interrupted by a masculine voice calling out loudly.

They stopped, searching the throng. Shane possessively drew Christa closer to his side as a tall handsome young man approached them.

"Christa, Christa Devereax? I can't believe it. It is you. My dear, what are you doing here in Jamaica?" The intruder was well dressed and spoke in clipped British tones. Then without waiting for an answer he drew her into his arms and kissed her soundly, and Shane jealously realized, not for the first time.

"Richard what a surprise," she gasped, "I thought you were still in Canada. Oh, but you do have a sister here don't you."

"Yes, I decided to come visit her and see if she wanted to go to New Orleans with me. She's a widow you know." Then as if noticing Shane for the first time he said, "I suppose you've gone and gotten married and this must be the lucky man."

"No, not yet" Christa laughed then explained, "This is Captain Shane Coulter, a friend of my family. He's taking me home." Then she explained to Shane how she knew Richard.

Shane forced a smile and politely extended his hand. With a slight nod of his dark head he said, "Mr. Fontaine, we were just on our way to find a hotel."

"Oh no, I won't hear of it. Please you must be my quest," Richard insisted. "We have a house not far up on the hill. There's plenty of room and then you can meet my sister Laura. She'll be thrilled to have a women of near the same age to talk to, come along."

"No," he said, holding up a hand, when Shane started to protest, "I insist, and my carriage is just over there. We'll send word to your ship and someone can fetch your things later."

He moved to Christa's other side, took her free arm and lead the way. When they were all comfortably seated he told his driver to take them home.

"All right my dear, now I want to know what you're doing here without a proper chaperon. Oh, I know you want to go home, but why now and under these circumstances."

"Well Richard, to put it bluntly, my Uncle William was trying to marry me off to Robert Wolf and I simply despise the man."

"I knew it. I always thought he had his eye on you. I believe he used some of his influence to get me out of the way. My commission was almost up and then suddenly my regiment was ordered to Canada."

"Well, now after such a close call surely my proposal will look better to you," Richard teased, with a challenging smile at Shane Coulter who was wondering why she had never mentioned Richard before.

"Christa my dear, you never told me about Mr. Fontaine." Shane chided innocently, but his tone of voice implied some kind of intimate relationship. He wanted Richard Fontaine to wonder if there was one.

Christa was saved from an explanation when the carriage turned through the wrought iron gates of a beautiful white mansion and all conversation turned to admiration of the architecture.

A few hours latter Christa had washed her hair and had a bath and now sat at the dressing table in a borrowed robe brushing out her long auburn strands.

She felt much better and looked it too, she thought, as she walked out onto the balcony and stood watching the magnificent sunset.

She wondered where Shane and Richard were now. It was obvious Shane didn't trust Richard but she felt sure that he wouldn't turn them in because one look at him, at the joy he had displayed at seeing her again had convinced her that he was still attracted to her.

There was a knock at the door and thinking it was another servant she just called out, "come in," and didn't even turn around until she heard a soft feminine voice say her name.

"Miss Devereax?" I'm Richard's sister, Laura. "May I call you Christa," she inquired.

" Yes, of course," Christa smiled.

"I'm sorry I wasn't home when you arrived. I went for a ride. Do you ride?"

"Yes, I love horses."

"I see you haven't dressed yet. Didn't any of the clothes I sent fit you?"

Christa knew that she was going to like this friendly young woman who was a petite and feminine version of Richard. She had his same clear blue eyes. Her blond hair was pulled back into a chignon, with short wispy curls framing her heart-shaped face.

"The gowns were too short but the maid that brought them said she would merely add a ruffle at the hem. I picked out a yellow one to wear to dinner, and she's working on it now. Thank you so much," Christa said, feeling she had found a true friend.

She was hoping to get a chance to talk to Shane privately but she didn't know what room he was in, and besides Laura stayed with her while a maid helped her dress and fix her hair.

Shane had taken a bath too, and now he was looking forward to a good meal. He didn't plan to stay in Jamaica very long, but he sent a message to Adam, so the crew would be ready for anything.

Now there was another danger. He wanted Christa, but she wasn't the kind a man could take to his bed and leave. She was Charles Devereax's daughter. She was the marrying kind but that wasn't all.

The moment they met he knew Richard Fontaine felt the same way.

He inhaled deeply of his cigar, and cursed himself for not taking her the other night when she had come to talk to him. He watched the sun sink into the sea, and remembered her sweet, wanton response to him, and he knew she wanted him too, at least she did then. Or was she just using him to get to Richard Fontaine? Should he trust either of them?

Chapter 4

While Christa was still upstairs, Shane found his way down and was now ensconced in a comfortable chair in the large salon, with Richard still playing the gracious host as they sipped fine French brandy.

They were interrupted by the sound of the women's voices as they descended the stairs. The men stood and waited expectantly.

It never ceased to amaze Shane how each time he saw Christa she looked more beautiful then the time before. He had expected his attraction to fade quickly, but it seemed to become more intense as each day passed.

Laura was just the kind he would have pursued, until a short time ago, now he could hardly take his eyes off Christa. She was wearing a yellow gown with a large yellow artificial rose tucked in on one side of her glorious auburn hair. He wanted to be alone with her and soon.

Christa hoped her attraction for Shane would fade when she saw him again but now she felt that same familiar excitement, that same joy at just being in the same room with him. He was so handsome standing beside Richard.

Richard was handsome too, but there was something almost too perfect about him. He was almost as tall as Shane, but he lacked the large muscular frame. Richard's hair was cut in the very precise manor that would be fashionable in any London drawing room. Shane's hair by contrast was a little too long as it touched the high white collar of his ruffled shirt.

Laura Sims was very impressed with Shane Coulter, but wondered what her brother was up to, entertaining these two Americans. Of course he was smitten with Christa, but she seemed to be taken with Mr. Coulter.

Laura was a bit jealous as both men rushed to escort Christa into dinner when it was announced. Shane remembered his manners and deferred to Richard who was their host after all. Then he offered Laura his arm and devastated her with a full smile as if seeing her for the first time.

All through dinner they made diplomatic small talk and it was all Christa could do to concentrate on the conversation, she was so aware of Shane's controlled politeness. She knew he was suspicious of Richard, but she was sure Richard could be trusted.

"Captain Coulter, I think we should talk," Richard said, pushing away from the table, when the meal was finally over. "Would you come with me? Ladies, if you'll be so good as to wait for us in the drawing room, we shall join you shortly."

Now we're getting somewhere, Shane thought but said, "of course."

Pushing his own chair back he stretched his body out to it's full six feet two. Then adjusting his cuffs he smiled and bowed to the ladies and followed Richard, who had just done the same thing, into the hall.

Richard opened a door at the back of the house and they entered a room that could have served many purposes, a den perhaps or an office, although Richard didn't appear to have a need for either.

When they were seated and had been given wine by a servant, Shane challenged, "all right Fontaine, what do you want?"

"Ah!" Richard chuckled very amused," you're always so direct, I like that very much. Well, you're right of course." Setting his glass down and leaning forward he looked Shane right in the eyes. "I want you to take us with you to New Orleans."

"Or you'll tell the authorities that we're here, is that it?"

"Of course not, Captain Coulter, but if you don't take us we'll be stuck here till the war is over."

"All right. Be ready in two days," Shane told him and added, "as long as you admire directness so much, stay away from Christa Devereax."

At that Richard got to his feet. "Are you saying you're lovers?" he asked, curious and jealous at the same time.

"No, not yet," Shane conceded.

At this admission Richard relaxed a little. "Have you proposed to her?" he asked next.

"No," Shane admitted beginning to feel very uncomfortable.

"Well then, seems to me she's fair game and you have no right to tell me to stay away from her," Richard reasoned.

"Perhaps after I get her home…, I don't have to explain to you," Shane almost shouted in frustration.

The two men stood glaring at each other. Each man sizing up the other, each unflinching, ready to do battle. They were saved from doing any bodily harm to one another by a knock on the door.

Richard tore his eyes away from Shane's as a servant entered.

"There's a person who wishes to speak to Captain Coulter, sir" he announced.

Shane had retrieved his drink and after throwing the liquid down in one gulp, said, "take me to him," Then with a wink and a smug smile at Richard as he turned to leave, he suggested, "why don't we let the lady choose for herself."

Shane was lead to where Harry Patch stood waiting with his hat in his hand. A smile of relief broke over his worried face when Shane approached him looking well fed and healthy.

"Oh. Cap'n, am I glad to see you. Is everything all right?"

"Yes, Harry, I'm glad you're here, Shane said, putting his arm on Harry's shoulder and turning him to face the door."

Christa and Laura were a little surprised when Richard joined them and announced, "Captain Coulter has graciously agreed to let us join you for your trip home. Isn't that wonderful news?"

"Yes that's wonderful," Christa smiled and thought Shane must have changed his mind about Richard.

"I've always wanted to live in America, ever since we visited our relatives in Boston and Virginia, before Laura was married," Richard explained. "If it wasn't for this blasted war we would have done it already."

"Besides, I intend to renew our friendship," he said giving Christa a knowing look as he bent to kiss her hand.

Turning his attention to his sister, who was more surprised than Christa by his announcement, he inquired, "Laura, my dear, won't you play something for us. The good Captain is consulting with one of his men. I'm sure he'll join us shortly."

Christa had the feeling he didn't want to be questioned further, so she waited, wondering why Shane would risk taking an Englishman through the blockade.

A few minutes later Shane walked into the drawing room, where Laura was playing the piano. Seating himself near Christa, he sat quietly and let the music wash over him, soothing the beast that was always warring within.

For a little while he wanted to forget the war and just relax and enjoy the evening.

He saw Christa's dainty eyebrows lift in a silent question when their eyes met. She looked so serious, he couldn't help winking at her and was rewarded when she blushed and smiled, but then turned her eyes to Laura. He wondered if she played the piano too. He realized he wanted to know everything about her.

After Laura had played a few more melodies she rose gracefully from the bench and straighten her gown, then lifted a small hand to her mouth to cover a yawn. "Excuse me," she apologized, "I haven't played this much at one time, since I was a student. I hope everyone has been sufficiently entertained by my meager offering."

"My dear Laura, I don't remember when I've heard such a magnificent concert," Shane smiled as he placed a light kiss on the back of her soft hand.

Taking a cue from Laura, Christa yawned and was compensated by Richard Fontaine's attention.

" Christa," he said sympathetically, "you must be tired. It has been a long day for you, and although I hate to end this wonderful evening, I suppose we should all turn in now. There will be a lot of arrangements to be made in a short time and we'll be seeing a lot of each other from now on." The others quickly agreed and Laura lead the way up the long staircase.

Christa found a maid in her room waiting to help her get ready for bed, but she dismissed her. She needed to think.

She was looking forward to being in her own room again at La Fleur, but to get there she would have to endure another sea voyage.

Glancing around she noticed that the bed had been turned down and the lamp had been turned up. A pretty blue night gown had been laid out for her. She held it up admiring the quality of the white lace trim, but she really wasn't tired yet, so she laid it carefully back on the bed.

Moving to the dressing table she took the artificial yellow rose from her auburn hair, and then pulled out the pins that held it up in the back.

She blushed at her refection in the mirror as the memory of that day on the ship flashed into her mind. Shane's kisses had thrilled and excited her. What would have happened if they hadn't been interrupted?

Absently, she began stroking her long hair with the silver hairbrush she found in front of her. She tipped her head forward letting the silky strands fall over her shoulder, reaching almost to her waist. While she brushed, she wondered how she could find a way to talk to Shane.

Should she take a chance and go to his room? He had been very angry the last time she had tried to talk to him alone. He was unpredictable.

He might tell her what he had in mind, but on the other hand he might try to kiss her and …

She closed her eyes, no it would be better if she just let it go, then to take that risk, because when she was in his arms he was in complete control of her senses and she couldn't think straight.

Putting down the brush, she wondered over to the bed and sat on the edge. Kicking off her kid slippers she removed her silk stocking and let them drop to the floor.

Turning the lamp down very low, she walked to the open French doors and looked out at the silver waves rippling in the moonlight.

Slipping out onto the wide balcony, she leaned against the guard rail and sighed softly. This place was so beautiful, with it's tall palm trees swaying in the warm flower scented air.

It was so romantic or at least it could be, if she had someone to hold her, someone who really loved her.

The sound of footsteps on the tiled patio below ended her musing. Stepping away from the railing into the shadows, she watched as Richard crossed the patio. After pausing to look around, he quickly made his way to the opposite side of the lawn to some steps that led down to the beach.

Christa saw that he was glancing around again as if to make sure he wasn't being followed. That's strange, she thought and wondered if perhaps he was going to meet someone down on the beach. Someone that he didn't want to be seen with but before she could follow him, she heard more footsteps and stayed where she was, in the shadows.

This time it was Shane and he too crossed the tiled patio and stopped to look furtively around, then continued on across the lawn and down the steps to the beach. It was obvious he was following Richard.

Christa was overwhelmed by curiosity so she decided to take a walk on the beach herself. Maybe she would get a chance to talk to Shane, and besides she wanted to walk on the beach anyway.

She found stairs at the end of the balcony that led down to the patio, and was soon hurrying across the cool green lawn in her bare feet. Giggling, she lifted the hem of her gown, delighting in the feel of the soft grainy, white sand. Waves splashed happily on the shore as a playful breeze tugged at her long loose hair.

She had lost sight of Shane and now she stopped. Looking around she noticed a large outcropping of rocks a short distance ahead. The dark shadows sent a shiver of fear down her spine. Don't be silly she chided herself. Shane and Richard are near-by. What could happen?

As she neared the rocks she thought she heard voices and paused to listen, but before she could move to let her presence be known a hand was clamped over her mouth and another one was pressed around her slim waist. She felt herself pulled back against a hard chest.

"Be quiet," a man's husky voice whispered into her ear. It had happened so quickly that she didn't have time to be afraid, but from the way her body was reacting she knew it was Shane Coulter.

He was very strong, and could easily overpower her so there was no use in struggling.

Richard was talking to another man a little ways down the beach from them. Apparently Shane wanted to find out who Richard was meeting and why and so did she.

Shane felt her relax against him and they listened.

"Well, did he agree to take you with him?" the stranger asked.

"Of course, he didn't have much choice," Richard laughed then added, "we leave in two days."

"Alright, now when you get to New Orleans, you're to contact a man by the name of Dominic Sabastian. He should be easy to find. Make a way to talk to him alone, then give him this."

"Sounds easy enough," Richard admitted, "but where's my money? After all that's why I'm doing this."

"Where's your loyalty man? Don't you know there's a war on? You should be doing this for your country," the other man admonished.

"Maybe I left it in Canada, when I saw my friends dying for their country while other men stayed home living in comfort trying to steal their women, or maybe it was before that, when my father married my sister off to a man she hardly knew and let him take her away."

"It doesn't matter, I'm doing this because there's nothing left for me in England anymore. I intend to make a new start and that's why I want the money, and I want it now."

Richard's voice was low, but the man felt the treat in it, and reluctantly reached into his coat once more.

"Alright, I guess you're as good as anyone for the job."

With a slight bow of his head Richard turned and started back towards the house. When he got near the rocks, Shane dragged Christa further back into the shadows with him. They watched Richard until he was up on the lawn and then Shane told her, "Keep your voice down and I'll take my hand away."

When she nodded her reply he took his hand away from her mouth. By now the other man had disappeared into the night.

"Why are you spying on Richard," Christa asked as Shane turned her to face him, but didn't release her.

She felt so good he wanted to keep her with him and make love to her.

"If you don't trust him, then why did you agree to take them with us?"

"He might turn us in if I don't."

"I can't believe it, Richard's not like that, he wouldn't do something like that."

"My dear Christa, he may have already done something like that," Shane reminded her. "Just how well do you know him?" His tone was cold as the thought of Christa with Richard flashed into his mind, and not for the first time. "Are you in love with him?" he demanded and wished he hadn't ask that. What if she said yes?

Christa was speechless for a moment. "How dare you suggest such a thing?" she said. Her voice quivered angrily when she realized what Shane was thinking.

"Then why were you coming to meet him just now," Shane asked huskily as the feel of her firm women's body in his arms began to weaken the anger and stir the embers of his passion.

"I wasn't coming to meet him," Christa defended, her voice raising, feeling weaker now herself.

Breaking free she turned from him and stomped out of the shadows and into the bright moonlight. She turned back again and her eyes widened in appreciation as she watched Shane walk slowly towards her.

He moved with sensual grace and she felt the pull of his masculinity. He had removed his coat and the neck cloth that he had worn at dinner.

The balmy breezes had mussed his dark hair making one lock fall across his forehead.

She deliberately avoided looking into his eyes. Her gaze drifted down to the hairy chest revealed by his open white shirt. She wanted to touch him, but that was something good women didn't want and she a good woman. Wasn't she?

Then she remembered how she had let him touch her breast on the ship and now they were alone again.

She stood frozen, excitedly waiting as he drew nearer. She knew she should run, but she couldn't move. He was dangerous. If she let him kiss her, she would be lost. To be honest, she had to admit at least to herself, that she wanted to be with him, but she was afraid of him too, and her heart pounded wildly now as he stopped in front of her.

The gentle breezes played with her long burnished hair making it fly out around her head and shoulders and Shane forgot every other woman he had ever known. "Are you saying you were following me then, Christa?" he asked. "That you wanted to be alone with me again, the way I've been wanting to be with you."

Watching her heaving breast he reached out and touched her hair, smoothing it down, keeping his hand on the back of her head. Before she could answer he pulled her into his arms tipped her face up with one hand and looked deeply into her eyes as if searching for some elusive answer, but Christa didn't know the question. She finally came to life.

"Don't touch me, please," she begged weakly.

"Why not, this is why you followed me out here isn't it? I've denied myself too long to stop now." His eyes dropped to her lips and she knew he was going to kiss her, then his seeking mouth swallowed the sound she tried to make.

She didn't want to feel that same wild response, the same giddy weakness that she felt before.

When it happened then, she thought it was just her inexperience that caused her to respond so wantonly to him, but the tantalizing touch of his warm mouth on hers sent a spark darting through her igniting into a flame of desire as he crushed her against his hard chest.

As Shane continued his tender assault, kissing her over and over again, it didn't matter if he was a bold privateer or if he wanted to marry her. The only thing that mattered was that she was in his arms and he was kissing her senseless.

"I'm drunk with desire for you, Christa. I want you now." His voice was husky against her mouth. The hand that had been holding her face, now slipped over to caress her neck and then he moved it to tug the neckline of her gown down lower.

She closed her eyes and sucked in her breath as he bent his dark head and laid light fiery kisses across the tops of her ripe breast.

His warm tongue flicked out, licking then gently sucking her nipple right through the thin material of her gown. His mouth sent shivers of pleasure through her.

He raised his head as she moaned softly and that mouth she loved and feared came up and turned her half formed protest into a sigh. His mouth, gentle at first became more demanding and somewhere in the corner of her mind a small voice was trying to tell her this was wrong.

She tried to push away from him, but she was to weak.

She struggled and squirmed, and as her body rubbed against his Shane felt a stirring in his loins. He grabbed her arms and pulled them behind her, holding both wrist in one of his larger hands he returned his other hand to her jaw and held her face. Like a moth drawn to a flame her eyes locked with his and she saw his raw desire there.

"Why are you fighting me Christa. I know you liked it. Would you fight Richard Fontaine if he kissed you?" he demanded.

Before she could answer he was kissing her again and his tongue was pushing against her lips forcing them open. His probing tongue shattered the last of her meager resistance, and she clung to him. He felt her relax, and hugged her closer.

The cold wind of reality blew through her mind with panic on it's heels as she was lowered to the sand. His hand slid exploringly up under her skirts and over her thigh.

They were gasping for air when he finally took his mouth from hers.

Do something before it's too late she scolded herself. She tried her voice.

"Stop!" Was that her voice? That ragged shrill cry? She swallowed and tried again. "Stop!"

Her voice was stronger now as anger and fear again took hold of her. "How dare you put your hands on me this way. Release me at once," she demanded on the verge of tears.

Her voice was like a bucket of cold water. Shane knew the sweetest torment of his life as he removed his hand from it's contact with her lovely body.

Finally gaining control of himself, he wondered shy he lost that control every time he was alone with this luscious beauty.

Looking into her teary eyes and then moving his gaze down to her trembling lips, as if he would kiss her again, he breathed out softly, "If that's what you really want, then you'll have to release me too."

To her horror and shame Christa found her arms were around his neck and her fingers were tangled in his soft dark hair.

Embarrassment flashed through her from head to toe and she quickly withdrew her arms.

Placing one hand on the sand on either side of her, he lifted his long muscular body up and away from her. She had won the struggle and kept her virginity. Then why did she feel this sense of loss?

Gazing down at her as she sat up, Shane was ashamed of himself.

He had always been able to get any woman he wanted with just a smile.

In most circles he was considered a good catch, and he didn't like being so out of control. After all she was no tavern wench. She was a well bred young lady, the daughter of a good family.

He had been holding back, denying himself because of that, but when he thought that perhaps Richard Fontaine had already tasted of her many charms he was jealous and angry.

Could he be wrong? Just now she had certainly acted like a scared virgin, but was she? The way she returned his kisses and caresses wasn't very virginal. Dam it. He was sure she wanted him too.

Was she fighting it because she was a virgin or was it because she wanted to marry Richard Fontaine. "Here let me help you," he offered, giving her his hand.

"It's the least you can do," Christa snapped, taking his hand and springing lightly to her feet. "You, you animal, she sputtered, "you bully."

Christa was very embarrassed by her own part in the situation, and didn't understand how she could react so wildly in his arms. "Do you always attack women when you get them alone?"

Releasing her hand and folding his arms across his broad chest, he took a step back away from her. "No, I only 'attack' the most seductive ones," he answered with an amused smile.

"Shane Coulter, are you laughing at me?" she was angry now and went on before he could answer, "all right, I admit that there does seem to be a strong physical attraction between us, but I'm not a fool. If you think you can just lay me in the sand and take me against my will, then you're the fool."

"When I take you, you'll be willing," Shane told her boldly.

"Why, you arrogant, conceited," furiously she drew back her arm, but before she could slap his handsome face, he grabbed her wrist and twisted her arm behind her back.

With his hand on her supple waist, he pulled her against his chest then gathered a handful of her long silky hair and pulled her head back forcing her face up.

His pride stung by her rejection, he fought back with his only weapon, the fact that he knew she wanted him too.

"It's your pride that makes you deny you want me as much as I want you, and it's my pride that keeps me from taking what we both want right now, but someday soon, you'll come to me willingly, Christa Devereax. After tonight I won't force myself on you again. Just remember this the next time you let Richard Fontaine kiss you."

His mouth was hard this time, melting her, branding her, and she knew he was right. She wanted him, but not like this, and he still hadn't spoken of love or marriage. Could she, should she settle for less.

Her senses reeled as he sensually moved his warm lips on her hungry mouth. He gently slid his lips from her mouth over to a spot just below her ear, where he trailed light fiery kisses down her neck to the crevice of her shoulder and she couldn't fight him anymore.

She felt weak and the fire was starting in her blood again, burning down every obstacle, in spite of her anger and hurt pride. Only now Christa realized that it wasn't Shane that she was afraid of, but herself.

Shane smiled triumphantly as he felt her go limp and snuggle her head against his chest.

He held her close and savored the feel of her in his arms, then turned his nose into her hair and breathed in its fresh fragrance.

" Go now, before I change my mind," he advised, releasing her.

Remembering why she was here, Christa asked, "What are you going to do now?" Are you going to tell Richard what you know?"

"No, I don't think so, there's a war on Christa," he shrugged, "this is a British port and he's an Englishmen. There are spies on both sides. I don't trust him, but I don't see any harm in taking him and Laura with us to New Orleans under the circumstances."

As he spoke he took a step closer to her.

He wanted to reach out and pull her back into his arms again, but he only reached out and touched her lips with his finger.

Christa closed her eyes and thrilled to his touch. What's the matter with me, he touches me with a finger and I go limp with desire, she thought. He's dangerous. I seem to lose control when

I'm alone with him. "What now?" she asked hoarsely, as he pulled his finger away.

"Now," he repeated lost in her nearness and fascinated by her pretty mouth.

"About Richard, " she prodded.

" Oh, there's not much we can do, except keep an eye on him," Shane confessed.

Christa didn't want to go, but how could she stay. After the way she had fought him, if she didn't go now she would probably throw herself into his arms and beg him to have his way with her.

Gathering her strength about her, she sighed and said, " Perhaps we can talk some more when we get to New Orleans."

Richard returned to his room to find Laura waiting for him. He wasn't surprised.

She was startled by the opening of the door and jumped up from the winged back chair where she had been dozing. "Oh Richard, where have you been? I don't know how long I've been waiting for you. Will you please tell me what's going on? I know you've been waiting for an opportunity to go to New Orleans, but with an American privateer?"

Richard smiled, holding up his hand as if to stop her questions, amused by her bewilderment. "Alright, alright, I'll tell you every thing, but first you tell me something. How do you like Christa Devereax?"

"I like her very much but," she paused as she realized Richard's meaning.

He looked in her eyes and said simply, "I'm in love with her, and I intend to marry her and live in America. Laura, I've changed since we last saw each other."

"Oh, I guess I'll always be a bit of a gambler, but I've learned some hard lessons in these last few years since father died. I know now that there's more to life than fast horses and even faster women."

"I started to court Christa when we were in London but her Uncle William didn't seem to approve of me. I never did find out why, until I was fighting in Canada."

"I was drinking and playing cards with some of the others one night, where we were camped, when one of them made a remark, something to the effect that everyone knew I had squandered most of my inheritance. I asked him what he meant by that and he said he had overheard Robert Wolfe telling someone else about it at White's. I was already pretty sure that he was the reason my regiment had got shipped out so suddenly."

"But, Richard, why would he do such a thing?"

"He wanted Christa for himself, that's why," he explained, taking off his jacket and tossing it on the bed behind him.

"But he's married, isn't he?"

"He was, his wife died last year."

"And what about Captain Coulter? I couldn't help notice that she's traveling with him without a maid or woman companion or even a suitable wardrobe."

"After I was out of the way her uncle was about to accept Wolfe's offer for her in marriage. She wants to go home to her father and brother."

"And what about the war?"

"It will soon be over. The Americans can't hold out much longer."

"And what about me? I love you Richard, but I resent your freedom. Father arranged my marriage and told me I would learn to love my husband in time. Well, they're gone now, and I'm not so sure I want to just let you take over where they left off," she said, crossing her arms in front of her. "Oh, alright," she relented, "I'll go to New Orleans with you, there's nothing here for me now, and I do like Christa Devereax."

"You won't be sorry Laura," Richard beamed. "You're only twenty-two and you're a very rich and beautiful widow. Well, maybe not rich, but you're well off and you seemed a bit attracted to the good Captain. Surely, you've thought of getting married again. After the mourning period is over, of course," Richard suggested pointedly.

"I think Shane Coulter is after Christa too, and if he is, I'm telling you right now, I won't do anything underhanded to keep them apart."

"Laura, my dear," Richard answered, with mild shock. "I was only hoping you might keep him occupied while I court Christa." They smiled a knowing smile at each other and said good night.

After he watched Christa disappear into the shadows of the mansion, Shane made his way to the waterfront tavern where he was to meet Adam Michaels.

He stopped after entering to let his eyes adjust to the dim light and smoke. Slowly scanning the room he spotted Adam sitting at a table near the back. Shane's face collapsed into a broad smile, and he chuckled to himself.

Adam wasn't alone. He was in the process of kissing a comely serving girl seated on his lap.

Coming up for air just in time to see Shane's approach, he released her, whispering, "I'll see you later sweetheart, but first bring my friend here a drink. We have some business to discuss."

With a sensuous smile she left them, hoping he would keep his word.

Taking a chair across from Adam, Shane grinned, "I should have known it wouldn't take you long to find a woman."

"I didn't find her, she found me," Adam winked. "Harry told me you ran into some old friend of Christa's from London. "Now tell me what else you've found out, if anything. No, wait, here comes your drink." They waited for the girl to leave before speaking again.

"I followed him to the beach, where he met another man, an Englishman. I didn't recognize him, but I overheard their conversation. He gave Fontaine something to give to Dominic Sabastian," Shane confided, lifting the cup of rum to his lips.

"Well, your old rival. It's a wonder to me that the two of you have never been in a duel. You were both after Angela Stanton for awhile, weren't you," Adam asked over the rim of his cup. It amused him, the way Shane always seemed to come out on top of things.

"For a while, but then I lost interest, when I realized how much like her mother she was, and I couldn't stand that woman," Shane chuckled, as a picture of Mrs. Stanton came to mind.

"He might be dangerous," Shane speculated, "no one knows much about his background before he came to New Orleans a few years ago. Some people seem to think he's the bastard son of some one close to the royal family, because he's well educated, has a lot of money and seems to know a lot of people in high places both in America and in Europe.

I met him in London at a gambling club. You remember when we went to visit my grandfather a few years ago. Then I met him again in New Orleans, when he opened his own hotel and gambling club.

"I've never met Dominic Sabastian but I have seen him around. He seems a little high and mighty to me."

"A very good description Adam," Shane agreed.

"I'm surprised Fontaine hasn't turned us in yet." Adam observed.

"That's because he's in love with Christa Devereax and he talked me into agreeing to take him and his widowed sister with us to New Orleans."

"Oh, I see," Adam said slowly, raising his thick eyebrows and nodding his head. " What do you want to do about it?" He inquired as he finished his drink.

"If Fontaine's got any business with Sabastian it should be investigated," he added.

"Just what I was thinking," Shane agreed again. "We better be ready for anything. Alert the men and be careful what you say to your lady friend. There are spies every where on both sides and she could be a friend of Fontaine's" Shane warned.

"I'll be careful," Adam assured him absently, as his mind turned to thoughts of being alone with the exotic Annie.

"It's late. I suggest we get some sleep," Shane said, finishing his rum, letting the sweet liquid relax him.

He stepped out into the almost deserted street and looked around. After walking a short distance, he stopped. He had the eerie feeling someone was following him.

Continuing on, he inhaled deeply of the clean fragrant air and thought about Christa Devereax. She was so lovely with her flame streaked hair dancing around her head in the moonlight.

He wondered if she might be thinking of him. He remembered holding her lush curves in his arms not an hour ago. The way she had answered his passion with her own, she couldn't be in love with anyone else. He fought down the urge to go find her.

He had to forget her for now. His country was at war and it was ironic that he went around accusing others of spying, when that was exactly what he was, a spy.

Oh yes, he was a privateer, but when the war started he had made a commitment to help his country in any way he could.

That included gathering pertinent information wherever he could and then passing the information on to a government agent in New Orleans who would pass it on to Washington, if he decided it was important enough.

A little information from him and a little from another source and pretty soon, they might be able to tell where the British would strike next. Some thought Washington, but most like himself, Jean Lafitte and Andrew Jackson thought Mobile or New Orleans.

He would have to put his personal wants and desires aside for now he decided. He found his way back to his room by way of the back stairs and sat on the edge of the bed, noting it had been turned down.

He pulled off his boots and stripped off the rest of his clothing, turned down the wick of the lamp and lay back. The clean cool sheets felt good on this warm night. He ran his right hand through his dark hair and rubbed both hands over his face, then yawned and stretched. It was good to lay down.

It occurred to him that Christa was in a room just a few doors away, and again her beautiful face appeared before his mind's eye. It hit him very forcefully that he couldn't just take her for a night or even for a mistress. If he wanted Christa Devereax, he had better be willing to marry her.

The bright silver moonlight poured into the room where Christa Devereax tossed and turned on the large bed. She raised herself up and pushed back her hair, poked and fluffed at her pillow and lay back down.

She was beginning to wonder if she had jumped from the frying pan into the fire. She had thought for so long that Shane Coulter was married to someone else that when Richard Fontaine began his pursuit she was ready to except his proposal, but he left England suddenly, and then Shane came back into her life and Richard and now she had two men after her.

When she was alone with Shane on the ship, she thought his intentions were honorable, but the way he acted on the beach tonight made her wonder just what kind of woman he thought she was.

When she closed her eyes she saw his handsome face just the way he looked before he kissed her and in spite of everything she wanted to be in his arms again. She remembered the night on the *Falcon* when she went to his cabin to talk and he had been so angry and called her a fool.

Was he trying to resist the strong tide of his own passions. If that was the reason than why had he changed his mind. He was jealous of Richard. He had said something along those lines. *Remember this the next time you let Richard Fontaine kiss you.*

She wondered what she was going to do now? She would have to walk a fine line to keep Shane and Richard from dueling over her. She was sure it wouldn't be long before Richard proposed to her again. She would just have to put him off until she could sort out or get over these feelings for Shane.

At least she would have the company of another woman for the rest of the voyage. That thought brought another set of problems.

Should she tell Laura everything? How she felt about Shane and Richard? Laura was Richard's sister and might feel obliged to inform him of her feelings. She didn't want to hurt him but didn't see any way to avoid it. She wrestled with these thoughts most of the night and finally slept towards dawn.

Laura Sims was up earlier than usual the next morning to supervise the packing of the things they would take with them.

She planned to see Mr. Alden at the bank to make arrangements for the transfer of funds New Orleans, and had already sold the house thinking Richard would want to return to England.

She looked good in black, she thought, pausing to glance in the mirror at the foot of the stairs, but she was tired of wearing it.

She could very well fall for that handsome Shane Coulter, she mused, tucking in a loose hair pin, but she was sure he was more interested in Christa Devereax. She would try to get his attention as Richard suggested but, if Shane and Christa were in love then she would bow out.

Her marriage to Henry was arranged but there was an atttraction between them at first until she found out he had a roving eye. His taste ranged from the servants to the older married women of their acquaintance. She was bitterly disillusioned, but she hoped it was just because he was young and he would settle down to her when he got older. She'd never know now, she thought, as tears blurred her pretty blue eyes.

This time, for the first time in her life she was free to choose for herself and she would make sure the next man would have eyes only for her.

And so the preparations continued. Christa, who seemed to be the only one with nothing to do, tried to help with the alterations of the gowns Laura had so generously given her.

When asked if Christa would like to join her for the trip to the bankers, she jumped at the chance.

Shane and Richard left the house after breakfast each with many arrangements to make. They would return for the evening meal.

The women stopped at the Colonial Hotel, the largest on the island for a light lunch on the patio overlooking the bay. A balmy breeze blew gently bringing with it the scent of the flowers and trees around them.

They were friends enough by now for Christa to confide how her Uncle William had threatened to give her hand in marriage to Robert Wolfe and how she had masqueraded as a boy to work in the galley of the *Falcon*. She decided not to tell about her feelings for Shane.

Laura discussed her marriage with Christa. Then said, "It's good to have a woman close to my own age to talk to, Christa. I have no sisters and Richard is my only brother. Well, we do have an older half brother in England, from our father's first marriage. He inherited the family estate, Ashmore. We never really knew him."

"When we were small he was away at school and then he married. His wife Hester, is the original snob, so we didn't see much of them. They had their own life in London. I was married there, so they did come to my wedding."

"I was young and I thought things would work out. We came here to Jamaica so Henry could run his fathers sugar plantation."

"His younger brother runs it now. His family never approved of our marriage. They'll be glad to hear I've gone."

"How did he die? I'm sorry, if it's painful you don't have to answer. I have this habit of talking first and thinking later," Christa explained.

"That's all right," Laura graciously replied. "He was coming home from a night of carousing. It was a dark, stormy night. He should have taken a room at the hotel, but for some reason he didn't. He was thrown from his horse and broke his neck. They told me he died instantly."

"How awful for you," Christa sympathized.

"I'll be all right now that Richard is here."

"I have a brother too," Christa said, deciding to change the subject. His name is Jamie and he's twenty three years old. I think you'll like him."

"My mother died when we were young too, but my father is still alive and I can't wait to see him again."

"Of course he may be angry at first, because he sent me a letter telling me to stay in England until the war was settled, but once he sees me I think he'll be glad."

"You must have a very good relationship with him." Laura surmised.

"Yes, very good," Christa answered, frowning. "I take it that you weren't close to your father."

"No. After my mother died he went to London and we were left in the care of servants and tutors."

"We didn't see much of him except on holidays. He never married again but after his death we discovered he had a series of young mistresses."

They wondered if there was such a thing as true lasting love or were they overly romantic and naïve. As they talked they discovered they had much in common. The subject of horses came up and Christa told Laura about La Fluer and the beautiful horses her father raised there.

The next night, after a busy day of supervising the loading of fresh water and supplies as well as some new cargo to be sold in New Orleans, Shane and Adam made their way to the same tavern they had met at before.

They compared notes and agreed the only thing left to do was collect their passengers and their luggage in the morning.

Chapter 6

As the tide left the shores of the sun kissed island behind the next morning it took the *Falcon* with it into the blue green Caribbean.

Standing at the rail, watching the wake, Christa Devereax's spirit soared like the sea gulls she saw flying about the ship. I'll soon be home, her heart sang.

One afternoon, after they had passed into the golf of Mexico the wind died. The sea was still as glass, and the air was hot and humid. As the women stood at the rail, Christa was reminded of the phrase, *The calm before the storm.* And storm it did. Just a few hours later the sky began to darken and the wind started to howl with a vengeance.

Shane barked orders and the crew scrambled to do his bidding. Some climbed high into the rigging, ready to furl or unfurl the sail as ordered.

By late afternoon the *Falcon* was in deep trouble and Shane fought to head her into the wind.

He hoped to ride out this storm as he had so many others. Lightning bolts ripped apart the blackened sky and thunder rumbled ominously. He ordered the women to go below fearing for their safety.

The ship was heaving and tossing so much they clung to any place they could get a good hand hold. After considerable slipping, sliding and staggering they reached their cabin.

Harry Patch secured everything as best he could in the galley and went above to offer his help.

Huge waves slammed over the deck sweeping men into the ocean. Fear gripped every heart. An awesome cracking sound was heard above the thunder. Then the top of the main mast came smashing down on to the deck and scattered those who weren't crushed.

Christa thought of Shane and wanted to be with him. She knew she could die unafraid if she could do it in his strong arms. Time ceased, and water was raising in the cabin Shane had given the women.

After a while the lighting and thunder began to strike with less frequency and the wind let up a little, but the air was much cooler now. The women wrapped themselves in blankets and huddled together on Shane's bed waiting for one of the men to tell them all was well but that word never came, because huge waves still buffeted the ship.

Shane and Adam and, yes even Richard Fontaine, took a turn at the wheel, as Richard had some experience with sailing.

Suddenly a gigantic wave lifted the *Falcon* and slammed the ship into the rocks that appeared out of the blackness before them.

With an agonizing screech she lurched onto her side as if seeking rest from her labor.

Shane gave the order to abandon ship and the men scurried for the long boats.

The women were already trying to make their way up the stairs when Shane opened the door of the hatch. The men gallantly led the frightened women to one of the waiting long boats when another huge wave washed over the world.

The blazing tropical sun rose above the low mountains of the lush green island. Sea gulls and other strangely beautiful birds darted and dipped and flew away.

On the beach, the warm blue-green water lapped at numerous pairs of toe's belonging to the bodies strewn at random on the shore.

Christa Devereax smiled at Shane Coulter before he kissed her, and his arms tightened around her. "Christa?" Why did he sound so far away when he was holding her close, she wondered. "Christa?" Why was he shaking her. Realizing it must be a dream she struggled to open her eyes.

"Thank God, you're alive," he whispered. "For a minute I thought…" And then he was really kissing her. She slid her arms around his neck, and joy filled her heart as she realized they were alive, and on dry land.

Richard Fontaine was furious as he watched, and in a blind rage he hurled himself at Shane. Grabbing a handful of the thick dark hair in one hand then circling Shane's neck with his other arm he forcefully pulled Shane away from Christa, who was dropped back onto the sand as Shane struggle to keep Richard from choking him to death.

Shane fell to the ground taking Richard with him twisting his body as he did so, forcing Richard to loosen his hold. Shane jumped to his feet and Richard followed.

The two men with their shoulders hunched and feet spread, sized each other up. Then Richard threw a punch at Shane's jaw, which Shane effectively dodged.

By this time Adam Michaels and Harry Patch and several of the crew had gathered around and Laura was helping Christa to her feet.

When Christa had awakened to find herself in Shane's arms that was all that mattered, but now she was humiliated by her own wanton behavior and to make matters worse Shane and Richard were fighting over her.

Richard lunged for Shane again, going for his throat but Shane stepped aside and landed a blow that caught Richard in the ribs.

Horrified, Christa shouted, "Stop!" Please stop." The men momentarily moved apart and she tried to step between them only to be pushed aside by both of them.

Without breaking his eye contact with Richard, Shane growled, "Stay out of this, Christa."

She turned to the others standing around and pleaded, "Won't someone stop them. Adam? Harry?" They just looked at her as if there was something wrong with her. She slid a glance at Laura and saw she was helpless too.

"Well, just because the two of you have decided to act like uncivilized savages, doesn't mean I have to stand here and watch," she shouted indignantly.

With this she picked up her torn and wet skirts, pushed back her bedraggled hair, stuck her nose in the air and stomped off down the beach.

Harry's first instinct was to step in, but Adam stopped him from doing so, and later explained that at least it was a temporary diversion from their problems.

Shane and Richard continued to throw punches, sometimes drawing blood from a cut above an eye or the corner of the mouth. Although Shane was the larger man, they were weak from the previous night. With little food or sleep both men were tiring quickly now. When Laura realized maybe they weren't going to kill each other after all she decided to join Christa.

Shane was gaining new respect for Richard, whom he had dismissed at first as a limp wristed dandy. Richard was hardly able to see clearly now because his left eye was beginning to swell, never the less, he valiantly decided to try one more time to knock Shane down.

As it happened, Shane was planning to do the same to Richard.

The simultaneous blows found their marks and the two fell rather heavily to the ground. Adam motioned for Harry, finally deciding both men had had enough. "All right, now if you two are through having your fun, we should get organized and see if we can salvage anything from the ship."

"I for one am starving, and could use a drink of something, even water," he said, giving Shane a wink and a hand up while Harry helped Richard to his feet.

Richard was beginning to realize he didn't want to make Shane Coulter his enemy, at least not yet, so he slowly walked over to Shane, and offered his hand in apology.

"I'm afraid I saw red when I saw you a…, embracing Christa in such an intimate way. After all she is a lady."

"Let's just forget it, seems we're all going to be here for a while, so we'd better try to get along," Shane conceded, rubbing his jaw.

Shane took charge and was shocked to find only about half of his crewmen were there, and some of them were in bad shape.

The *Falcon* didn't have a doctor aboard on this voyage. Doctors were scarce anyway and not many wished to be at sea for any length of time leaving their wives and families behind. Especially when the ship was a privateer, so the women were put in charge of the sick and injured.

Shane and Adam divided the men into work parties with some swimming out to the wreckage of the *Falcon*, while others were sent in search of fresh water and food.

When Shane swam out to the damaged ship he noted she was hung up on a reef that formed a natural barrier to the beautiful bay.

Later Tom Harvey, the ship's carpenter, reported to Shane that it would take a lot of hard work to make her seaworthy.

"The rudder is badly damaged, and the main mast is broken and the sails are in shreds, then of course there's the hole in her side, Capt'n."

"Do your best Tom, and we'll hope for another ship to come to our rescue, preferably an American ship."

A long boat was found still intact so blankets, clothing and some personal belongings were brought ashore.

Richard and Laura took their valises a little apart from the others and checked to see if their money and letters of credit were still safe. "Here Laura, take this and put it with yours for safe keeping, will you," Richard asked, handing her his letter of credit.

By nightfall things were looking up and when everyone had eaten their fill of fish and fruit, Shane passed out some of the fine French wine and brandy he had intended to sell in New Orleans, although they had discovered a spring a little ways in-land with good tasting fresh water.

The huge fire cast bizarre shadows on the sand as the forlorn group decided to just sleep on the beach for the night. Shane studied his charts that had been preserved from the water by the leather case he kept them in. After gazing intently at the night sky, he told them, "The best I can tell is we're on some small uncharted island. We're in the gulf of Mexico, so I'm sure we'll be rescued soon." Then he added to himself, but will it be by friend or foe.

Richard was sitting cross legged next to Christa. "How can you act as if nothing happened. Just this morning you were trying to kill each other. What made you change your mind about him," she asked.

"I was rather upset when I saw him mauling you, but I can't help admire him at the same time. He seems to be a natural leader. Haven't you noticed," Richard inquired. "He said we might be here for a while and we should try to get along and I agree with him, that's all."

"Oh. I see," she said, and wondered why it bothered her.

She picked up her blanket and moved to the spot where she had left her valise earlier and lay down.

The next day as the relentless sun climbed higher in the sky, the men erected shelters. They consisted of a roof made of palm fronds with tall polls at each corner. Most of the men had discarded their shirts as they cut the fronds with swords that had been brought from the ship.

They took the longboat back and forth bringing back tools and rope and anything that would make life more comfortable.

The first few days passed quickly with so much to do just to survive. Soon, they were all straining their eyes trying to spot a sail on the horizon during the daylight hours. At night they kept a huge signal fire burning.

Christa often found herself searching for Shane, as the men did their work, and just as often she longed to be in his arms. Her eyes followed him as he worked and she watched in fascination when he took off his shirt and his muscles rippled under the dark tan of his back and shoulders.

"Christa, are you alright?"

"Of course, why do you ask?"

Laura was amused at the flush that came to her friends face at being caught watching Shane. "You didn't hear a word I said, did you?" Laura smiled.

"Oh! I'm sorry," Christa apologized. "I guess my mind was wandering."

"That's all right, it wasn't important anyway." Laura grinned.

The women fell into a pattern of helping Harry Patch with little chores, such as gathering kindling wood for the campfires and although Christa and Laura had no experience in such task they found they really didn't mind and even enjoyed learning new things, besides having something to do made the time go by faster.

Some of the men made snares and set traps to catch small game, having quickly tired of fish and then they would have rabbit or some exotic bird to eat.

One day, near the end of the week, while Adam Michaels was telling Laura and a few of the wounded men stories of his childhood in Tennessee, Shane saw Christa walk down the beach, a little apart from the rest of the group.

Knowing Richard had gone hunting with Harry Patch and some of the other men, he decided it would be a good time to talk to her alone without causing trouble again, so he slowly followed her.

As he approached her she leaned against a large gray rock and waited and he marveled again at her beauty. Her long auburn hair hung half way down her back and a playful breeze ruffled the wispy strands. She was wearing a blue muslin gown with a border of small flowers that was very attractive, in spite of being wrinkled and slightly soiled.

He stopped about four feet away, feeling awkward now that he was so close to her.

"Come here, Christa," he commanded. His low husky voice reached out seductively tempting her, making her want to throw herself into his arms.

She glanced around and closed her eyes, then folded her arms across her body trying to fight her own desires, struggling to gather the strength to resist him. Slowly she opened her eyes and looked over his shoulder when she answered. " No I can't, everyone will see us."

Lifting a questioning brow, he asked, "Are you afraid of what everyone will think or are you afraid of what Richard Fontaine will think?"

"When I knew Richard in England and yes even now, his actions have always been honorable and I see no reason to jeopardize my relationship with him now," Christa explained, as she nervously watched the foaming waves swirl up on the golden sand at her feet.

"All right," she went on, looking him straight in the eyes," I admit I'm physically attracted to you but from the way you behave when we're together it's obvious that you," and she emphasized the word, "you" don't have honorable intentions and I won't be just another notch on your bed post." She put her hand over her mouth, shocked at her own bold outburst.

She hadn't planned to say those things, but she couldn't hold back her anger any longer. With a withering look at Shane she turned and ran back towards the tree where the others sat laughing in the shade.

"Christa, please, wait, let me explain," Shane called as he started after her. A shout from the beach stopped him in his tracks.

Shading his eyes from the sun, he saw Tom Harvey jumping out of the long boat.

"Capt'n, Capt'n Coulter," the burly carpenter called again.

Shane hesitated and looked from Tom, who was coming quickly towards him, to Christa who was by this time seating herself beside Laura under the shade tree.

"Dam, what an exasperating woman."

"What. What woman, Capt'n. We got more trouble than any woman. I just spotted a sail on the horizon."

"Is it British then, Tom?"

"Yes sir, I believe it is, and she must have spotted the wreckage because she's headed right this way."

"Go tell the others, and get every one together Tom. I'm going up there, on the hill to have a look."

It only took one short glance into his spyglass for Shane to recognize that the ship was indeed a British vessel and was fast approaching the entrance to the bay. By the time Shane made his way back down to the beach everyone was there anxiously waiting.

"Well, is it British?" Adam asked.

"What are we going to do, try to put up a fight?"

"No, Adam, we're hopelessly outnumbered, we'd probability lose anyway."

Harry Patch stepped forward, "Capt'n I think I can speak for everybody when I say we don't want to just give up with out a fight."

"Oh we're going to fight Harry, but we're going to pick our own time."

"What do you mean Shane?"

"Well Adam, I was just thinking that if we use the right argument maybe we can persuade them to give us their ship."

"Give us their ship," Adam repeated, then he realized what Shane meant. "Oh! Yes, of course, the right argument," he smiled.

Then Shane turned his gaze to Richard. "Mr. Fontaine, why don't you look after the ladies and the injured. They'll probably lock me and my men up."

"If you're planning something Coulter, I want to be in on it. I want to get to New Orleans as much as you do. Let me help."

"Just take care of the women and stay out of the way if any trouble starts, Mr. Fontaine, after all I wouldn't expect you to fight your own countrymen. "Richard nodded his consent and led the women back to their shelter.

As Shane talked strategy with his men, Christa was restlessly pacing in front of the shelter with her arms crossed in front of her. Of all the luck, she thought, just when I was almost home. First, the shipwreck and now the British.

It's almost as if God himself is preventing me from going home and yet I can't believe that, I won't believe that. She stopped her pacing and gazed down the beach where men stood in groups discussing the situation. She had to do something.

Lifting her skirts she walked purposely to where Shane and Adam stood watching the two long boats that had been launched from the frigate bouncing closer with each incoming wave.

"Give me a gun," she demanded, placing her hands on her shapely hips.

Shane and Adam turned at the same time. They looked at her and then at each other and then they laughed.

"And just what may I ask, is so amusing," Christa snapped, highly offended. "I assure you, I do know how to use a gun."

"I see, Shane said as he tried to compose himself. "And how many men have you killed?"

"None yet, but I won't be taken back to England after I've come this far."

The amusement was almost gone now except for the twinkle in his big brown eyes, and Christa couldn't help think of the girls she knew who would kill for such long dark lashes.

"Don't worry, I'll get you home," Shane promised her.

"How can you do that aboard a British sh…, she started to ask, then realization flickered in her brain, just as if someone had lit a lamp. She smiled and crossed her arms, relaxing a little now. "You have something planned don't you? Mind telling me?"

Shane studied her lovely face and cursed himself again for letting her go that night in Jamaica.

"Don't worry, Captain, you can trust me," she said, answering the unasked question in his eyes.

He shrugged his wide shoulders, and with a roguish smile that tugged at her heart he confided. "Well not really a plan. I was just thinking if we could take some of their weapons then perhaps we might persuade them to take us to New Orleans instead of back to Jamaica."

Of course," she chuckled, much relieved. She knew if it could be done Shane would do it.

"Now, be a good girl and go pretend to be scared," Shane told her. He stopped her with a hand on her arm as she turned to go. "Please don't tell your friends what you know. I still don't trust Fontaine."

Laura Sims brushed back the stray lock of blond hair that kept falling down over her eyes with her left hand while her right kept vigorously manipulating the black lace fan that had been salvaged from the wreck, and wondered if there was a breeze outside.

"Laura listen to me," Richard said, from where he sat in the sand in front of the shelter, "I know the Americans can't put up a fight, so we'll soon be on our way back to Jamaica."

"Yes, and how are we going to explain our presence to the authorities?"

Richard hadn't told her he was carrying a message and decided it was better if she didn't know now. "Leave that to me, Laura, I got us into this and I'll get us out."

Chapter 7

Captain John Perkins stood on the bridge of the British ship Mermaid, and watched as his men herded the American prisoners aboard.

What the hell? Two women among them and young beautiful women at that. He waited patiently for his first mate's report, then walked slowly down the steps to the main deck and began a careful inspection of his captives.

Richard Fontaine smiled to himself as he recognized John Perkins, a friend from his school days. He couldn't remember how many times they had gotten drunk together and fought over some pretty face and then made up again when the pretty face was fickle enough to choose some one else. Richard had always been able to talk John into following his lead in any situation. Now, he wondered if he still could.

"Which one of you is or should I say was the Captain of the wreck?"

At this question Shane took a step forward, casually hooked his thumbs into the wide leather belt at his waist, and proudly stated, "I am."

"And just who are you?" There was a note of hostility in Perkins voice when he asked the question.

"My name is Shane Coulter."

"Ah yes, the privateer. Or should I say pirate?"

Shane's answer was an indifferent shrug of his broad shoulders.

Richard knew John Perkins well enough to know he was intimidated by Shane's height and good looks and when he felt threatened he could get very nasty.

Perkins was very conscious of his short stature and tried to make up for it by being a bully.

At school he was always involved in a brawl. That's how they met. When some bigger fool made a remark about his height, John started to beat him to death, but Richard stopped him.

At first John started to turn on Richard until he realized that Richard was saving him from a worse fate. That being, to be expelled and sent home in disgrace.

"John. John Perkins? It is you. I can't believe it, here we are in the middle of the ocean and I find myself rescued by an old friend from my school days. It's me. Richard Fontaine."

"Richard, my God, what are you doing with these Americans?"

"Why I was just escorting my fiancee home." Then smiling broadly, Richard moved over to stand beside Christa. He put his arm around her shoulders, and pulled her closer, then beamed, "May I present Christa Devereax, of New Orleans, Louisiana. She's been visiting her uncle's family in England for almost two years, but she prefers to be married at home. We were in Jamaica when we discovered Captain Coulter and we persuaded him to take us home with him."

Christa raised her eyes and was chilled by the coldness in Shane's return gaze. She was helpless, to do anything. She couldn't very well deny what Richard had told the British Captain, it would only make matters worse.

John Perkins, always a man to appreciate a pretty woman gave Christa his full attention. That is until Richard introduced him to Laura.

Shane was surprised at first by Richard's announcement, but thought Christa was surprised too. But she must have known, she must have said yes to his proposal.

Or was Richard just trying to save his own skin by using the engagement as a logical reason for his going to the United States.

After a flirtatious exchange of flattery with the ladies, Perkins gave orders to his men, and a cabin was made ready for the women. Richard was invited to share the Captain's quarters.

Shane and his men were put to work helping with repairs to the *Mermaid*. There was considerable damage from a run-in with another privateer. One of LaFitte's ships.

The lamp light threw grotesque shadows as it swung from its chain above the table. Christa wondered if she would ever see LaFleur or her father or brother again. She glanced around and wondered what she was doing here on this ship going back toward Jamaica instead of home.

Some way, some how, she had to talk to Shane Coulter. She knew if they could get weapons, Shane and his men would have no trouble taking over the Mermaid, but how?

When they were finally allowed to rest and eat Shane and Adam sat on the deck with their backs braced against the bulkhead. They had been put to work along with the English crew because like all British ships the Mermaid was short handed.

To make matters worse, she had lost about half her crew in the scrimmage with the American privateer.

"I'm surprised we haven't been tied up or put in the hold," Adam told Shane in a hoarse whisper.

"Like all Englishmen Perkins is still underestimating us," Shane smiled. "They are keeping an eye on us." He paused, and waited for a guard to pass before continuing. "Just follow my lead and when we get the opportunity we'll take this ship home."

The night passed slowly for the rescued captives. The silver moon climbed up to take the place of the sinking sun and brought with it a cool refreshing breeze that ironically filled the sails and persisted in taking them in the direction they did not wish to go.

The next morning, Christa wondered what sin she had committed that warranted this kind of punishment. Hadn't she always been kind to animals and little children and servants? There must be a way to turn this ship around, but how?

She casually looked around her. Slowly she scanned the men gathered in small groups about the deck. Where were Shane, and Adam? Where was Harry Patch? Oh good, she sighed, when she spotted Harry. They exchanged a smile and a nod.

"Looking for me, I hope," Richard Fontaine smiled, as he approached the railing to stand beside her.

"Oh, Richard how are we going to get out of this and why did you tell that awful Captain I was your fiancee?"

"Well, to answer your first question, I don't know and as to the second, it's been my dearest wish since we met. I had to give him a valid excuse for being with you, didn't I?" Besides, I do want to marry you."

"I thought I had lost you forever when I was shipped to Canada, but I knew when I saw you arrive back in my life that day in Jamaica that my luck had changed and I don't intend to let you go again. You will marry me, say you will," he pleaded, as he drew her into his arms.

"Richard, please, this is no time for this kind of discussion. I want to go home. I was so close and now I'm being forced to go back and I…"

"I see," Richard pushed her a little bit away from contact with his yearning body but kept his hold on her arms.

"And if I were to help you get home, then would you marry me?"

Christa had hoped to avoid answering this question, at least for the time being. Now she didn't know how to answer him.

He saved her the trouble by saying, "That's alright you don't have to give me your answer now, however let me remind you that we are making good time towards Jamaica.

"By the way did you know Captain Coulter and his mate have been put in the hold. I don't think Perkins trust them," he joked.

"Oh no. I wish we had more time to think of a good plan, but I'll think of something."

"Richard if you help me get home I'll consider your proposal very carefully, I promise," she pleaded.

A few months ago she was ready to say yes, but she hadn't and now he was asking again and she still wasn't ready. Why? She closed her eyes for a moment and the answer appeared in her mind. Shane Coulter.

Even now, she missed his presence. How had she grown so used to him in such a short time. He was a magnet, drawing her to him, even when they were apart.

Why couldn't she break his hold even after he had made it clear that she was just a foolish female to be used for a night's pleasure and then put aside, to be used again when the mood took him.

"Christa, my dear," Richard pressed, "do you realize that what you're asking of me amounts to an act of treason. I am still an Englishmen, although my sympathies are with the Americans. If I were to help you escape, I could be hung and what about Laura? You're asking a lot of me and giving nothing in return. Look at me," he ordered softly, placing a hand under her chin, turning her face up. "I love you Christa, and I know I could make you happy." Then he kissed her.

It was a warm sweet kiss, and she did feel comfortable in his arms, but when she closed her eyes she saw Shane Coulter.

Remember this the next time you let Richard Fontaine kiss you, his memory reminded her.

"I know John Perkins very well, Christa, just say yes and I'll get him drunk and out of the way," Richard whispered into her ear, as he buried his face in her silky hair.

"I could do that on my own, he seemed quite attracted to me," she suggested and then wished she hadn't when Richard slowly released her.

"I see. You don't want to marry me, is that it? Well, that's all right I don't want to be hung for treason either. Good luck and do be careful. Perkins can be very dangerous," With a slight bow he turned and walked away.

"My dear Miss Devereax, why don't you just confess why you're here," John Perkins leered at Christa. Acting deeply offended, he asked, "Do you take me for a fool?"

Christa almost choked on the sip of wine that she didn't really want to swallow. "Why, Captain Perkins what ever do you mean?" she asked innocently.

Perkins rose from his chair and moved around the small table then bent over her. He lifted a stray lock of her hair and tested it's softness by crushing it in his hand helping himself to a view of her cleavage as he did so. "You've come to bargain haven't you?" I have something you want and you have something I want. It's as simple as that."

Christa's eyes followed his hand as it gently laid her curl back where it had been nestled on her breast and with a shock she realized what he was suggesting.

If she would allow him to take privileges, he would let them go.

She had sought to get him drunk and maybe steal his weapon and keys, but the man obviously had a hollow leg. Now he was making advances that she dare not refuse.

She jumped to her feet, throwing Perkins off balance. When he fell he grabbed her arm trying to catch himself. The next thing she knew she was sprawled on top of the good Captain. She struggled to get up, but he clutched her about the waist and held her to him.

Although he wasn't a big man she could feel the power in his sinewy frame. This is insane, she thought, and pushed her hands against his chest trying vainly to pry herself out of his grasp.

He laughed and rolled taking her with him. Now she was beginning to feel some fear. Her arms were pined to her sides so she tried to bring her knee up, but he successfully blocked that move.

"Why Miss Devereax, where ever did you learn such un-lady like tactics?"

"From one of the girls at school. She said her brother told her to use it if a man ever tried to take advantage of her."

"If you want your friends to arrive alive at our destination, then I suggest you be a bit friendlier."

"Please, John, you don't have to use force, I fully intend to be friendly," she lied, desperately trying to gain some control over the situation.

"However, I find this floor very uncomfortable, why don't we get up then we can start over again."

"Why should I let you up now, when I have you right where I want you?"

Christa's fear turned to anger, and she struggled again.

Perkins ignored the weak pummeling blows to his shoulders and continued placing slobbering kisses on her face and neck. He was moving his attention and his hands to her heaving breast when he suddenly collapsed on top of her.

Then he was jerked away from his awkward position. Looking beyond him Christa was relieved to see Richard. After depositing Perkins in a chair he returned to stand above her.

Richard stood momentarily frozen, he could understand what Perkins had done as he watched her struggle to a sitting position.

"Oh, Richard, I'm so glad you changed your mind. Now help me up and we can get his… I don't know what got into him."

"Well I do . Don't pretend you don't know how beautiful you are, your effect on men. It's all I can do not to take up where he left off."

"Richard, please, I thought you came to help me." As she spoke she reached out her hand and Richard gallantly helped her to her feet.

She brushed her tangled hair out of her eyes and pulled her gown back into place.

"I must look a fright."

"You look magnificent. You're the most beautiful women I've ever known." In one step he took her into his arms and to her surprise he just held her gently.

She sighed deeply, she owed him something. Something more than just a "thank you," She relaxed against him and closed her eyes, and as always Shane Coulter's face appeared before her. She couldn't help but compare these two men.

Shane Coulter had kissed her and awakened some sleeping passion that she feared and at the same time wanted to know better.

She wanted to be free to follow that enticing yearning that flared into a fire when he was near. Perhaps it was to hot and would die quickly, but she had to know.

Richard Fontaine was charming and handsome and she liked his company, but there wasn't any passion in his arms. What she felt for him was a little more like the way she felt about her brother Jamie.

The thought of Jamie made her homesick and she wanted to go home.

Pushing away from Richard, she looked up into his blue eyes and was uncomfortable when she saw the desire there.

"Richard, I want to go home. Are you going to help me or not?"
"Yes, of course."

"By the way, what did you hit him with?"

"The empty wine bottle that was on the table. I was waiting outside, just in case of something of this sort happened."

"Should we tie him up?" Christa asked, as Richard discovered a pistol in Perkins coat pocket."

"Yes, although I think he'll be out for the night. Christa, I want you to do as I say. I want you to go back to Laura. Tell her what's going on, then lock your door and stay there until one of us comes for you."

"What are you going to do?"

"First, I'm going to find out just exactly where Coulter and his mate are, and how well guarded. Then I'll find Harry Patch and with any luck we'll turn this ship around with-in the hour."

Richard left her to search for Harry Patch, who had been put to work in the galley and not locked up with the rest of Shane's crew.

Shane Coulter prowled the tiny room like some caged animal. Perkins had ordered them locked up just before dark.

There was no way of contacting Harry or any of the others. If they were going to take control of this ship the sooner the better. There was only one guard at the end of the hall, but he was a big bull of a man and well armed, and worse yet he was loyal to Perkins.

Shane kept trying to think of a plan of escape. The trouble was he couldn't keep his mind on the subject.

All he could think of was that Christa Devereax was betrothed to Richard Fontaine and right now they were probably enjoying a fine dinner and even finer wine at the Captain's table or perhaps they were alone up on the deck with only the blushing moonlight to witness their embrace.

He dropped down to the pallet opposite Adam. When he closed his eyes he imagined Christa smiling at him and he remembered the feel of that sweet mouth responding to his kiss. Dam. How could he still desire her after the way she had used him to get to her lover.

She said she wanted to go home and she did but some how she must have known that the *Falcon* would put in at Jamaica first. He must have mentioned it to her uncle William.

He cursed himself for not taking advantage of the opportunity when he discovered her aboard his ship. He had thought then that the witch was an innocent virgin.

Maybe she was, if she could fool him maybe she had fooled Richard Fontaine as well. But there was nothing innocent about the way she had melted in his arms. Her beautiful body gave her away. Why had he let her go that night on the beach in Jamaica. He could have had her then.

Well the next time he wouldn't be so noble. If he got another chance he wouldn't deny himself the pleasure again.

After bribing a few of Perkins men, Richard found Harry Patch and together they located the small room, in the hold of the ship, where Shane and Adam were being held. Now they had to get rid of the guard.

"Have you got any money?" Harry asked in a husky whisper as they peeked into the dimly lit hallway.

"A little, but I doubt he'll take a bribe, I think we should try to overpower him."

Taking the sight of the big gorilla in again, Harry said, " ya, but how?"

"With this," Richard said with a pleased smile at Harry's reaction when he drew a pistol from his coat pocket. " I barrowed this from my old school chum Captain Perkins."

Harry chuckled, "Why, Mister Fontaine, I do believe there's hope for you yet."

"Ready?" When Harry nodded, Richard lowered the pistol. Then taking a deep breath he opened the door and lead the way. The guard, who had been dozing came to with a start and was about to jump up from his chair when he saw the pistol in Richard's hand.

"What do ya want?" The guard asked, as he eyed them suspiciously.

"Nothing much, just open that door and I won't shoot you." Richard was careful to stand back away from the man's long reach as the giant stretched himself up out of the chair and reluctantly dug a key from his pants and put it into the lock.

A strong wind filled the sails of the *Mermaid* as she sliced her way through the heaving waves of blue green sea.

Christa watched from lowered lashes as Adam Michaels handed a cup of coffee to Shane. She brushed the hair from her face and quickly looked away as their eyes met.

Ever since the night they had taken control of the ship and turned back towards New Orleans, his every look held a silent question.

She stirred restlessly feeling trapped as she sat on the deck beneath the tarp that had been erected to protect the women from the blazing sun.

Drawing her knees up and her gown down, she wrapped her arms around them, closed her eyes and lay her copper head there. Soon, she would finally be home again.

They were well into the golf now and although she liked Laura she savored thoughts of sleeping in her own room and going riding where ever she wanted, and eating in the big dinning room a La Fleur, with her father and Jamie. But the first thing she wanted was a long luxurious bath with scented soap and big fluffy towels and then…

Laura interrupted her thoughts, when she spoke. "I like going places, but a ship can be so confining. I'm glad Captain Perkins is an educated man, so we at least have the use of his books. I do enjoy reading."

Christa giggled, "I imagine he wishes he had the use of them right now."

"Most of the time I like being a women, but there are times when I wish I were a man, so I could do something more physical," Christa confided to Laura.

"Yes, even Richard seems to be enjoying himself, working about the ship. I believe that's him now, coming down from some perch up there," Laura observed, as she squinted and put up her hand to shield her eyes from the sun. "Yes it is. Well I never thought I'd see the day. I think he really likes the physical work."

Christa watched as Richard dropped down gracefully to the deck close by. He seemed different, freer, not so stuffy as before. His hair was longer and although he was blond his skin was turning a light tan.

It was very becoming and she couldn't help notice that he had a very nicely built upper body, as he pulled on his shirt. He lacked a large muscular frame like Shane Coulter, but still he was very handsome, she could do worse.

The thought of Shane made her eyes seek him out and her heart skipped a beat as she saw him at the wheel with the wind playing with his dark hair, his feet planted apart, his white shirt open half way down revealing his broad hairy chest.

Richard Fontaine had seen Christa watching him and as he tucked his shirt in he was pleased with himself, thinking perhaps he had impressed her a little, but now she was watching Shane Coulter and there was a light in her eyes that wasn't there when she looked at him.

Jealousy welled up from deep inside and he determined to win her.

After all she had been quite taken with him in London, before Robert Wolf saw her and pulled a few strings to get him sent away.

"Christa, my dear, come, the sun will soon be setting, let's watch it together over there by the rail," he urged. Christa answered him with a nod and soon they stood awed by the beauty of the sunset.

The sun was like a huge orange and gold ball of fire, tinting the clouds radiant shades of pink and coral.

The air was much cooler now and when Christa shivered Richard put his arm around her and drew her close to his side. He knew Shane Coulter was watching them and he wanted to show Shane that Christa was his, so he slowly and deliberately bent his head and kissed her.

Richard's kiss though sweet and gentle, had taken Christa by surprise and she remembered Shane Coulter's hot sizzling kisses that night on the moonlit beach in Jamaica.

Chapter 8

The word spread quickly through the city that Shane Coulter the American privateer had arrived back in New Orleans. Shane hired a man to find Charles Devereax and ask him to meet the ship at the wharf.

The authorities had come aboard and were in conference with Shane for the better part of an hour and now it was finally over, and they were gone, taking charge of the prisoners and officially turning the *Mermaid* over to Shane.

Even now Adam was transferring the guns and ammunition to one of La Fitte's warehouses for safe keeping.

Christa stopped her pacing when her father came aboard. "Christa, how dare you defy me. You must have received my letter. I specifically ask you to stay in England until the war is over. And Shane Coulter I thought I could trust you. What's the meaning of this foolishness."

Charles initial anger at seeing Christa soon turned to concern for her comfort and now he hugged her close and kissed her forehead.

"Oh, Daddy, can we please go home now, she pleaded.

"Of course, " he smiled, then added, "we'll talk later."

Charles was shocked at seeing Christa. After two years in England the headstrong young girl he remembered had turned into a headstrong beautiful young women. If he had known that the war would be declared so soon he never would have let her go to England in the first place.

"Shane, thank you again for everything, we must get together soon to talk," Charles said pointedly. He could see clearly now though he hadn't before that except for having the reputation of being a ladies man, there was nothing wrong with Shane Coulter.

"I had a letter for you from your brother William, but I'm afraid it was lost with the *Falcon*," Shane explained, wishing he could get Christa alone and wondering why. Why did he still want her, still remember the way her luscious curves fit into his arms and the passionate way she had returned his kisses.

How could she look so dammed tempting with her hair mussed and her gown soiled and wrinkled. As if she felt his hot gaze she looked up and as their eyes locked, he could see her own puzzlement. There was something between them, but why was she fighting it so hard and why did he even care.

Christa was the first to break the silence that had fallen. "Captain Coulter, thank you for bringing me home. You must come visit us at La Fleur soon," she said, hoping to keep her voice steady.

"Thank you, Miss Devereax," Shane responded in the same formal tone. Then grabbing her hand he bent over it and she felt a shock as his warm moist lips came into contact with her skin.

Oh, the devil, she thought, what evil power did he have that could make her body yearn for more. She wanted to touch his hair, and she closed her eyes for a moment, a big mistake because with her eyes closed she suddenly remembered the feel of his hand on her breast and his lips too.

She caught her breath, and was glad Charles still had an arm around her. Her father felt her slump against him and asked, "Christa, are you all right? Come on, I'm going to get you home. I think the ordeal is catching up with you."

"Shane, thanks again. See you soon. Mr. Fontaine, Mrs. Sims come along. We'll get you all settled in no time and then we'll have a nice long talk." Charles Devereax was the personification of the jovial host, as he herded the group into his carriage.

A feeling of nostalgia swept over Christa as the carriage approached the long curved driveway of La Fleur Plantation. She wondered why she hadn't seen the slaves working in the fields on the way. It must be because there was no way of shipping the goods to market. Well the war would soon be over and so would that problem.

Richard Fontaine watched in admiration as an angelic smile lit Christa's face, she was glowing and only then did he realize how much La Fleur meant to her. As she saw again the big house with it's long white columns and the wide veranda she became very excited. She could hardly wait to go into the house.

When the carriage stopped, Christa jumped down without waiting to be assisted. All the years of drilling about how a lady should act, when she attended Miss Allen's Academy for young ladies in Richmond, were forgotten. She flew up the wide steps and into her brother Jamie's waiting arms.

Jamie laughed at the childish delight on her face and wrapping his arms tighter around her waist he picked her up and swung her around.

"Well, well if it isn't my prodigal little sister come home at last. What took you so long? I'd have thought you would have charmed your way aboard a ship before this," he teased.

"Oh, Jamie, I'm so glad to see you. I don't care how much you tease me. As a matter of fact I didn't realize how much I missed it until now."

By this time Charles, Richard and Laura had exited the carriage and were quickly ascending the stairs behind Christa. Jamie put Christa down and she turned to the others. After introductions were made, Jamie gallantly took Laura's hand then looked into her clear blue eyes. Laura blushed, no one had looked at her that way for a long time and she was flattered. Her heart jumped when he kissed her hand.

"Mrs. Sims, I hope you like our country," he drawled. "I know our country will like you. Though I have much against your country,

I must say your beauty covers a multitude of sins. I'm sure we can be great friends," he added, with a smile.

Richard cleared his throat, "I'm sure we will Mister Devereax." Richard liked Charles Devereax immediately and had been prepared to like Jamie, but he was a bit offended at Jamie's remarks about England and thought him a bit bold. He glanced at his sister's hand which Jamie was still holding. Jamie got the message and reluctantly let it go.

"Well, shall we go in, I'll order some tea, and have the servants get your rooms ready," Charles said, as he lead the way with Christa and Richard close behind. Jamie offered Laura his arm and they brought up the rear.

Home, I'm home at last, Christa thought happily as she looked up at the huge crystal chandelier in the entrance way.

Excitedly, she swung open the double oak doors of the library, then paused on the threshold. She scanned the room quickly noting the portrait of her beautiful mother above the mantel.

Everything was just as she remembered, or was it? Was something missing? Oh, probably not.

"Christa it's everything you said and more. We're very impressed," Richard said as he came up beside her.

It was a few hours later, after they had eaten and she had had a long leisurely bath. Christa sat at her dressing table as a servant brushed her long auburn strands. "What did you say your name is," she asked the young slave girl.

"Abby, Miss Devereax, my name is Abby."

"I don't think I remember you."

"No. I guess you wouldn't remember me, Miss."

"I used to work in the fields with my family and we lived in one of the cabins out back, but that was before your daddy done sold 'em off," the girl explained.

Christa turned, surprised, "Sold them off?" she asked, looking the girl straight in the eye.

"Yes,' em, he been sellin' off some of the land and sellin' a lot of the slaves."

"So," Christa sighed, "is that why you're here instead of Cora, my old maid?"

"Yes 'em, I guess it is."

Taking the brush from the girl, Christa dismissed her for the night. She got up and continued to brush her hair as she wandered around the room.

Why was Charles Devereax selling land and slaves? Did he need money so badly? She stopped her pacing and leaned against the frame of the opened French doors and watched the moonlight spread a silver sheen over the lawn and garden below. She closed the doors reluctantly and went to bed.

A knock on her door wakened Christa with a start. She sat up quickly, then smiled as she enjoyed the feel of her own bed in her own room at her beloved La Fleur.

"Miss Christa, it's Abby. I brought you some coffee."

"Ah, yes come in, put the tray down here," Christa said, indicating the night table beside her. After doing what she was told, Abby moved over to the French doors and opened them. Bright sunlight flooded the room, while a light breeze played with the curtains.

"Abby, what time is it?"

"Why, Miss Christa it's almost noon."

"Noon? It can't be that late already."

"I wanted to talk to my father this morning. Do you know if he's still in the house?"

"Oh, Miss Christa, your father went into the city 'bout a hour ago."

"Did he say when he'd be back?"

"Not to me, Miss, but maybe your brother knows. They all had some breakfast together. You know your father and your brother and them English people that come back with you."

Putting the empty coffee cup down, Christa threw back the sheet and swung her feet to the floor. With Abby's help she was soon dressed and in search of Jamie.

After questioning several servants she found herself approaching the cook house. She could hear the head cook Hanah giving some poor young girl a tongue lashing for some offence in serving the food.

"Now, I tol' ya before and I ain't gona tell ya again," she was scolding, but stopped in mid sentence as she heard the squeak of the screen door as Christa pulled it open and stepped into the oppressive heat.

A smile of joy replaced her stern countenance. "Miss Christa, I heard you was finally home. Now you get in here and tell me everything. You hear. But first you come over here and let me have a big ol' hug."

Hanah was one if the reasons Christa had missed La Fleur so much.

After her mother had died, Hanah was the one who took care of her and comforted the lonely little ten year old girl.

Hanah happily clasped Christa to her ample bosom then pushed her to arms length. "Girl, let me get a good look at you. Well if that don't beat all. I do believe you got even more beautiful, if that's possible."

"Oh Hanah, it's so good to see you, now I really feel I'm home."

"Miss Christa you sit down in this here chair and you tell me all 'bout England while I fix you something to eat," Hanah said, smiling broadly as she pored Christa some coffee.

Meanwhile Jamie Devereax was in the stables with their English guest. Richard Fontaine was duly impressed as Jamie hoped he would be.

"We're very proud of our horse flesh at La Fleur," he boasted.

"And you should be, if this magnificent animal is an example," Richard said over his shoulder as he eyed the golden stallion in the large stall before him. As if he knew he was on display the horse lifted his head and his ears and nickered, flicking his long white tail.

"Oh, Jamie he's just beautiful, the most superb horse I've ever seen," Laura smiled, her eyes lighting her face.

"Jamie, are you in there?"

"Christa, we're over here," Jamie called.

"Good morning everyone," Christa bubbled feeling exuberant at being home at last. "Magic! My God it is you, and all grown up," she gushed stroking the animal gently. "I'd know you anywhere. Isn't he beautiful. You were only a frisky young colt when I left. Weren't you boy?"

The way Christa was giving her attention to the horse, prompted Richard to speak.

"Christa, I do admire a good horse but I must say you are the most beautiful thing I've ever seen. You're absolutely radiant this morning."

"Thank you Richard," Christa answered, blushing. "I guess it's just the excitement of being home at last."

"Magic's more than a pretty face, we've been training him for the races. He can run like the wind. You should see him. He's already won some large purses," Jamie continued, as if he hadn't heard Richard.

"By the way Jamie, do you know where father's gone. I wanted to talk to him this morning."

"Yes, he's gone into the city. He'll be back soon, after all we do have guest."

Jamie's right, Christa thought, her father would be back soon and then after lunch they would have a long talk.

Playing the gracious host Jamie led the way as they left the stables and headed for the cooler side terrace that over looked the well tended flowers and spacious green lawns of La Fleur Plantation.

They strolled leisurely down a stone path that took them by a small pond where white swans glided smoothly by on the sun dappled water. The sun was higher now and so was the humidity. After passing another large oak tree, they saw a white gazebo at the end of the path.

Why don't we rest a few minutes,. It's so pleasant here. I can see why you were so anxious to get home Christa."

"I'm glad you like it too Laura and remember you're welcome to stay as long as you like."

As the two men hung back a little to let the ladies go up the three steps into the gazebo, Richard was trying to think of a way to get Christa alone. Jamie was having the same thoughts about Laura.

A few minutes later Christa suggested they return to the house for something cool to drink. They were soon sitting on the wide veranda sipping lemonade and making small talk.

Although she was home at last and enjoying pleasant company, Christa had the nagging feeling that something was missing. Her mind began to wander. Here she was where she had longed to be and yet she wanted to get up and run away.

She finally let herself think about the reason. Shane Coulter was what was missing.

"Shane Coulter, just the man I wanted to see," Charles Devereax's friendly voice called out. "Over here," he directed as Shane paused on the bottom step of the bank he was just leaving and where Charles had been earlier that morning. " Step into my carriage and I'll take you where ever you wish."

"Good morning, Charles, I was just heading back home, but I would like to talk to you," Shane smiled.

Shane Coulter had never taken to plantation life, where slaves were kept to do the work. He much preferred to hire free men as servants and usually treated them kindly. He knew Charles well enough to know that he too would prefer it that way.

But Charles had bought his land as a young man and did what everyone at that time did, he bought slaves to work his fertile fields and prospered.

There was little conversation as the carriage wove through the crowded streets. They finally turned onto the residential street where Shane lived in a comfortable town house.

Shane had decided not to go back to sea. He wanted to pursue Christa Devereax and he could be just as useful here as far as the war was concerned.

Harry Patch had taken up the duties as cook and valet, while Adam was a temporary house guest. Most of his men had already joined the crews of other privateers.

"Do you remember the first time we met," Charles asked, quietly.

"Yes, of course." Shane answered with raised eyebrows that quickly relaxed when followed by a knowing grin. "As I recall I was leaving some din of iniquity on the waterfront late one night and interrupted some river rats who had you surrounded."

"Yes, the scum would have robbed me and left me for dead if you hadn't come to my defense. You saved my life that night Shane. I owe you."

"I'll remember that," Shane smiled, as the carriage stopped.

As the two men approached the door of Shane's house, it swung open to reveal a smiling Harry Patch. "Why Mr. Devereax, it's good to see you again sir. Come right in, let me get you some of that fine French brandy we brought back with us. You'll love it."

After Harry scurried away, Shane threw his hat in the general direction of the coat rack in the hall, and lead the way through the drawing room and out the open French doors to the blue tiled courtyard and motioned Charles to a white painted wrought iron chair.

"How's Christa this morning," he asked hoping to sound casual.

"Well enough I suppose. She was still in bed when I left the house."

The thought of Christa in bed with her hair spread out on the pillows and her luscious body clad only in some flimsy night gown, sent a flash of desire surging through Shane.

Not wanting to look Charles in the eye he left his chair and walked over to the small fountain in the center of the courtyard and pretended to examine the statue of a mermaid in it's center. Then he impatiently covered the few steps back to the French doors. "Harry, where's that brandy?"

"I'm a coming, keep yer shirt on. I had to wash the glasses. It's been awhile since they been used," Harry explained defensively, as he sat the tray down on the table.

He poured the brandy, licking his lips, hoping Shane would ask him to join them. He had brought an extra glass just in case.

Charles Devereax looked at Shane and then rolled his eyes towards Harry indicating he wanted a private conversation.

"That'll be all for now Harry, thanks," Shane said. Harry's face fell in disappointment as he turned to leave.

Shane caught the look and knew what it meant. "Wait a minute Harry. Why don't you take a glass of this brandy with you, "he offered.

A broad smile split Harry's face. "Don't mind if I do," he said, and after filling his glass and taking a sip he smacked his lips and left them.

When they were alone again, and had tasted the brandy, Shane took his seat once more. "So, what did you want to talk to me about?"

Putting down his glass, Charles decided to get right to the point of his visit. "I want to know what happened between you and my daughter."

Shane had expected something like this when Charles made a point of wanting to talk to him. "Charles, I don't know what to say."

"Alright, I'll make it easy for you. Have you taken any liberties with my daughter."

"No, of course not, but why are you asking me. Why aren't you asking her fiancé?"

"Fiancé? They didn't say anything about that to me. I could sense that there's something between the two of you."

Shane took a swallow of brandy, then calmly offered, "cigar?"

"I believe I will," Charles answered, letting Shane light it for him.

"Now, tell me what happened between you and Christa," he said as he blew out the smoke and examined his cigar.

Shane pushed out of his chair and began pacing. "Well, all right, I kissed her," he admitted, remembering the feel of her warm sweet lips and how she melted in his arms. He stopped his pacing and waited for the next question, like he was waiting for the hangman.

"Are you telling me that you had my beautiful young daughter on your ship and all you did was kiss her? You expect me to believe that you didn't try to seduce her."

"Well, if you put it that way. Of course it crossed my mind. I'm a man, and she's about the loveliest women I've ever seen, but she is your daughter. Every time I looked at her I saw you looking back at me just like you are now. You stopped me from having my way with her just as if you were there in person."

"Then I believe you. You're my friend and I know you're an honorable man." Finishing the last of his brandy, Charles got to his feet and reached out to shake hands with Shane, then patted him on the back as they headed back into the house. "Come to dinner tonight and we'll celebrate your safe return."

Shane excepted the invitation quickly, grateful for a chance to see Christa again."

"Let's go home Jubal," Charles ordered his driver as he stepped into his waiting carriage. "I have a lot to discuss with my prodigal daughter."

Pushing herself away from the table, where they had just finished a light lunch, Christa turned to her father. "Daddy, may I speak to you alone, please?"

"Of course, my dear. I have a few things I wish to discuss with you too." Turning to the others the picture of the perfect host he said, "you will excuse us, won't you."

Richard Fontaine watched Christa leave the room with her father and wished he could be a fly on the wall of the library so he could hear what was said.

As soon as they were alone, Christa threw her arms around her father and hugged him. "Oh, daddy I missed you so. Uncle William looks a lot like you, but he's so bossy. Did you know he was about to give my hand in marriage to Robert Wolf. A man I despised. That was the last straw."

"And what about young Fontaine?"

"Richard had a commission in the army. Then his regiment was called to Canada. I was surprised to find him in Jamaica. When his time was up he went there to visit his sister only to find that her husband had died."

They had always wanted to come to the Untied States, so Richard asked Shane if they could join us." Then she explained about the engagement.

"What about Shane?"

Christa chewed on her lower lip and shrugged her pretty shoulders."What do you want to know," she asked. Then she turned away and pretended to examine the picture of her mother above the mantle.

"How do you feel about him? Did anything happen between you and Shane Coulter before you got to Jamaica?"

"I think he's much too bold and reckless and," she turned to face her father, " he kissed me, that's all."

At least they told the same story, Charles concluded, but he still wasn't satisfied. He was sure there was something more.

"I'm glad you're all so friendly and that nothing happened because I invited him to dinner tonight."

"You did. How nice," Christa said, trying to keep the excitement out of her voice.

"Now daddy," she went on trying to change the subject. "I want you to tell me why you've been selling some of the land and slaves."

"Come, sit down over here beside me and I'll tell you why."

Christa made herself comfortable beside her father and he began to explain his actions to her.

"Christa honey," he started, then picked up her hand and held it in both of his. "I never liked the idea of keeping slaves, it was always a matter of economics."

"If you want to succeed as a planter you must have cheap labor. That's how it's done, but I never had the stomach for it. There's been a lot of talk up north against slavery you know. I believe some day it will be abolished."

"But daddy what's to become of La Fleur without slaves?"

"'That's why I've been gradually getting rid of a little here and there. I've been putting the money into my stables, and acquiring some good horse flesh. Do you remember Magic. The golden colt that you liked so much?"

"Yes, I saw him just this morning. Daddy he's so beautiful."

"Yes, yes, but more than that he can run. We've been grooming him for the races and he's ready. I expect to make a lot of money from that horse and then use him for stud."

"But daddy you're not going to sell La Fleur, are you?"

He looked at his young daughter and then at the portrait above the mantle. She was so much like her mother. He sighed, and sought to reassure her. "Of course not, my dear. Don't be alarmed."

"I intend to keep a good part of the land and the buildings but it takes a lot of money to support such a large plantation now a days. It's not so easy as it was when I started out.

You must remember that soon you'll be getting married and your home will be with your husband."

"Married. Yes. You're right." Christa smiled at her father, but inside she was shaken. Some how she had always thought of La Fleur as her home.

She had taken it for granted that even if she married, she would still live here. She had never considered that a husband might want to take her to some other place. But now Richard was here and she could tell that he loved La Fleur too. If she married Richard she was sure he would want to stay here with her.

"Well, what about Jamie? La Fleur is his inheritance. How does he feel about your decision?"

Charles put his hand under her chin and looked her straight in the eyes. "Jamie knows my feelings and he knows that everything I have will be his some day and that includes the stables. It was his idea. He's the one I'm doing it for. Now, give me a smile," he said, and Christa knew the discussion was at an end. "That's my girl."

He got to his feet and walked to the door, then paused and turned back again, looking her over carefully. "The first thing tomorrow I want you and Mrs. Sims to go into the city to a dress maker. Your wardrobe is woefully lacking."

When she tried to protest, he silenced her with a hand. "Don't worry about the expense. Let me worry about that. If we're to find you a proper husband then you must look your very best." At her stricken look he began to laugh. "Christa, my dear, I was only joking."

Later that evening, Christa looked up expectantly from the piano keys when the butler announced that Mr. Shane Coulter had arrived.

Laura Sims eyes followed Christa's gaze to the handsome figure entering the room.

"Ah Shane my boy, so good of you to come."

"My pleasure, Charles. I couldn't turn down a chance to dine with the two most beautiful women in Louisiana."

Christa blushed at the way Shane looked directly at her when he spoke. A shiver of excitement ran through her. All afternoon she had waited to see him again, wondering if she would feel the same at the sight of him now that she was home again. She did. And now she wondered if that was good or bad.

"Why, Mr. Coulter, what a charming thing to say."

"But true none the less, Laura." Shane spoke the words to Laura but his eyes never left Christa's face.

Richard Fontaine stood by the mantle and observed the way Shane and Christa looked at each other and decided to make his presence known.

"Shane, good to see you again," he said as he offered his hand and stood beside Christa, forcing Shane to break the eye contact. Reluctantly Shane took Richard's hand and was then greeted by Jamie.

"Care for something to drink?" Placing his hand on Shane's arm, Jamie led him to a side table.

Christa watched him in quite conversation with her brother. It seemed so right somehow. He always fit in. Whether it was on a ship with the wind whipping his dark hair about his head or in a fashionable drawing room in London with his hair neatly combed.

Chapter 9

Christa didn't eat much at dinner that night and afterwards she couldn't have said what was served, but she remembered the conversation very well.

Shane Coulter on the other hand, remembered both the food and the conversation. Because it was his favorite meal. Crisp fried chicken, potatoes, tender cooked vegetables and apple pie.

The conversation he remembered because every word he spoke was carefully planed to make Christa admit at least to herself that she was in love with him not Richard Fontaine.

"How does it feel to finally be home. Is it everything you expected?"

Dam, leave it to Shane to cut right to the heart of the matter. What was she supposed to say? No. It's not the way I expected. There's something missing. Instead she answered very politely, "I'm very happy. I don't ever intend to leave again."

"That's hard to believe," Shane persisted.

"What do you mean?"

He shrugged his shoulders and said, "It's just that you're engaged and you'll probably be married soon. And as a married women you would go where your husband wanted, wouldn't you?"

"Yes, of course I would, but La Fleur will be our home."

Still he wasn't satisfied. "But what if your husband preferred to live somewhere else? Maybe even leave Louisiana."

What did he mean by that? Was he suggesting that he might offer marriage? Was he testing her? To see if she would ever give up living without servants and fancy gowns? But this is what she wanted. Wasn't it?

"Then I guess I'd have to choose between La Fleur and the man I love, wouldn't I? But I hope I'll never have to make that choice. After all, most men would consider themselves fortunate to gain a wife and a plantation at the same time."

"Of course, you're right," Shane finally conceded.

Richard came to her rescue by changing the subject. "With you for a wife, a man wouldn't need any more fortune. What about you Shane? Will you be going back to sea soon?"

"I've given up privateering," Shane informed them. There was confused silence, with everyone looking surprised, and Shane looking amused.

"What will you do now?" Christa ask, and everyone waited for his answer.

"I'm in pursuit of another objective. If all goes well everyone will know about it soon enough."

"It's common knowledge Shane's an adventurer," Jamie remarked.

"But don't you ever feel the need for a permanent home, some land and a family?" Christa asked.

"It's because of my adventuresome spirit that I've learned home is where the heart is. It's not a piece of land or a house." If Shane had wanted to give her something to think about he had. It was some time before she got to sleep that night.

Shane wondered if she understood what he was trying to say. Maybe he should just propose and let the chips fall.

The next morning Christa had almost decided to confront Shane and ask him directly what his intentions were or if he had any intentions towards her at all, but something happened to make her change her mind again.

Jubal drove her and Laura into the city. She was browsing through a pattern book while Laura was being fitted by Elaine, one of New Orleans best dress makers, when she heard the bell above the door tinkle and looked up.

"Goodness! If it isn't Christa Devereax. My dear, I heard you were back. It must be two years. My how you've blossomed," Angela Sabastian said, looking Christa over carefully as if she really didn't believe what she had just said. "Of course you know you're the talk of the town."

Christa took in the elegant blond goddess. Yes, elegant was the word.

A little taller than Christa and blessed with a slim perfect body. She was a vision in a pale blue gown. A petty straw bonnet with blue and white flowers and ribbons famed her perfect oval face.

"Angela, how are you?"

Angela Sabastian was still smarting from the hurt she felt when Shane Coulter hadn't proposed. It was humiliating after the way she had told her close friends that he would momentarily.

To cover her embarrassment she had made up a story about his womanizing and gambling and the fact that he did have Indian blood. So of course, she had turned him down.

"Everyone is talking about how Shane Coulter ran the blockade to bring you home. He's notorious you know. Especially with young nubile women like yourself."

Christa didn't miss the light in Angela's eyes or the lazy smile, as if she was savoring the sound of Shane's name when she spoke.

"How fortunate that you had your fiancé and his sister with you to protect your reputation." Angela let the words sink in. There. She could see the things she said about Shane had stung as she meant them to. She wanted to hurt Christa for having spent so much time with Shane.

"I can't wait to meet your guest. You are coming to my mask ball next week aren't you?" It was a statement rather than a question.

"You will be receiving a formal invitation."

"My goodness, yes. Wouldn't want to miss that," Christa drawled sweetly.

"Good. Now be a dear and tell Elaine that I'll be back for my fitting later. I have to meet my husband now. He hates it when I'm late."

She was gone as fast as she had come and Christa just stood looking after her, then walked over to the mirror in the corner of the room and studied her reflection. Turning from side to side she decided that she was just as attractive as Angela. Maybe that's why Angela didn't like her.

If they were going to go to the mask ball, she was going to make sure she had the most beautiful gown ever and Laura too. It was sure to cost extra. After they picked the patterns they would have the gowns sown at La Fleur or they would never be ready in time.

The next night found Shane Coulter at Dominic Sabastian's casino in the back room of his fancy new hotel. "You win again, Coulter. I've never seen such luck. Have you made a deal with the devil or something?"

Dominic Sabastian didn't like losing especially not to Shane Coulter. The man was a thorn in his side. Shane's smug answer only served to strengthen Sabastian's ire.

"Perhaps I am the devil," he grinned, showing even white teeth.

As they threw their cards on the table Shane turned to the dealer and said, "Deal me out Jim, I've taken enough money from these gentlemen for one night." He pushed back from the table and swallowed the liquid in his glass, stood up and collected his winnings.

"But you can't quit while you're ahead ol' man, isn't done. Play another hand and let us try to get even."

Richard Fontaine was a very good gambler himself and he hadn't really lost that much, still it galled him that Shane was the winner.

Did he always win at cards and with women. Maybe he was the devil after all.

"No, it's late and I have to take care of some unfinished business," was the excuse Shane gave when he left.

Once in his bedroom he undressed down to his breeches and poured himself a drink. He paced back and forth then wandered out onto the balcony. It was a beautiful balmy night. The sky was clear and a million stars shown down on him.

He sat down and gazed at the moon and wondered if Christa Devereax ever thought of him like this. Was she on a balcony at La Fleur thinking of him in the moonlight or was she in the moonlight thinking of Richard Fontaine. Dam. Where was his luck now? Here he sat like a frustrated schoolboy while Richard Fontaine was an honored guest at La Fleur.

There must be some way for him to spend some time with her. If she could get to know him better she would see that he was a nice enough fellow. Not the rowdy womanizing savage he must have appeared to be.

Someone knocking at his door brought him to his feet. It was Adam. "Shane I saw your light and I wondered if we could talk."

"Yes. Adam, I'm glad you came. I've got some things on my mind too."

"I can guess what your problem is, Shane. It's either Carista or the war. Am I right?"

"I think I'm in love with Christa Devereax."

"I don't understand. How is that a problem?"

"I think she loves me too, but she won't admit it. Maybe she thinks I'd take her away from La Fleur or something."

"You've never had any trouble getting a woman What did you do to impress a lady before?"

"I gave expensive gifts. I don't think I ever really cared before," Shane said, running his hand through his hair.

"That's all right for a mistress, but not for a respectable young lady."

"Well, that's not the only problem. There's Richard Fontaine.

He's in my way. I could challenge him to a duel but if I killed him, Christa would never forgive me. I really don't think she's in love with him."

"Yes, even I can see there's something between you two," Adam teased.

"That's what Charles said."

"You've discussed this with Charles?"

"Yes. He's on my side, but he wants to let Christa make up her own mind. I, on the other hand have decided to give her a push in my direction," Shane smiled.

"How, may I ask are you going to do that," Adam inquired, amused at Shane's problem.

"I'm going to buy a new horse."

"I don't see how…"

"Who do we know, who has the best horse flesh in this part of the state?"

Adam smiled, "Charles Devereax." He watched as Shane paced the short distance of the room, his left arm across his chest and his right hand rubbing his chin.

He finally spoke, "I think a change of scene is in order. I really should go see Lafitte. Come with me. We'll be back in time for the Sabastian's masked ball."

"All right. It will give us both a good diversion," Adam said, somewhat relieved and glad to have something to do. "What about your plan to buy a horse."

"We'll be back, in a few days. There'll be plenty of time. I've let my feelings for Christa take my mind off the war. It's not like me, is it?" She's the reason I decided not to go back to sea. But that was different because I knew I could be just as useful here."

Early the next morning found Shane and Adam down at the quay, where the *Mermaid* was in dry-dock. After making a few inquires they found a privateer headed for Barataria.

Richard Fontaine sat alone on the terrace of La Fleur plantation, sipping his third cup of tea. Christa and Laura were getting more fittings for their new gowns, and looking forward to the Sabastian's masked ball.

Richard had already been to a tailor himself, so now he had some time on his hands. He remembered the night at the casino. After Shane left that night Sabastian took him into his office and Richard gave him the packet he had been hiding so carefully since he left Jamaica.

"How much do you know about this?" Sabastian asked suspiciously, after looking at the message that turned out to be nothing but a playing card. A joker.

"Nothing. I was told to deliver that to you, now I have. That's it as far as I'm concerned. Well, there was a note with it, but the sea water ruined it."

"Did you read it. Do you know what it said," Sabastian demanded, a worried look on his face.

"Yes. It was something about, 'The joker is always eliminated from the game,' or something like that." Richard was surprised to see a look of comprehension replace the worried frown on Sabastian's face.

Now as he slowly sipped his tea Richard wondered what that joker meant. It was obviously some kind of code or signal. Oh well, might as well forget it, even if he figured it out, it was for Sabastian any way.

Richard turned his thoughts to a new subject. How to get Christa alone. He mistakenly thought once she was home she would be so happy she would turn to him. But she had been very elusive.

Christa let the curtain fall and decided she might as well go riding with the others instead of watching for Shane Coulter to come riding up the long drive. She had already changed into her riding clothes. Downstairs she passed the library and saw her father behind his desk and decided to chat with him for a few minutes.

She walked around his desk and kissed his cheek and hugged him.

"Oh, Daddy it's so good to be home with you at last. How I missed coming into a room and seeing you there," she said, wiping a tear away.

"My dear, I missed you too," he said, stroking her hair," but I still don't like your boldness in talking Shane Coulter into going against my wishes to bring you and your friends home. Still, 'All's well ends well,' as they say. Going riding with Jamie and the Fontaines?" he asked noting the way she was dressed.

"Yes, I guess I will," she sighed listlessly.

"Christa, my dear, in spite of your words, I sense that there's something wrong. Why don't you tell me about it. I know you're unhappy about something. Is it Shane Coulter? What happened between you two? If he tried to take advantage of your innocence I'll call him out, the rouge," Charles said, his anger raising at the thought.

"No, Daddy, it's nothing like that. If you must know, we argued just before we got home and I have been put out," she lied. "I'm over it now and I wanted to apologize, but he hasn't come around again and it wouldn't do for me to go to him."

"Well, if that's all it is, you can do it the next time you see him. He may show up. We are friends after all. There's always the masked ball next week if we don't see him before then."

"Yes, I suppose you're right," she said forcing a smile.

The next day Shane arrived home and met with several other prominent citizens.

Returning home later, he found Charles Devereax waiting for him, comfortably seated at the wrought iron table in the court yard. Harry had served him some brandy and a Cuban cigar.

"Charles," Shane smiled and extended his hand as Charles stood to greet him. I've been meaning to pay you another visit but I've been so busy since my return."

Charles Devereax straighten his shoulders and waved a hand as if to brush away what Shane had just told him. Then nailing Shane to an invisible wall with his sharp blue eyes searching Shane's face, he asked, "Why have you been avoiding me? And why wasn't I invited to Edward's lunch today? Never mind," he said, returning to his chair. I guess I already know. It's because of the Englishmen isn't it? Richard Fontaine. The enemy in my house."

"Yes. The others thought it would be easier all round if you didn't know everything."

"Then I won't be able to let something slip," Charles said sadly.

Shane shrugged, "I'm sorry."

"Tell me the truth, Shane. Is Fontaine a spy? Have I been a fool to trust him so quickly."

"All right, Charles, I'll put my cards on the table, because we're friends and if I can't trust you I can't trust anyone. I don't know if Richard Fontaine is a spy yet, but he is an Englishmen and when we met I thought he might turn us in if we didn't take him with us. As long as I'm being honest there's another reason that I don't trust Fontaine," Shane started to say, as he lit up a cigar of his own.

"Christa," Charles said with raised brows.

"Yes, Christa," Shane repeated, smiling. "Is it so obvious?"

"Of course, to everyone but the two of you," Charles answered, laughing.

"You are in love with her, aren't you, Shane?"

Shane took a deep breath and stood, turned away for a moment, then slowly turned back and looked Charles straight in the eyes. "Yes," he admitted, and was relieved. He watched for a reaction.

"I'm delighted. I was hoping you two might get together," the older man said, then jumped to his feet and slapped Shane on the back.

"We're not together yet. As I recall you weren't so pleased about my interest in your daughter two years ago. That's why you shipped her off to England, remember? And that's where she met her fiancé, Richard Fontaine, who's company she seems to prefer to mine."

"Nonsense, she's mad about you," Charles said taking his chair again.

"Did she tell you that?" Shane put his hands on the table and leaned forward, hope lighting his face.

"No, but she's been moping around the house and avoiding Richard as much as possible. Which isn't much because he follows her everywhere. He's hers for the taking if that's what she wanted.

If you love each other, you should be able to work it out. I shouldn't have interfered two years ago, but at the time I thought you were too wild and restless for her and would soon tire of domestic life and I knew it would break her heart if you went off exploring or to sea and left her behind."

Shane decided to tell Charles about his plan to visit La Fleur to buy a new horse. Charles was pleased and told Shane it was a good idea and just might work. He even invited Shane to stay for as long as it took.

That settled, Shane took a chance and told Charles about his trip to Barataria to see Jean Lafitte and brought him up to date about the privateers there. They discussed the war and the news from Washington.

The stillness of the air and the humidity along with the gray sky foretold of an approaching storm. Still the group of riders pressed on undaunted.

Christa Devereax was angry, but she was determined to hide her feelings.

"I'm sure it will be considerably cooler by the river, then we can have our picnic," she said, cheerfully. She wasn't cheerful at all. She was nervous as a cat. Shane Coulter was here and yet he might as well be back in New Orleans. He had shown up yesterday, saying he was interested in buying a horse.

First, Charles and Jamie and then Richard had all gone down to the stables for the rest of the afternoon, returning for super, all pleased at Shane's choice of a filly Charles had recently bought at auction.

"And my dear sister, I suppose that if we get caught in the storm it will merely serve to cool us off," Jamie laughed.

"Of course," she teased back. I need something to cool me off she thought. And Shane wasn't much help. Just when she had half convinced herself to marry Richard because Shane was not the kind of man who would make a good husband, he shows up being his most charming.

They rode on without further conversation. When a slight breeze rustled through the trees, Laura said, "Oh! Did you feel that?"

"Yes, it seems Christa was right and just in time, I could eat a horse."

"Why, Mr. Coulter, what a big appetite you have," Christa said in an exaggerated southern drawl that made everyone laugh.

Her anger was suddenly forgotten. How could she stay angry, when his every look made her melt.

After the things he said before when he came to dinner that night, she had done a lot of thinking and then the things Angela said caused her to think some more.

But all the thinking, and all the sleepless nights compiling a list of his faults, his arrogance, his conceit, the way he seemed to enjoy showing her how easily he could make her forget that she was a lady, had all been for nothing.

When he was near her heart took over, leaving her mind in the dust. She wanted to be with him like a child playing with fire, she might get burned, but she had to touch the flame.

They reined the horses in and dismounted under a live oak tree by the river. Christa wasn't sure how to act, with Shane being the perfect gentlemen and showing a side of himself that she hadn't seen before. He was very polite and charming and she could find no fault in him today.

He was treating her as if she was only the sister of his friend and was being very civil to Richard as well. She let herself relax a little. Had she misjudged him? Or had he lost interest in her now that they were home at last?

If Christa only knew, Shane was more interested in her than ever, although he was doing a good job of hiding it. He was watching her every move, wondering if she was more impressed with him now, and how long he could keep his distance.

A large table cloth had been laid out on the grass and they were soon feasting on cold fried chicken and cheese with fresh baked biscuits.

As they were washing it all down with glasses of wine, and making small talk, the distant thunder grew louder. A flash of lighting followed.

"Perhaps we should leave now, I just felt a sprinkle," Laura said, standing up and throwing out the remains of her wine.

"Laura's right. If we go now we can make it back before the storm hits," Jamie concurred.

A few minutes later Christa adjusted her skirts about her and sighed. She hated to use this sidesaddle, but it was looked on as very unlady like for a young woman to ride astride.

If she were alone she would be wearing her split skirt or maybe even the old pair of Jamie's outgrown trousers she had hidden in the back of her closet years ago.

It was almost as bad as being in London with guest in the house all the time. She hadn't even been to her special spot yet because she wanted to go alone. Some how she would have to find a way to sneak off by herself soon.

Her musings ended and her eyes once again were drawn to Shane as his new filly danced away skittishly, frightened by the rumbling thunder. He spoke gently to her and stroked her and when she waited as if reassured, he swung gracefully into the saddle, then looked up just in time to see Christa watching him.

A loud clap of thunder was the signal that started the group on their way and Christa didn't have time to examine why her heart was galloping as fast as her horse. They were soon turning up the long drive that led to the big house.

Old Asa, one of the Devereax's oldest slaves, and in charge of the stables for many years, was just coming around the corner of the house with his hunting dog, Sparky.

Asa stopped abruptly. Sparky sat down at his heels with his tongue hanging out and his ears hanging down. "There they are now, Sparky. I knowed they be comin' home for the storm hit's." But Sparky wasn't listening, nervous and excited and afraid of the lightning and thunder he charged baking and snapping at the horses.

Every horse but Shane's new red filly was from the La Fleur stable and was used to the dog, and ignored him, but Shane's horse was high strung and well bred, which made her fast, but not calm.

When a flash of lightning struck nearby, her eyes went wild and she reared up on hind legs throwing Shane to the ground. Stunned, he lay there temporally, his backside aching as he tried to suck air back into his lungs. "Oh my God," Christa cried as she jumped down and ran to him.

Asa, by this time had grabbed Sparky by the scruff of the neck and was scolding him. "Now you bad dog, jes look what you done. Now you git back where you belong," he said, pointing toward the back of the house. Hanging his head, and looking duly chastised, the mongrel gave one last bark and did as he was told.

Chapter 10

"Shane are you all right?" Christa knelt beside him and laid his head in her lap. Shane had only had the wind knocked out of him, but when he saw Christa bending over him full of tender concern, he decided to make the most of it.

"If I could just rest here a minute to get my breath, I guess I'll be all right," he gasped leaning weakly against her shoulder.

"Of course," she smiled, relieved that he wasn't badly hurt, and content to hold him like this.

Richard swallowed his anger at the sight of Shane cradled in Christa's arms. "Here, let me help you to your feet," he offered, bending in closer. He put his arm under Shane's and wrapped it around Shane's broad back, leaving him no choice but to give it a try.

As they rose to their feet together Christa released her hold reluctantly, then followed as Richard and Jamie escorted Shane into the house. They decided to let Shane rest in his room until dinner.

A half hour later, Jamie stuck his head in the door and asked if he could come in. Shane nodded his consent, and Jamie seated himself in a chair by the bed where Shane lay comfortably propped against at least three fluffy pillows.

"Except for a few bruises you're healthier then I am Shane, so why don't you tell me what you're up to."

"Up to, me," Shane smiled innocently.

"It's Christa, isn't it? Well, I'm warning you if you're after my sister you'd better be serious or you'll answer to me."

"I know that Jamie. Why does everyone jump to the conclusion that I don't have honorable intentions?"

"Don't you know your own reputation man? They say you chase a women until she surrenders and then drop her to look elsewhere."

"Well, why not? I'm a healthy male. What's wrong with being choosy? Some women are beautiful and appear to be charming until you get to know them." A picture of Angela Stanton flashed into Shane's mind. So beautiful, but so selfish. He wondered if she had ever thought of anyone but herself.

Making up his mind he said, "I intend to marry your sister, that is if I can convince her not to marry that Englishman. I can't get her alone to talk to her. He's always around watching every move I make. As if I was going to hurt her or something."

"Yes, I know what you mean," Jamie acknowledged. I'd like to be alone with Laura myself, he thought.

The rain finally stopped after dinner. The men had their brandy and cigars and rejoined the women in the drawing room. Christa jumped when Shane spoke to her and asked nervously, "I'm sorry what did you say?"

"I was just asking if you were planning to attend the Sabastian's masked ball next week?" And why you chose to sit over there in that arm chair instead of on the sofa near me, he thought, watching the light dance in her hair.

Was he wrong in thinking she was attracted to him? He watched her closely.

Was it what Jamie had told him earlier about his reputation. Had she heard that drivel? If she had it would explain her actions. Was she convinced he was only after her body. He had never mentioned marriage to her.

But surely she knew that he would offer marriage if she gave herself to him. Or did she?

Well there was only one way to find out. He had his doubts about her abilities as a wife, but he had no doubts at all about her ability as a lover. He had gambled before, but never for such a prize. One thing he had noticed by coming to La Fleur was that she seemed to be avoiding Richard as much as she avoided him.

"Yes," Christa was saying, "it will be one of the biggest social events of the year. I wouldn't miss it for the world. I just love to dance." Oh, why did I say that, it sounded foolish even to me. And why does he have to be so handsome. Just look at that smile, it's so hard to resist him. Why am I even trying. After all, surely he knows that my father and brother would make him marry me if I, if we…

She had to get up and turn towards the open French doors to hide the flush that rushed to her face at that thought. She used her favorite little white lace fan and tried to regain her composure.

"I'm looking forward to it myself," Shane said, coming up behind her. I could use some practice though, would you care to," then he indicated an open space nearby.

"Oh, I suppose it will be all right," Christa said, looking around and finding no help. Laura was playing a nice slow waltz, lost in her own thoughts. Richard and Jamie were deep in conversation about the coming horse races and Charles had gone to the library to talk to his overseer.

She was lost. She couldn't fight the way he was looking at her. She wanted to be in his arms. The devil, he knew the effect his attention had on her and he was taking every opportunity to let her know he knew. She tensed when he placed a hand on her slim waist and drew her closer.

They stood gazing into each others eyes. "I want to kiss you" he whispered so softly she thought she was only imagining it at first.

Laura saw them and thinking they were going to dance started to play faster and louder. Shane drew her closer, gazing hungrily at her lips. Surely he wouldn't be so bold.

"May I cut in,?" Richard asked, a challenge in his eyes.

Shane reluctantly released Christa and turned scowling to Richard. "We haven't even started yet, Fontaine."

"Oh, I am sorry, I thought you had," Richard grinned with exaggerated politeness.

Embarrassed, Christa tried to ease the tension between them by saying lightly, "I'm sure you both are much better dancers than you would have me believe. Let's just wait until the party and then we shall see."

"If anyone needs practice, it's me," Laura, broke in.

"Why don't I play while you gentleman dance with Laura." Christa was grateful for the interruption and quickly traded places with Laura at the piano, while Jamie just as quickly claimed Laura for a dance.

Shane and Richard glared at each other then moved as one to the piano, only to find that Christa had seated herself precisely in the middle of the small bench, so there was no room on either side for anyone else to sit.

With a shrug at Richard and a slight bow to Christa, Shane drifted over to the French doors. Once again Richard Fontaine had interfered.

Shane knew that she wanted him too, he had felt it and seen it in her eyes, but for some reason she was fighting it. Maybe it was just because she was a virgin and afraid of her own sexual desires. He hoped that was all. He would just have to be gentle with her.

Later that night Christa lay in her bed unable to sleep. Every time she closed her eyes she saw the way Shane looked when he was about to kiss her. She got up and tried to read, but she couldn't concentrate and kept losing her place, so she put the book down, and wondered around the room, finally sitting down at her dressing table.

She stared into the mirror and wasn't surprised to see Shane's reflections standing behind her. Why couldn't she get him out of her mind? Sighing softly she stood and turned. He pulled her into his arms and kissed her gently. It was wonderful. She didn't know if this was a dream or real, until he spoke. Then she knew he must have snuck up to her balcony and come in the French doors.

"Christa," he whispered breathlessly against her cheek. I had to see you alone. I had to hold you in my arms again and kiss you. I can't get you out of my mind I close my eyes and I see your face. I look for you everywhere I go. It's been hell not being able to touch you. Please don't send me away until I have my say."

"No, I'm glad you're here," she confessed. "I think we should talk about this, but kiss me first." She was rewarded for her bold request when he quickly did as she asked.

It was a long, slow, sweet kiss that was followed by another and then one more. Lack of air finally drew them apart and Shane smiled knowingly. "I knew you liked it. I'm glad you're finally admitting it." This time he kissed her more passionately, and pressed her closer.

She was only wearing a thin cotton night gown and her auburn hair was loose the way he liked it. That burning desire that she always evoked in him burst into a flame that he fought to control. He didn't want to frighten her again. He loosened his hold and took her face in his hands. "Christa there's something I want to ask you."

"No," she whispered hoarsely pulling away from him. She walked a few feet then turned to face him. Her voice shook with indignation when she spoke. "I won't be your mistress, how dare you even suggest such a thing." Her hope that Shane might really care for her after all had evaporated now. After the way she acted she could hardly blame him if he had no respect for her.

"And how dare you assume that I would," Shane almost shouted, but caught himself and lowered his voice.

"Well, what are we going to do then," Christa demanded. "I can't go on like this."

"Neither can I. I think you should break your engagement and marry me."

Christa froze. "Marry you?" She was confused and didn't answer right away. He hadn't mentioned love. Was she ready to settle for less?

Shane was puzzled. "What's the matter. Isn't that what you want?"

"I, yes I guess so, I..., " she hesitated.

"You guess so?" Shane was getting angry now. He was hoping for more enthusiasm. "You won't be my mistress and you don't know if you want to marry me? Then let me help you make up your mind." He quickly closed the space between them and stopped just in front of her. But before he could say any more they were interrupted by a soft knocking at the door.

"Christa, it's Laura. Is someone with you? I just got a book from down stairs and I thought I heard voices coming from your room."

"Think it over Christa, and give me your answer at the Sabastian's masked ball," Shane whispered. He kissed her forehead and turned her towards the door.

She took a deep breath and opened it a crack. "Laura, still up?"

Laura moved into the room and looked around. "I could swear I heard voices."

"I was just reading aloud," Christa lied, crossed her fingers behind her back then picked up the book she had tried to read earlier. "I do that sometimes," she explained nervously, hoping Laura believed her.

"So do I," Laura smiled and seemed to be satisfied. "Well, I'll leave you to your reading and go do mine."

After closing the door, Christa searched the room for Shane thinking he was hiding somewhere, but he was gone. She sat on the edge of her bed. The room seemed big and empty now. She felt empty.

Had she dreamed the whole thing? Had he been here? She closed her eyes and remembered the feel of his lips when he kissed her. Yes he had been here. He proposed marriage, but never mentioned love. Did it matter? If he wanted to marry her, did it matter if it was from love or desire? She loved him and perhaps he could learn to love her in time.

Tomorrow she would talk to Richard and explain that she couldn't marry him. She didn't want to hurt him, but she had no choice now.

The next morning when Christa came down to breakfast she found the others had started without her and Shane had gone back to the city. She knew he was giving her time. But she was sure now. She would have to tell Richard later because Jamie had taken him to another horse auction this morning.

There wasn't much for young unmarried women to do except primp and plan for the next party, so Christa and Laura helped the maids make the mask that they would wear to the Sabastian's ball. It would be their first official public appearance since their arrival home.

Finally after lunch Richard asked Christa to go riding and she quickly agreed. She was relieved when Laura said she had a headache and Jamie said he had to check on a mare that was ready to foal. No one believed them. It was obvious that they wanted to be alone together.

Charles was still in the city taking care of business. Shipping was slow but now and then a ship got through and the cargoes had to be checked and distributed.

The cooler breezes that felt so good told them they were approaching the river. Richard suggested they walk the horses for awhile. Christa agreed and Richard followed as she lead the way to a pretty spot.

They sat on a fallen log and watched some ducks float leisurely by. She took a deep breath and sighed, she wanted to take off her shoes and socks and if she were alone she would go for a swim, something she hadn't been able to do in two years. The water looked so inviting.

Richard moved closer to her and picked up her hand, then gazed into her eyes. "Marry me, Christa," he said simply.

The wind rustled the leaves of the big live oak tree that rose imposingly above them, and made the Spanish moss sway lazily.

Christa took a deep breathe and sighted wistfully. The time had come.

When she started to speak, he stopped her. "No, let me finish. I like it here in America. I like the people and the land. I want to be a part of it. Be my wife and together we could do anything."

Tears gathered in her eyes and she turned away trying to find the lace edged handkerchief in her reticule. Richard turned her slowly back around to face him, overwhelmed by feelings he couldn't name, tenderness, love.

He put his hand under her chin and gently wiped a tear from her cheek. "Come on now, show me that lovely smile," he coaxed. "It's Coulter isn't it?" She dabbed at her eyes and sniffled then nodded. "I don't like it, but I want you to be happy my dear."

Christa stood and walked a few feet away then turned again to face him. "I didn't want to hurt you, Richard. I do care for you, but the way I feel about Shane is different."

"You don't have to explain Christa, I love you but I'll get over it," he smiled weakly. He couldn't help the bitterness that seeped into his voice. "I guess we should get back, they'll be wondering what's happened to us."

They rode back in silence. Christa felt awful and yet she felt wonderful too. Now she was free to go to Shane, and Richard would find someone else in time.

They entered the house together and went up the stairs. When they reached Christa's door they stopped.

"Does Shane know how you feel about him?"

"In a way, I haven't actually told him, but he did ask me to marry him."

"I see and of course you said yes."

"No, I'm to give him my answer tomorrow night at the masked ball. I'm sorry, Richard. I know you only came here because of me. You're welcome to stay as long as you like, you and Laura are like part of the family."

"What I said earlier about liking it here, I meant that. I have some thinking to do, some plans to make. I need to be alone for a while. I'm going into the city." To get drunk, he added to himself.

"I hope we can still be friends," Christa offered hopefully.

Later that evening Shane decided a game of cards might be in order and where else to gamble but Dominic Sabastian's club. He might pick up some bit of useful information concerning the war.

He paused to pass a few friendly words with his host, then spotted Richard Fontaine at the bar, and made his way around and through the tables and men, stopping now and then to speak to someone of his acquaintance.

"Fontaine, I'm surprised to see you here," he lied, slapping Richard on the back. "Feel like playing a game of cards? I feel lucky tonight." Shane was still suspicious of Richard and Sabastian, so he wasn't a bit surprised to see Richard there but he was surprised to see him drunk.

Something must have happened. Christa must have broken the engagement. By this time Richard had worked himself into a lather and seeing Shane's smiling face was all it took for him to unleash some of his anger.

"I think you've won enough for one day, Coulter," he said and without further ado he drew back his fist and aimed it at that smile with all the force he could muster, which wasn't much considering the amount of liquor he had consumed. Nevertheless, it had enough force to make Shane stagger back a few steps bumping the arm of the poor fellow next to them at the bar. The man's drink splashed and spilled and dribbled all over his new clothes and his chin.

Dominic Sabastian, who had been watching Shane and expecting trouble, stepped between them quickly.

"Perhaps you had better leave, Coulter. I don't want any trouble here tonight. Can't you see he's drunk?"

Shane's anger died as quickly as it had come, and was replaced by a pang of pity.

"I'd call you out," Richard growled, flexing his sore hand, but she'd only hate me if I killed you."

"Funny, I was just going to say the same thing about you," Shane replied, discovering blood in the corner of his mouth.

As he left the club, he was elated. Christa had chosen him. He fought the urge to go to her. He could wait until the ball and let her tell him. He wanted to make her come to him this time. If she did then she would be his forever.

When Shane was gone Dominic asked," would you come with me to my office Mr. Fontaine, I'd like to talk to you in private."

Curious, Richard raised a golden eyebrow. "We've already done our business Sabastian. Oh all right, lead the way." Richard was reluctant to get involved in any thing to do with the war and suspected that was what his host was interested in talking about.

After ordering some food and coffee from the bartender they went up stairs to Sabastian's office, which was really just a hotel room with a desk instead of a bed in the center. "You better eat something, you'll feel better," Sabastian suggested, when they were seated.

Richard had some cold fried chicken and drank some of the coffee. He did feel better so he reached for one of the apple tarts, just to appease his sweet tooth. He slowly wiped his mouth and threw the napkin at the tray on the desk. "All right Sabastian, now that you've played the gracious host, what the bloody hell do you want to talk about," he asked, cynically.

Amusement danced at the corners of Dominic's mouth. "Still angry? Why don't you tell me about it?"

"Why should I? We're not friends, and I'm not too sure if I want to be."

"That's all right. I think I know. It's that Devereax girl isn't it? She turned you down because of Shane Coulter. God's gift to women. They just seem to fall at his feet," he said, spreading his hands in a sweeping gesture toward the floor. "Well, no matter. That's not what I wanted to talk about." Richard stirred restlessly, and Sabastian went on. "I have a proposition for you. You can't very well stay on at La Fleur now. How are you fixed for money? What are your plans."

"I don't want any part of spying for you if that's what you're getting at. I like it here and I plan to stay and make a life for myself. I have some income from my fathers estate, although my half brother inherited the title and lands in England. I'm not rich like you but neither am I penniless."

"Yes, I am rich. I own this hotel and ships and warehouses and land too." Sabastian stated factually. He pursed his lips thoughtfully, then got up and came round to the front of his desk directly in front of Richard, and said seriously, "I want you to come to work for me, or are you too much of a gentleman to do common labor?"

"I told you I'm not interested in spying."

"That's not what I had in mind."

"What then?"

"I'd like you to manage the casino for me. I need someone I can trust. I had a man, but I found out he couldn't be trusted so I fired him. Think it over, take your time. I hope to see you at the ball tomorrow night. I'm looking forward to meeting your sister. I hear she's lovely.

"Yes, she is." Richard had sobered some what now and decided he had better mend fences. "I apologize for my behavior earlier. You understand."

"Of course, don't give it another thought. It's a long ride back to La Fleur, why not take a room here for the night?"

"Thank you, I believe I will."

Just before he fell asleep Richard remembered Christa's last words to him. After turning him down for another man, she had the nerve to want him to still be friends.

Chapter 11

The carriages clogged the streets around the Palace Ballroom, and like a flood they poured into the long circular drive way. The elite of New Orleans society coming together for an evening.

This was not a costume ball but rather a masked ball. Each lady was a queen and each man a king for this night. Everyone wore a mask, and every mask was different. Mask of velvet and silk and leather. Most decorated in fantastic colors and jewels and feathers. Mask of papier-mâché, painted to imitate clowns and various animals.

Angela and Dominic Sabastian, resplendent in white and silver stood just inside the open double doors, and greeted their guest, while the orchestra played softly.

"Charles Devereax, I recognize you," Dominic chuckled, shaking hands vigorously. "You devil you" he added making reference to Charles mask and red satin cowl with small horns sewn on the top. The rest of his clothing, plain black and white must have given him away. Charles presented Laura and Richard, both in sapphire blue with gold mask and trimmings.

A tall figure in black and gold, Shane Coulter watched the arrivals from the balcony on the second floor and smiled as he beheld the auburn haired beauty in pink satin trimmed in black lace enter. She had stopped to greet the wife of one of her father's friends.

Christa's half mask was stiffened pink satin covered in black lace and trimmed with black and pink feathers that swept back into flaring wings. A black lace stole was draped over her shapely arms.

Shane started for the stairs and then stopped. No, he would make her seek him out.

Christa danced with her host first and wondered where Shane was. When they first arrived she thought she had seen him on the balcony, but perhaps it had been someone else after all.

She scanned the room now, as the dancers formed a square for the quadrille. The fiddles struck up the music and she was absorbed in forming the patterns and rhythms of the dance.

Her next partner was Jamie and she spotted Shane talking with their host, but by the time the dance ended he was gone. Was he deliberately avoiding her? The music was good enough and the food and champagne were adequate but she was very disappointed in the evening. She felt like Cinderella with no Prince Charming.

She nodded her head again when the chubby little Frenchman she was dancing with paused in his conversation. A Creole from one of New Orleans oldest families, his youngest daughter, Celeste, was two years older than Christa and had been married for five years, but still he seemed to think of himself as some sort of a ladies man.

She begged off when he would have claimed her again, using thirst as an excuse. Spying a liveried waiter treading his way through the colorful throng, she grabbed a glass of champagne and was looking for a place to sit, when she almost dropped her glass.

There was Shane dancing by with Angela Sabastian in his arms. He did give Christa a nod and a smile. The cad, just as if he hadn't proposed to her the other night.

It appeared to Christa that he wasn't very interested in her answer.

What she didn't know was that Shane already knew her answer, but some perverse devil on his shoulder wanted to make her jealous.

He wanted her to know, really know that she loved him. That it wasn't something that he was making her do. If he had meant to make Christa a little jealous then he had mistaken her temper. Christa was furious.

"Christa, I must say you look ravishing tonight," Richard Fontaine said from just behind her. She turned, "Richard, so do you," she grinned, perhaps I've chosen the wrong man after all, she thought. "Dance with me?"

"Don't tease me Christa," he told her seriously. "Why aren't you dancing with Shane? Now that I think about it I haven't seen you dance with him yet. What happened, I thought you and Coulter would be inseparable tonight but I doubt you've even talked to each other?"

"I don't know, but I'm going to find out right now," she said as the music ended. She followed Shane slowly, as he handed Angela back to her husband. He turned, and when he saw her he couldn't play hard to get any longer. She had danced with half the men here tonight and hadn't even smiled in his direction. Maybe Fontaine was wrong about why she broke the engagement. He had to talk to her.

The orchestra was just starting again. He reached out and pulled her into his arms before she could protest.

He could feel the tension in her rigid spine, and the anger by the way she was looking around the room and not at him. He had to get her alone so he could ask for her answer.

"You look magnificent tonight," he said, just to break the ice and because it was true.

"I'm surprised you even noticed, the way you've been avoiding me."

Christa was so angry she was shaking.

"I think we need to talk," Shane suggested and danced her out the open French doors.

The music ended and she pushed out of his embrace and took a few steps away from him. "Why are you so angry?" he asked, bewildered.

"Why have you been ignoring me all evening? Christa shouted, unable to hold her temper any longer. "First, you practically beg me to marry you and then when you think you've got me, you don't even speak to me. I'm glad I haven't told my father and Jamie about it yet."

"I was wrong to do that. I apologize. I just wanted to make you came to me, that's all. I thought that I might have been pushing you too hard."

"Why, is it so important that I come to you. Just so you can add me to your list of broken hearted females and then you can go on to someone else."

"Why do you think I would do something like that. I asked you to marry me because I love you. If I've broken a few hearts in the past then I'm sorry, but I swear that I've always had honorable intentions towards you."

"In all this time that we've known each other this is the first time you've mentioned love," Christa said incredulously.

Shane smiled, and then began to laugh, and then he threw back his head and roared. "Is that all?" Is that what's been sticking in your craw," he asked at last still smiling.

Christa clenched her lips and crossed her arms indignantly in front of her. "Well, I'm glad you find it so amusing, Mr. Coulter." She was on the verge of slapping his face when he pulled her into his arms.

"I thought you knew. Could these feelings be anything but love? Oh, I admit I didn't trust you at first. I thought you were just using me to get home. Then later I thought you might have used me to get to Richard, so I tried to stay away to give you some time."

"To give us time. Now it's your turn Christa. As long as we're being honest. You've fought me at every turn and you've never spoken of love either." He couldn't hold back any longer. He found her mouth quickly and covered it with his own.

Christa drew back her head and gazed into his longing eyes and smiled through tears of joy. "I love you, Shane Coulter."

"Then prove it. Marry me now, Christa, marry me tonight."

"Shane, there you are. We've been looking all over for you," Edward Livingston said, as he approached them with Adam Michaels by his side.

"So sorry to interrupt, but could we talk with you privately. It won't take long."

"I'll be with you in a minute," Shane said then turned back to Christa and told her. "Think about it, be sure this is what you really want, because I won't let you go. If you give yourself to me you'll have to be ready to go where I go and live where I live. That might take us a long way from La Fleur. Wait here for me. I'll be back soon."

It was a night made for love. The air was warm and the breezes balmy and who really knew how many assignations were made from behind the mask. It was nearing midnight, but the ball showed no sign of winding down. The orchestra had taken a break and couples poured out onto the terrace and into the gardens to get some air and refresh themselves.

The word had spread quickly that the handsome young Englishman, who was a guest of the Devereax's wasn't engaged to Christa, as everyone thought, but was very free and eligible.

Richard found he had the attention of some very lovely young ladies and was beginning to enjoy himself in spite of his broken heart.

Jamie had introduced him and Laura to his friends and of course Laura was getting too much attention to suit Jamie.

When the musicians began taking their places on the platform, the couples slowly began to drift back inside. Christa was wondering what was taking Shane so long.

Across the hall from the ballroom, Shane was in a meeting with Charles and Edward and some of the other prominent citizens of the city. But, of course their host wasn't invited.

"Gentlemen, I'll make this quick," Edward started. "As you know it's looking more and more like New Orleans will be the target of the British before winter. To be blunt, I'm asking for your pledges of financial support. Some of you have already spoken to me about this, but I want you to know that guns and ammunition must be stockpiled and also food and medical supplies. It doesn't look like we can expect any help from Washington." A murmur went through the group. It was the thought that they couldn't expect help from Washington that was so upsetting.

"Edward I was born in England, and as you know my brother and his family are still living there," Charles Devereax said, "but I love this country and I will pledge all that I have for her freedom."

"I think you know how I feel," Shane said. The others quickly offered their support and the meeting was adjourned.

"Getting anywhere with Christa?" Charles asked Shane as they left the room together. Shane paused. Might as well tell Charles now.

"I proposed to her."

"I know. She told me she turned Fontaine down. Well, what did she say?" Charles asked impatiently.

"We were discussing that when I was ask to join you for this meeting. If I can get her alone long enough I think I can persuade her."

Christa was happy. Shane loved her and wanted to marry her, and all was right with the world. She hummed and swayed to the music and danced down the few steps from the terrace to the garden. Then danced down the stone path. She closed her eyes and whirled and twirled. When she opened them again she saw Shane coming towards her and smiled.

She was about to speak to let him know her location when a shadowy figure stepped out of the shrubbery between them. Shane stopped abruptly. Christa screamed as the moonlight revealed the knife in the shadows upraised hand.

Shane lunged to the side and by the time he recovered his balance the shadow was gone. Christa threw herself into his arms. "Oh Shane, who was that? Why would someone try to kill you?"

"Yes it is rather hard to believe, isn't it," Shane smiled.

Christa drew back trying to see his eyes. "How can you make light of it? I couldn't bear it if he killed you."

"I'm glad you've finally come to your senses," he said, pulling her into his arms. Keeping one arm around her waist he lifted her chin and ran his thumb lightly and slowly across her lips. She closed her eyes and waited because she knew he was going to kiss her. She felt his warm breath on her cheek as he kissed her there, and then on her earlobe.

"Christa, Christa." he whispered at the corner of her mouth and at last he covered her yearning lips with his own. It was a long passionate kiss, a kiss of desire and fulfillment. Christa gave herself up fully to the feelings she had been trying to hold in check all this time. He had proposed and he loved her. She wanted to spend her life showing him how much she loved him.

Voices spilled across the terrace and washed over them like a cold wave of reality.

Shane looked around. "We better get back inside now before he tries again," he murmured breaking away from Christa's tantalizing embrace. "I've got more to live for than ever now."

"Do you think he's out there in the dark watching us, just waiting for another chance," she asked, trying to keep the fear out of her voice.

"Probably not, but I'll feel better if I know you're out of his reach."

Shane took her by the arm and led her quickly back to the house. When they neared the French doors he stopped. "Let's get married now Christa, tonight."

"But Shane, we can't. What would everyone think?"

"They'd think we were too much in love to wait for a proper wedding."

She smiled. How could she argue with such logic.

"I'm comin', I'm comin'," Harry Patch called as he hurried to answer the persistent knocking at the high wooden gate on the street side of the house. "Why, Miss Christa, what are you doing here?" His surprise was multiplied when Shane appeared behind her after paying for the hired coach.

"Close your mouth Harry," Shane laughed. "Here take these will you?" he asked, handing Harry their discarded mask. "I know it's late Harry but I'm expecting another guest," Shane said, sweeping Christa up in his arms. "He'll be here in about an hour."

Harry was a little shocked, when he realized their intentions.

"Now wait, Capt'n just where do you think you're going?" he demanded, alarmed, as Shane carried Christa to the stairway.

"It's all right, Harry," Shane reassured.

"No, it ain't," Harry said solemnly," "I'm sorry Capt'n , but I can't let you take Miss Christa to your room in the middle of the night."

"Harry, Shane has asked me to marry him and we're just going to discuss plans for our wedding," Christa explained, smiling happily into Shane's amused face.

Harry's concern faded quickly and his grizzled leathery face split into a delighted grin. "Marry, why that's wonderful. I'm so happy for you." At Shane's impatient glance, he added, "well, I'll just go now and let you two a …" he hesitated, "talk." He took a deep breath and turned towards the back of the house. He chuckled, "they're going to get married, that's wonderful."

Reaching the landing Shane took the few steps to his door, and stopped. "Well, Christa Devereax, this is it. If we cross this threshold there'll be no turning back or running away. You better be sure this if what you want, because you'll have to bare your body and your soul if you go in there."

Christa closed her eyes and swallowed, she remembered the upraised knife in the shadowy hand and the fear she felt for Shane. She opened her eyes and tightened her grip on his broad shoulders then smiled, "open the door."

The only light in the room was a small candle on the table next to the huge bed as he kicked the door closed behind them.

"Shane, I…"

"You talk to much," he whispered, and she forgot what she was going to say anyway, when he covered her mouth with a passionate kiss.

Pleasure filled her senses as she let herself taste and feel him.

He pushed his tongue past her lips and slowly explored the taste of her.

She tasted tobacco and wine, and smelled his fresh clean scent as he pulled the pins from her auburn hair and combed it with his fingers.

He quickly found the fastenings of her gown and pushed at the puffed sleeves until it slid, rustling softly to the floor. She stood mesmerized and let him untie the pretty little pink ribbon at the top of her chemise. Soon she was naked and he took a step back to admire her beauty.

Desire flared in his eyes when he scooped her up and carried her to the bed. After putting her down gently, he discarded his own clothing and lay beside her.

"You're so beautiful it takes my breath away," he said dipping his head to taste the breast nearest to him, while he cupped the other one in his hand. A deep longing for him filled her, and she ran her fingers through his thick wavy black hair. He kissed her on the mouth again, driving her mad with a hunger she had never known before.

Shane continued to fuel the fire that he had started in her soul leaving hot little kisses on her nose and cheeks. Growing bolder, she kissed him in return, on his shoulders, his cheeks, his eyes.

"I've wanted you for so long I don't know if you're real or a dream," he said, sliding his hand over her round hips and her flat belly.

"You talk to much," she whispered, then gasped, when his wandering hand found the triangle of hair between her thighs and she let him spread her legs apart.

"Oh!," she sighed as surprise mingled with pleasure when his fingers began to message and then gently probe her silken flesh. He wanted her to enjoy their joining and tried to hold back as long as he could, but when she cried out," Shane, please, I feel like I'm going to explode," he knew he would have to take her now.

"It will probably hurt at first, but only for a minute, I promise," he whispered against her cheek. He slowly entered her soft moist core and caught her cry in his mouth. She tensed up and he held still, savoring the hot feel of her and when he felt her relax a little he began moving slowly, pumping himself into her.

Christa was swept up into a sensual fire storm, and she clung to Shane and they were as one, her heart overflowed with love as well as desire. It was as if some primitive instinct was taking over her body. A tension was building and she didn't think she could take much more without flying apart into a million little pieces.

They flew up on the wings of pleasure and then exploded together and floated back down to earth again. Sated, they slept in each others arms for a while.

Shane woke up and wanted her again when he saw her sleeping beside him, but he decided to wait. Judge Stone would be here any minute and after tonight he would never have to wait again.

Christa woke in Shane's arms as he kissed her tenderly. "It'll be better next time," he told her as he stroked her hair.

"Better, how could it be any better?" she asked incredulously, smuggling closer with her head on his chest, a blush staining her cheeks.

"You're right," he smiled and kissed the end of her nose. "How could it be any better," he repeated huskily. "Come get up. We have a wedding to attend. Get dressed and join me down stairs. Judge Stone is waiting for us."

She caught his face in her hands and kissed him passionately.

"Maybe we could wait until morning to get married," he suggested, as desire stirred in him once more.

"Well, as long as the judge is already here, why don't we just get it over with." Amusement danced in her turquoise eyes. She pushed at him playfully. "You've had your fun, now you must pay the price by making an honest women out of me." Springing lightly to her feet, she went on, "just give me a few minutes. You asked me to marry you and I'm going to hold you to it. When did you get dressed?"

"Just before I woke you."

Discovering water in the pitcher on the washstand she poured some into the basin. "Now get out of here and let me clean up a bit," she ordered, conscious now of the blood on her tights.

When she heard the door open and close, she gathered up her clothing and wished she had worn something white with lace, but did it really matter what she wore, she felt radiant.

Shane would probably wait for a proper wedding if she insisted, but now that she had tasted the delightful fruit of his loving she wanted more. This was her home now. Not his house or this room, but with Shane.

Those years she had dreamed of getting married and living at La Fleur and raising her children there seemed strangely childish now. It must be true that home is where the heart is. Before her heart was at La Fleur, but now it was with Shane Coulter.

He was waiting for her at the bottom of the stairs and her heart pounded wildly. It would be nice if her father and Jamie could be here, but she knew they liked Shane and would understand. Crooking his arm, he smiled at her. "Ready?"

She took a deep breath, smiled back and nodded, slipping her hand through his arm. As they entered the living room, Harry and Adam joined them and Shane led the way through the French doors, into the courtyard.

They greeted the judge, who Christa knew as an old friend of her father's.

She blushed as she realized that they knew she had just come from Shane's bed. She lowered her lashes feeling shy and self conscious.

"Here, Miss Christa, I picked these for you," Harry said, handing her a bouquet of white magnolias.

"Oh Harry, thank you, that's so sweet of you," she said, wiping a tear from the corner of her eye.

So Christa and Shane were married in the courtyard in front of the splashing fountain, by Judge Franklin Stone, with only Harry and Adam for witnesses. They said I do at the right time, but afterwards they couldn't remember the rest of the ceremony.

The men all kissed the bride and congratulated Shane then Harry served champagne and Adam gave a toast to the newlyweds. With one arm wrapped around his lovely bride, Shane kissed her on the temple and promised to buy her a proper wedding ring as soon as possible.

Noting that Shane and Christa couldn't take their eyes off each other, Judge Stone congratulated them once more and then took his leave.

Adam and Harry found that they had things that needed attention, leaving the lovers alone in the moonlight.

Sweeping Christa up in his arms, Shane said "God, I thought they'd never leave," They laughed and Shane whirled around the room with Christa in his arms, pausing at the foot of the stairs. Their eyes locked. "Happy, Mrs. Coulter?" he asked, softly.

"Deliriously, Mr. Coulter."

He kissed her, taking her breath away and sending little shock waves radiating through her. She held him tightly, stroking the back of his head.

He carried her quickly up the stairs and kicked the door shut behind them. Letting go of her legs he let her body slide slowly down his length, while his hands slid down hers. He kissed her hotly on the lips and then trailed little light kisses down her neck. "I love the feel of your mouth when you kiss me," she told him.

"And how do you like it when I kiss you here," he asked, grazing the tops of her breast above her low cut neckline. "I love everything you do to me," she admitted breathlessly.

Shane unhooked the back of the gown, letting it slip softly to the floor. She stood in her chemise before him.

"You can sleep all day tomorrow if you like but this is our wedding night Mrs. Coulter and you have a lot to learn. I'm a harsh teacher and I intend to make you repeat your lessons over and over and over," his voice faded away as Christa stepped out of the chemise, and proceeded to help him out of his coat.

The next thing she knew he carried her back to the bed and laid her there, and he finished his own disrobing. After putting out the light, he lay down beside her. Moonbeams streamed in through the open French doors. Shane drew her into his arms and took her eager lips, fondling and feeling her everywhere. He sucked and played with her full firm breast and ran his hands down the curve of her waist and hips.

He had planned to take a long time with her this time but felt his body hardening with desire and knew he couldn't hold back much longer. When she felt his hand on her thigh she spread her legs for him.

Moving back on this hunches he raised her knees up and ducked his head between them, as his fingers began to probe and play and massage her, Christa knew that her private parts were no longer hers alone, but she didn't mind sharing.

Just when she thought she could stand no more, as she twisted and moaned and clutched the covers, she felt his tongue take the place of his fingers and she cried out his name.

That passionate sound shattered his restraint and he quickly mounted her, sliding his throbbing manhood into her soft, moist core. They soared up over a rainbow of colors and landed on a star that exploded beneath them, then floated back slowly down clinging to each other.

Christa had never been so happy or fulfilled, never dreamed anything could be so exciting and wonderful. Shane smiled, he had never been so satisfied after having sex before and he knew it was love that made the difference. "You're mine now, Christa, all mine," he whispered, rolling off her a little, as sleep over took them.

Chapter 12

The sun was high in the sky the next morning when Abby discovered her mistress hadn't slept in her bed and went to inform Charles Devereax, who was seated at the head of the table in the dining room, having a late breakfast with his English guest.

"Not in her room," he repeated then shrugged and sipped his coffee. "Probably got up early and went for a ride, before it gets to hot," he reasoned. Then Abby told him that she was sure Christa hadn't returned after leaving for the Sabastian's masked ball the previous night.

Alarmed, Charles jumped up, knocking over his chair. "Nonsense, where could she be, she came home with you didn't she?" he asked his son. Jamie looked guiltily at Laura.

"No," he answered. At Charles scowl, he explained. "Well, you see Laura had a headache," he lied, "and I escorted her home." When we left Christa was with Shane."

"Perhaps you should check with Shane Coulter," Richard suggested.

"What are you insinuating?" Charles demanded turning to Richard.

"Just that I have reason to believe that she may have spent the night with Shane."

Charles had a hard time not showing his delight at this bit of news, but managed to pretend great indignation. "Well, we'll just see about this," he barked. Then ordered a carriage to be brought around.

The noise of vendors pushing their carts and shouting their wares in the streets woke Shane. He smiled at the sight of Christa sleeping peacefully beside him.

This late July morning promised to be another hot humid day. Everything was the same and yet it was forever changed. He had to think of someone else beside himself and make his plans to include her from now on. It seemed an easy task at the moment.

His stomach growled and he realized he had another kind of hunger. He got up and opened the door a crack, he knew Harry wouldn't be far away. Sure enough he saw him going about his chores below. He called down and asked Harry to bring up croissants and coffee and water for baths. Still naked he slipped back in bed and gathered Christa into his arms. She snuggled closer and kissed his hairy chest. "I'm glad you ordered food, I don't think I've ever been so hungry," she murmured sleepily.

"My dear Mrs. Coulter, after we eat and make ourselves presentable, I'm going to take you shopping. The first item of course will be a wedding ring," he said, kissing her left hand. "I'm not the richest man in the world but I'm rich enough to keep you in the fashion to which you are accustomed." Before he could say anymore, there was a great commotion below with loud voices and footsteps on the stairs. Christa sat up. "Oh, Shane, it's my father."

"Sounds like Jamie and Richard as well," Shane smiled.

Harry Patch was heard to say, "wait, you can't," but it was too late. Jamie threw open the door, just as Shane and Christa drew the covers around themselves. Christa turned scarlet but Shane seemed very amused.

"Good morning, gentlemen. What brings you visiting so early," he inquired, feeling very contented and smug because he knew he had done the right thing.

Richard Fontaine wanted to beat that smug look off Shane's face when he saw Christa, her creamy shoulders bare and her hair all disheveled. He thought she had never looked more beautiful and she had never been more out of his reach.

"Christa, how could you?" Jamie asked, astonished. Charles looked almost as amused as Shane. Then Adam Michaels appeared behind them, holding a pistol. Everyone turned towards him when he spoke. "Gentlemen, won't you join me downstairs for coffee, so Mr. and Mrs. Coulter can get dressed."

"Mr. and Mrs. Coulter," Charles repeated, no longer able to hold back a smile, as he turned to the bed. "Shane, I knew you'd do the honorable thing. We'll wait for you down stairs, we want to hear all about it."

When they came down a while later, Charles gave Christa a big bear hug and kissed her cheek, took Shane's hand and shook it vigorously, then beamed, "welcome to the family my boy."

He turned back to Christa and said, "No need to ask, I can see you're happy. Richard is gone, he ask me to give you his best wishes, so we can talk freely. Why have you done this?"

Christa shot Shane a helpless look. "What do you mean? We're very much in love and we wanted to be together, that's all." Suddenly she realized what he meant and flushed. Coming to her rescue, Shane put his arm around her shoulders and smiled down at her. "It was to prevent such an occurrence that we married so hurriedly, but I suppose people will talk anyway."

"Well let them," Charles said, dismissing the thought with a wave of his hand. "It'll only last for a few weeks and then something new will come along for them to chew on."

"Yes of course, you're right Daddy," Christa smiled weakly. She hadn't really thought about the fact that everyone would think she was with child when she agreed to this hasty marriage, but it was done now so she would let the chips fall.

They had a long visit with Charles and Jamie and promised to visit La Fleur often. The city was so hot in the summer and then there was always the fear of the fevers that made a periodic sweep, leaving many dead in their wake.

The cooler air of the country, it was agreed, was much better for ones health. Most people retreated to their plantations as much as possible, only those with business or some important engagement ventured into the city.

"Perhaps a visit would be all right, but I would like to be alone with my wife first. I was thinking of a short trip. Just the two of us, you understand."

"Of course, and when you return I intend to give a big reception for you, after all I missed the wedding," Charles smiled happily.

He was a burly man, still attractive but his once blond hair had faded to a silver brown and there were small lines around his eyes, Christa noticed as she watched him. She was surprised that he seemed pleased with her marriage to Shane, after all two years ago he sent her to England to avoid it. Before he left he offered to see that the wedding was announced in the papers.

Richard Fontaine had made his way back to La Fleur, where Laura waited anxiously.

"Tell me what's happened," she said, fear in her voice.

"It's all right Laura," he soothed, taking her in his arms.

"They got married last night, that's all."

"Married! Oh, I'm so relieved," she said putting her hand to her breast. "I was afraid someone might get killed."

Richard released her and poured himself a drink from the side table, threw himself into a chair and snapped, "I'd like to kill Shane Coulter. I can still see that smug look on his face."

"Richard, please don't do any thing rash," Laura pleaded.

"Pack your things Laura. We can't stay here now after this," he said, pushing to his feet.

An hour later found them in the hall, while a servant loaded their valises into a carriage.

"We'll send for the rest of our things when we're settled," Richard said.

"Wait Richard, I'd like to say good-bye to Jamie."

"Well, just leave him a note, I'm sure he'll understand."

"Dominic Sabastian offered me a job the other night, I've decided to take it."

"A job. What kind of job?"

"He wants me to manage his gambling casino. Gambling's something I'm pretty good at, you know that. Come on, the carriage is waiting-"

Laura was reluctant to leave, she was sure Jamie cared for her and she wanted a chance to explore her own feelings-

The newlyweds spent the day shopping. Their first stop was the jewelers where they ordered a ring for Christa. Shane insisted on buying his bride more new clothes. People stared at them everywhere they went. They stared at each other all through the supper Harry served them, and didn't even notice Adam's absence. Again Shane carried Christa across the threshold of his room.

Harry prepared a bath for them and they bathed together. Shane washed Christa's hair and they played in the tub like children. When the water cooled and their blood got hotter they dried each other off with large towels.

Christa slipped away for a moment and started to put on the beautiful silk night gown she had purchased for just such an occasion but when Shane saw what she was doing he grabbed it. "Very pretty," he said, "but I don't think you'll need it tonight Mrs. Coulter."

"But darling, I just wanted to look nice for you," she protested sweetly.

"Believe me, nothing could make you look better than you do right now," he grinned, slowly advancing on her. She pretended fright and backed away from him until her bare legs touched the side of the bed, then she fell back laughing and held out her arms to him.

The sight of her laying there eagerly waiting for him, both thrilled and inflamed him. He bent over her and gathered her into his arms, pressing her lush silken body to his chest.

Christa wrapped her arms around his broad back and savored his hardness. She closed her eyes and let him slide his hands down her back to rub and cup her firm buttocks and she could feel his swollen manhood pressing against her.

He ran his hand down her body slowly feeling each breast and rubbing her flat belly. She moaned in anticipation, knowing what delights lay ahead.

Shane's roaming hand found the pleasure spot between her parted thighs and she sucked in her breath as his probing fingers sent her into a frenzy of rapture.

Bowing his head over her he began to gently lick and suck her throbbing nipples, and as his hand was working it's magic between her legs, his mouth covered hers and he kissed her passionately.

Shane knew she was more than ready as he eased himself slowly into her, then stopped for a moment, just content to feel her hot moist flesh as it received him. Christa couldn't seem to get enough of him and her hands ran over his hard muscled shoulders and back and then down to his buttocks.

When he pumped himself deeper into her, she rocked her hips up to meet his downward thrust. Shane felt the growing tension in his loins and knew that he was about to erupt like a volcano and spill his seed inside her.

Christa soared up on a rainbow. Her release came in a burst of fire that sent flames of ecstasy radiating through her. When she felt Shane's body shuddering at the same time, her joy was complete.

Before dawn the next morning Shane woke Christa. "Come on sleepy head, get up and put these on," he grinned down at her. When she moaned in protest and rolled over he sat on the edge of the bed and rolled her back again then lifted her to a sitting position with his arms around her. She snuggled against his chest like a trusting child in it's mother's arms, and his heart swelled with love.

He wanted to protect her and take care of her, but there was so much she didn't know and he had to teach her some of them if they were to have a life together. He stroked her hair and then shook her until she protested again.

"Why do we have to get up so early. It's the middle of the night,"

"It's time for your initiation, Mrs. Coulter."

Thinking he was referring to their love making she teased, "why Mr. Coulter, what an insatiable appetite you have."

"Yes, but that's not what I want right now," he told her, nuzzling her neck.

"Then what?" she asked, finally starting to come to life.

"We're going on a little trip."

"And where are we going may I ask?"

"To Paradise. Here, now that you're awake, wear these," he said, letting her go and handing her some clothes that he had laid on the foot of the bed.

"But I don't understand I thought that's where we've been. These are the clothes I wore aboard the Falcon. You saved them?"

"Not on purpose. Somehow they got mixed in with my things, and as you know when Captain Perkins rescued us from the island, there wasn't time to sort through anything. "I just grabbed my valise and …

"But you must have known, Shane," she cut in, her eyes searching his face.

"All right you caught me," he shrugged, and took her face in his hands. "I kept them, because they made me feel closer to you. I was thrilled when you came aboard the Falcon pretending to be the new cook's helper and I wanted to keep you with me from the first. I almost did if you remember, but then we were interrupted and I knew if I wanted you I'd have to marry you first."

"That's why I tried to stay away from you. I wanted to wait until we got home and then court you properly. But when we got to Jamaica and Richard Fontaine acted like you belonged to him, I got suspicious and jealous and," he paused and dropped his gaze.

"And what?"

"Well," he sighed, "to tell you the truth, I didn't know if you would be a good wife for me. Now don't be hurt. It's just that you're used to being waited on and although I have money enough for servants there are times when I like to go see what's on the other side of a mountain and how could I ever leave you behind. So now that we're married I'm taking you to see how the other half lives.

"That's why I resisted you for so long. I was afraid that even if you married me, after a while you'd get restless and leave me behind."

"Christa, what about La Fleur?"

"Remember when you came to supper there and you asked me what I'd do if the man I married wanted to take me away. I wondered if you were talking about yourself. It made me do a lot of thinking and I know if home is where the heart is, then my home is with you."

"I want to make a home for us where ever we go. I know now, that's why I loved La Fleur, it was because I had all those good memories of my childhood. Of my mother and father and Jamie. It wasn't the place itself. It was all the people that I loved, and now I love you, and we're going to make our own memories, with children of our own."

"I was hoping you'd feel that way, Mrs. Coulter," Shane grinned, kissing her soundly.

Without another word, Christa washed and dressed, then packed a few things in a cloth bag Shane had provided before he left.

Shane met her at the bottom of the stairs a few minutes later, and led her to the back of the house where he had three horses waiting. One was a pack animal. He took her bag and attached it to the mound of other things. They said good by to Harry, who Christa guessed, had helped Shane with the horses, then they were on their way.

They rode in silence through the still sleeping city, and then turned onto a dirt road running northward from New Orleans. It was a little after daylight when Shane turned off the road and stopped in a small clearing.

"I'm starving," he said, "so I thought you must be hungry too. See if you can find the food Harry packed, and I'll start a fire." This done, Shane patiently showed Christa how to cut strips of bacon and start them frying. He measured coffee and set the pot on the fire.

"Now all we have to do is wait," he smiled, laying against a tree with his long legs stretched out before him. Christa was hunched over the fire, feeling terrible inadequate.

How had she lived so long and not learned to do these things. Of course she had learned to cook fish and make some stew from Harry when they were on the island, and on the *Falcon*, but she had merely peeled some potatoes and a few carrots. Harry had done the bulk of the work. Now she wished she had paid more attention.

She couldn't help sneak a glance at Shane. He looked so at home here, dressed in buckskins with a pistol tucked into his wide leather belt and a long hunting knife in a scabbard tied with thongs to his thigh. He had laid his hat on the grass beside him, and closed his eyes, but now he sniffed and came over beside her. "Time to turn it over love," he said, taking the fork from her gently.

"Oh. How did you know. I was watching it and I didn't know."

"It just takes a little experience, you'll learn," Shane told her patiently. He kissed her cheek and put an arm around her. "It's just like any thing else. It just takes practice. I don't expect you to cook our every meal you know. It's just good to be prepared for anything. To be able to take care of yourself just in case you should get caught without a servant."

Shane felt Christa stiffen and then she stood and walked away from him. After setting the bacon on a stone away from the fire he went to her.

"Dam, Christa I'm sorry, I didn't mean that the way it sounded," he said, reaching out to pull her back against his chest.

"Is that really what you think of me. That I'm just a useless, shallow female who can't even cook bacon, let alone take care of myself? If that's what you think then why did you marry me?" She sighed and made an effort to swallow the lump in her throat.

Shane turned her around in his arms, and cursed himself when he saw the tears in her beautiful eyes. Wiping one tear away with his thumb, he smiled. "Well maybe you can't cook bacon, but you're certainly not useless. I married you because you took my heart from me and the only way I can be whole is with you."

"Oh, Shane, me too," she sniffed and wiped her own tears.

"Now let's eat, before I ravish you right here on the ground in broad daylight."

Feeling better now, Christa looked around and pretended to be frightened. "Goodness, and no one around to save me," she said, with a twinkle in her eyes.

"Here," Shane grinned, handing her a tin plate with bacon and a cold biscuit. "If we hurry we can still be there before night fall."

"Yes, you said you were taking me to Paradise. Is that a town?"

"No. It's the name of the farm where my grandmother lives."

Christa stopped chewing, although the bacon was delicious. "Your grandmother… I didn't know. I mean you never mentioned her before."

"I think you'll like her."

But will she like me, Christa silently wondered.

They were soon on their way again and she forgot to be anxious about meeting Shane's grandmother as they rode through the lush green country side. When they reached a meandering stream they stopped again and had a quick lunch of cold biscuits, left over from their breakfast, but this time they added cheese and apples.

Christa wasn't used to riding for any great distances and was nearly exhausted by the time Shane stopped ahead of her and turned back to tell her they were almost there. Her bottom was getting sore and she longed for a hot meal and a bath.

So much had happened to her in the last few days. It was less than a week ago that Shane had proposed and now they were married and she would have to change. Would Shane still want her if she became more independent and could take care of herself? Would she still want him? Would things have been any different if they had courted like other couples? If they had taken things slower. Well, she knew that she loved him and somehow that would have to be enough.

To the west, above a low ridge the sinking sun was painting the sky in shades of coral. They came out of the woods into a clearing and she saw the cabin. Smoke curled out of the chimney in their direction as if beckoning them.

The cabin sat in the middle of the large clearing. On the right side and a little to the back was a grove of fruit trees on the other side was a garden.

Chickens pecked and scratched in front of the barn, and a cow mooed somewhere in the distance.

When they got closer, Christa could make out the figure of a woman stepping out onto the porch. Then a man came from the back yard and joined her, putting his arm around her waist.

"Oh! Shane, it is you," the woman beamed, throwing herself at him, as he dismounted. He caught her in a big bear hug and lifted her off the ground then set her on her feet. "How's my best girl," he asked cupping her face with his hands.

"Perfect, now that you're here. But am I still your best girl?" she asked, rolling her eyes towards Christa, who had climbed down from her horse and come to stand beside Shane.

Keeping one arm around her he pulled Christa close with the other and grinned, "this is my other best girl, my wife Christa."

Without hesitation Christa was welcomed when she was introduced to Shane's grandmother, Maude Taylor, and her second husband Sam.

Christa discovered a different kind of life that she enjoyed. There was a friendly lack of formality, she couldn't help comparing to the rigidity of manners her aunt Harriet had insisted on in England.

Although the cabin was made of logs and the furniture was too, there was a cozy warmth that she had never felt before, except when her mother was still alive.

Each day she learned something new about Shane and his childhood and about his mother and father and of course, his grandmother, who was an amazing woman. She was a Cherokee, and had married an Englishman, Shane's grandfather at the age of sixteen. Over sixty now she was still a beautiful woman.

She ushered them inside, while Sam took care of the horses. "I've got a pie in the oven, Shane," she said, bending to open the oven door for a peek inside. Satisfied, she continued, "now you just take your pretty little wife and sit over there on the sofa. Sam made it just for company and I made the cushions myself," she explained to Christa.

"Sam why don't you take their things into Shane's room," she said when she spotted her husband coming thru the door.

"My goodness, just listen to me carry on. You two probably want to freshen up a little before supper. Shane, honey, show Christa where things are."

It was sometime later when the newlyweds were finally alone in the room that was built and kept ready just for Shane's visits.

"I love your grandmother, darling, but she's not what I expected."

"Oh, and what was that? A squaw in a buckskin dress living in a tepee."

"I'm sorry, but yes, I guess that's what I had in mind, but I'm sure I would have loved her anyway."

"It's all right as long as you love me," he said, taking off his shirt and tossing it in the general direction of the chair in the corner.

"You know I do," she smiled, slipping out of her trousers.

"Then come over here and prove it,"

She untied the black ribbon that held her hair in a queue and shook her head then started unbuttoning her shirt as she slowly moved towards him. She reached him just as she finished the last button.

He reached out and gently put his hands on her bare shoulder and pulled her against his bare chest.

They gazed into each others eyes and when his eyes dropped to her mouth she knew he was going to kiss her and her heart skipped a beat and then pounded with joy when he did.

Without stopping the kiss, he carried her to the bed. "The more I have you the more I want you," he whispered.

Chapter 13

Ten days later they were visiting La Fleur plantation. The hot August sun was promising another scorching day as Christa sat in the big bath tub in her own room. She couldn't help compare it to the small tub at Paradise.

It was kept in a small shed that leaned up against the back of the cabin, and was also used to wash clothes. It was round and wooden, and only big enough to allow for sitting with your knees drawn up to your chest.

The sound of someone moving about the room brought her mind back to the present. It was her maid Abby, who was arranging her clothes on the bed.

"All done, Miss Christa? I brought you some fresh towels," Abby said handing one to her.

With Abby's help she was soon dressed with her hair arranged attractively up in the back. Her gown was an off white muslin trimmed with lace and green ribbons. The low round neckline emphasized her full breast and she hoped it wasn't too daring as she admired the woman in the mirror.

"If I don't get down stairs soon they'll probably leave without me," Christa said, after waiting patiently for Abbey to put green and white ribbons in her hair.

She found Shane seated on the wide veranda at the front of the house with Charles and Jamie. He jumped to his feet and rushed to greet her, then held her at arms length and she could see the appreciation in his eyes.

"Mrs. Coulter, I believe you get more beautiful every day."

"Why Mr. Coulter, I do believe that marriage agrees with me," she answered with a slow drawl and lowered lashes. Then she opened her dainty parasol, lay it over her shoulder, and took a step forward. "Gentlemen, we all have appointments in the city, shall we go?"

Later Christa stood on a small platform in the back room of Madame Elaine's. The dressmaker was fitting her for the new gowns that Shane insisted on buying her.

When they heard the bell at the front door, Elaine took the pins from her mouth, and said, "Stay here and don't move, I'll be right back."

Christa had expected there would be talk about her hasty marriage, but it was embarrassing to overhear it first hand.

"Oh, Elaine I'm so excited," she heard the new arrival say. "Have you heard the latest news about that Devereax girl. The one who just returned from England. Well, my dear, of course everyone thought she would probably marry that handsome young Englishman she brought home with her, but she ups and marries that dashing rogue, Shane Coulter."

"And now," the gossip went on without pausing for air, "as if that weren't enough Charles Devereax is giving a reception for them at La Fleur. Now don't that beat all."

The speaker finally stopped, realizing Elaine was trying to silence her. "Oh, you have someone in the back room don't you, dear? Well, I'll just look over some of that lovely blue silk material. I want a new gown for that reception. What do you think," the lady asked, holding up the pale silk next to her face.

Trying to get rid of this customer as soon as possible, Elaine exclaimed, "Oh yes, I have your measurements but I can't get started today."

"Why don't you take these pattern books with you now and then stop in tomorrow morning and tell me the one you want."

Elaine pushed open the heavy curtain that served as a partition between the fitting room and the front of the store and apologized.

"I'm sorry you had to hear that, Miss, Devereax, a, er, that is, Mrs. Coulter. That Tillie Farnsworth is the biggest gossip in New Orleans. I'll bet she's on her way to her sister's house right now to spread this news."

"It's all right, Elaine," Christa sighed, "I expected something like this."

As Christa was leaving a while later, she bumped into Laura Sims.

"Oh, Laura, it's so good to see you," she beamed, giving her friend a hug.

"So you married Shane. I'm not surprised. I love my brother but I knew when I saw the way you looked at Shane that you were in love with him, not Richard," Laura admitted, with a knowing smile.

"Come with me for some coffee or tea or something, so we can talk, there's a place just down the street," Christa coaxed.

They were comfortably seated in the nice little French café, and had ordered tea and pastries, when Christa started the conversation.

"Laura, I hope we can still be friends. Richard will find someone else in time. I really didn't want to hurt him."

"I'm sure you didn't and of course we can still be friends," Laura assured her.

"Then you'll come to our reception won't you?" Christa pleaded hopefully.

"Oh, Christa, I don't know," Laura said, shaking her head thoughtfully.

Personally, I'd like to, but it might hurt Richard all the more. I don't want him to feel I've betrayed him." Laura smiled at her. "You must have done the right thing, you look positively radiant."

Christa lowered her lashes and her face turned pink. "Yes, I never dreamed how wonderful it could be to be married to someone you love."

Laura thought of Jamie when Christa said those things and asked, "How is Jamie?" Then blushing she added, "and your father."

Christa stopped stirring her tea when she heard the wistful note in Laura's voice as she said Jamie's name.

"Oh, they're doing fine," she answered, casually. "Happy for us of course. My father told me he always liked Shane and was glad we got together, and was sorry he interfered two years ago."

Christa watched Laura closely as she spoke. She had a hunch there was some attraction between her brother and Laura, so taking a chance she said, "Jamie seems a little lost since you left. I think he was beginning to care for you."

"Do you, really?" I did too, but I haven't seen him since the masked ball. He was certainly very attentive that night. Perhaps he's lost interest."

"If you come to my reception, you could find out."

They looked at each other and smiled knowingly.

"Well, I was on my way to the dress makers anyway. It's so good to be able to wear something besides black. I was beginning to hate it.

My father died shortly after my wedding and then I lost my husband so it seems like I've been wearing it forever." When she saw the sympathy in Christa's eyes, she went on, "Oh, don't feel sorry for me. I was never that close to my father like you are and my marriage wasn't like yours either."

She finished her tea, then continued. "We had some feeling for each other, but my husband was very handsome and he enjoyed having women chasing after him. I thought that when he got older he might settle down a bit and be content with me, but I'll never know now."

Christa reached out and put her hand over Laura's when she saw tears in the corners of her eyes. Laura sniffed and dug for the handkerchief in her reticule. "There I'm alright now," she said, forcing a bright smile. "Come back with me to Elaine's and help me pick some material."

"All right. I saw some lovely pink satin when I was there that would look marvelous on you."

They returned to Elaine's and had picked out the material and a pattern when Christa saw the clock on the high shelf at the back of the store.

"Laura, I've got to go now. Shane will wonder what's happened to me but it was so good to see you today. We're living in his town house when we're not at La Fleur. Let's get together often."

Laura arrived at the small town house that Richard had taken for them just in time to catch Richard, who was getting ready to leave, checking his appearance in the hall mirror.

She studied him for a moment then moved to stand behind him. "My don't you look handsome brother dear." She removed her perky bonnet. "I know, you've gotten a tan."

"Have I?" Richard asked as if he hadn't noticed, when if the truth be known he had worked at it. He had ridden out almost every day to take a swim in the nude, and then lay out on the grassy river bank to dry in the sun.

"Yes, it brings out the blue of your eyes, much more attractive than the pale face that's in fashion for men now."

"Trying to butter me up little sister? It's not like you to give out such great compliments." By the way, where have you been? I was beginning to worry that something had happened to you."

"I have something to talk to you about," she told him.

"Is everything all right?" he lead the way back into the sitting room. I think I'll have a glass of wine before I leave. Care to join me?" When she nodded yes, he filled two glasses and handed one to her. "Let's take them out to the balcony, shall we?"

After they were seated comfortably and each had taken a sip, Richard prodded, "We'll what did you want to talk about?"

"Richard, the reason I was late today was because I ran into Christa at the dressmakers. We had tea and talked."

A look of sadness came over Richard's face at the mention of Christa's name. He turned away as if to observe the passers-by and the vendors below them in the street. "I see, and how is she?"

"She looked very happy, of course." Laura didn't want to hurt him, but she knew he would have to except it.

"Of course," he said, absently. "If that's all I should be going," His voice was tight and his face a blank as he rose from his chair.

"No. wait, that's not all." You must have heard that Charles is giving them a wedding reception. Christa wants us to come. She really didn't want to hurt you, you know that."

He took a deep breath, and let it out slowly, then softened. "Yes, I know, but it hurts anyhow. You want to go don't you?"

"Yes, yes I do" she said defiantly, then got up and walked to the French doors and turned again to face him. "I want to have some fun. I want to flirt, Richard. For God's sake, I'm only twenty-two.

"Oh!" She put her hands up in front of her face in prayer fashion. "I'm so sorry. I guess I'm being selfish. It won't be fun for you." She couldn't keep the disappointment from her voice.

Richard had never really given much thought to whether Laura was happy or not, but now that his own heart had been broken he could feel her frustration.

"No, Laura, you're right if we're going to stay in New Orleans, then I have to face Mr. and Mrs. Shane Coulter sooner or later. We'll go." He smiled when she stood up, and led her back inside. "It'll be all right," He said. Then kissed her cheek and left.

The house he had rented for them was small but he had hired servants and it was in a good neighborhood. He was doing well as the new manager of Domino's and although he had been raised to believe that a gentleman didn't work for a living, life had taught him a different lesson.

He found he would rather pay his bills then always be one step a head of his creditors. One of the things he liked most about America was that people seemed to respect honest work. Oh, yes, they had a sort of snobbery in some circles, but Richard decided that he wanted to make a place for himself here.

As for the war, although he admired the American will power, England had the man power and would no doubt win in the end. Before long he looked up and realized that with his mind occupied he had forgotten to hail a hack and had walked all the way to Domino's.

Christa and Shane had an early supper with Adam and Harry at their townhouse, and they sipped wine in the blue flagstone court yard and watched the setting sun.

After a few minutes of silence, she realized they were waiting for her to leave them.

"Well I suppose I could go and admire the new bonnet I bought today. If you'll excuse me, gentlemen. I'll go and let you men talk about the war and smoke your cigars," she said, annoyed.

The men all stood as if giving their consent when she rose gracefully to her feet, and arranged her skirts. She resented this custom of the women leaving after the meal to let the men talk. She wanted to know what was going on the she intended to find out.

When she was gone Harry brought out Shane's box of good Cuban cigars and then poured more wine. No one spoke at first. Shane felt a peace and contentment that he had never known.

He had everything a man could want, he thought gratefully. He loved Christa more with each passing day and no one could ask for better friends than the two men sitting here with him.

The only fly in the ointment was the war. Though it seemed far away at the moment. "I saw Edward today," he reported after blowing a smoke ring.

They knew he spoke of Edward Livingston, a prominent lawyer and one of the city's leading citizens, and also a friend of both Jean Lafitte and governor Claiborne.

"Of course, Charles and some of the others were there. We discussed the possibility of the British attacking us, and what kind of defense we might provide."

"We haven't got enough ships in our small navy to withstand an all out naval attack, but with the privateers we might hold them off for a while.

"Our main chance is still the peace talks."

"I may have to go to Washington and find out what's going on in that quarter. Nothing definite was decided."

"We're to keep an eye on all the British born citizens. There's talk that someone must be giving or selling information about the American navy and privateers. Several ships have been taken lately almost as if the British knew their location in advance."

"But Shane, Charles Devereax was born in England and I'd trust him with my life."

"Yes Adam, I know, so would I. It's people like Richard Fontaine that need to be watched. One more thing. The English are stirring up the Indians and the slaves every chance they get.

It's like sitting on a powder keg with a lit fuse and not knowing where or how long the fuse is," Shane concluded. "Any questions?" he asked, raising black eye brows.

"Only one Shane," Adam said as he studied the tip of his cigar. "Why wasn't Lafitte at the meeting? We'll need his help if we are attacked."

"Yes, I know my friend, but some of the others don't trust him," Shane said, honestly.

"And we all know that those others are Governor Claiborne, and some of his friends, don't we?'

"Yes, Harry, but it can't be helped. We all know where Lafitte stands and Livingston trust him and Charles Devereax and most of the other plantation owners do too," Shane answered.

"Without the privateers many a household would be without cigars and wine and brandy not to mention all the other goods they provide," Adam added.

"I was thinking of taking another ship before my marriage, but now it's out of the question," Shane confided.

"All we can do is keep our eyes open and hope for the best. Speaking of marriage, I believe I'll go and see what my bride is up to. Good night, my friends. I'll see you in the morning."

Christa rushed up the stairs and was sitting at her dressing table bushing her hair by the time Shane came in. He closed the door and leaned against it, frankly admiring her.

He knew she had listened to his conversation with his men. When he stood up to leave the courtyard he had glimpsed a part of her white dress as she moved away from the drapes that covered the open French doors.

He really didn't mind that she wanted to be included, but it was for her own protection. It was better if she didn't know every thing and besides what she didn't know she couldn't worry about.

He smiled when she put down the brush, got up and came slowly towards him with outstretched arms. Her gown was white and had a panel of black lace trimmed with turquoise rosettes down the front. He liked it on her. But he liked what was under it even more.

Shane had taken his coat and neck cloth off on his way up the stairs and now he tossed them into a chair. His white shirt was open half way down and as she came into his arms she put her hand on his firm, hairy chest and kissed him there. He cupped her chin, bent his head and captured her lips. "Still dressed, Mrs. Coulter? Let me help you out of this lovely gown."

She turned and lifted her hair to give him access to the tiny buttons, which he quickly undid. When he gave the gown a tug, it slid impotently to the floor. He slowly caressed her satin skin, as she turned and put her arms around his neck.

He lifted her into the air and swung her around. They laughed happily.

He loosened his hold letting her slip back down to the floor. "Mrs. Coulter did I ever tell you I can never seem to get enough of you," he whispered.

"I'm glad, because I feel the same way about you," she said beginning to kiss and lick his bare chest again. He moaned feeling the now familiar stirring in his loins. Pulling her close his hands caressed her back and her round bottom.

"Come my dear, although you're a quick learner, I think you should practice your lessons as much as possible," he said, leading her to the bed. Christa lay back, and waited as he discarded the rest of his clothing and crawled up beside her.

"I wonder how I lived so long without you," she murmured, just before he started his tender assault on her senses and she forgot all about words. They rode the crest of a passionate wave until it threw them on the shore of sublime contentment that only lovers know, then slept in each others arms.

The next day they visited La Fleur and Charles chatted happily about the reception and how the preparations were going.

Christa told them about seeing Laura and the talk they had. Everyone agreed that Christa had done the right thing by extending the invitation and hoped that they would come. Jamie was especially pleased. He wanted to see Laura, but was afraid Richard might be offended.

Later that Afternoon Christa rode ahead of Shane leading him through some woods and high ground and finally down to the river.

She stopped just in front of him and he discovered they were in a secluded grove with a small water fall that cascaded down into a wide pool below.

They dismounted in the shade of a large live oak tree dripping with Spanish moss. She took his hand and led him to the edge of the water. "This is my favorite place. I used to come here as a little girl with my mother and father and sometimes Jamie, if he wasn't in school or something," she told him. "Will you help me with my gown?"

"Nothing I'd rather do, darling. Helping you out of your clothes is something I look forward to," he said, fumbling with her buttons again.

Just as Shane was about to reach for her she waded into the cool inviting water still in her chemise. She shed that garment quickly and dove into the deeper blue-green center of the pool.

Losing no more time Shane pulled off his own clothing and joined her. They swam to the waterfall, and climbed onto a flat rock that formed a ledge under the cascade.

"Remember when we were at Paradise and your grandmother made us a picnic to take to the river." When he nodded she went on. "I kept thinking of this place, and I couldn't wait to come here with you."

Shane smiled at the memory of that day. "Yes, I remember. I was a little surprised that you knew how to swim. I think I'm beginning to understand why you love La Fleur so much. You have so many good memories of your childhood. I wish I could say the same."

"Well, how do you like it?" she asked to change the subject. She had learned from Maude Taylor that Shane's childhood was lonely after his mother died. Her heart ached for the little boy he was then.

His father had been withdrawn and ignored him, leaving him in the care of equally detached servants and tutors. He ran away but was brought back and punished.

When he was fourteen his grandmother came for a visit and took him to live with her, until he went away to school at sixteen. Sam and Maude were his real family.

When she spoke Shane's face brightened. "It's wonderful, I think we should come here often," he said pulling her into his arms.

"When I was in England, I used to long for this place, and now I'm finally here again with the man I love." She sighed, and snuggled closer in his embrace.

He closed his arms tighter around her and found her eager lips with his hungry mouth. The scorching kiss sent a jolt through her and when his hand found a taunt breast she lay back on the hard rock ledge and let her eyes travel from his handsome head to his powerful shoulders.

She ran her fingers through his wet hair. She felt as if she was living in a fantasy of love. His tongue was a tormenting delight, and his hands were magic, as his fingers probed and caressed her.

When their desire had been sated, and he could breath again, he held her gently.

"I hope I didn't hurt you. I just can't seem to get enough of you. I thought once we were married this desire would cool down a bit, but I just want you all the time."

"Yes, I know," Christa agreed. "I feel that way too. Just when I think it can't get any better, you prove me wrong."

As they rode slowly back a little later, happy and contented, Shane teased, "Do you think it's time for dinner yet. I'm getting hungry again."

"My, my, what a large appetite you have," Christa giggled.

Suddenly, they heard a shot.

The frightened horses bolted and ran wildly down the dirt road. Finally bringing her horse under control Christa turned back to discover Shane slumped over in the saddle. She screamed.

Drawing closer she saw him straighten and she started to breath again. The shot had grazed his arm, she saw, as he pulled a handkerchief from the pocket of his coat and put it over the wound.

"Oh my God Shane," she cried anxiously, her face pale.

"It's alright, darling. It's jus a scratch I'll be fine. It just took me by surprise. Come on, let's get back to the house. Really, Christa it's nothing," he reassured her.

Just as Shane had told her earlier, it was not serious. The shot had gone through the flesh of his arm near the shoulder.

Charles and Jamie looked uneasily at each other as they stood behind Christa while she put a clean bandage over the wound.

"Did you see anyone around?" Jamie asked, suspiciously. "Perhaps when you first started out?"

"No, I don't remember seeing anyone," Shane frowned. He didn't want to get Christa all upset, but it appeared that someone was trying to kill him.

"Probably just a stray shot. Someone out hunting where they shouldn't have been, I imagine," he said, for her benefit.

Christa had been very frightened at first remembering the look on Richard Fontaine's face when he saw her in Shane's bed. For a few horrifying moments she had suspected him, but now with everyone else saying it was nothing she conceded to herself that they were probably right. It was a stray shot, just as Shane said.

They had dinner and went about the usual things, but Christa stayed by Shane's side even when he went to the stables with Charles and Jamie, and soon the incident was forgotten.

Chapter 14

The bright silver moon lit up the road that led to La Fleur Plantation a few nights later. It was the night of the wedding reception, and every one who had been invited was apparently coming.

Most, because Charles Devereax was well liked and respected by his neighbors and business acquaintances. The rest had come out of curiosity. They wanted to get a look at the young couple bold enough to defy the conventions of society and marry so quickly.

The chandeliers were all shining brightly and tables were laden with food and punch. Servants weaved their way around the salon offering drinks, while at the other end of the large room the musicians were tuning up their instruments.

The French doors were open and people moved freely in and out from the salon to the veranda, and even strolled about the lawns.

Charles had been informed that the musicians were ready, so stepping onto the platform that had been erected for them, he shouted for attention.

"Ladies and Gentlemen," he paused to smile happily, "as you probably are aware this party is to celebrate the marriage of my daughter Christa to Mr. Shane Coulter. He gave a glance in their direction.

The audience gave some polite applause and when the sound died, he went on. "I won't bore you with any more talk, I think the newlyweds should start the dancing." He gave a nod to the leader and stepped off the platform as they came to life.

Christa had been looking forward to dancing with Shane, and as they glided around the room they only had eyes for each other, so they missed the four people who entered just then, but Tillie Farnsworth didn't.

Because she was plain and dull and so was her life, she took pleasure in pointing out the social mistakes of others.

Her husband, Thomas Farnsworth, was a prominent banker in New Orleans, so she was automatically included like it or not by every hostess whatever the occasion.

"Look at that Mary," she said to her sister, "that's the handsome Englishman I was telling you about, the one she brought home with her. Oh," she continued, giving her sister a poke, "that little blond must be his sister. I heard she was a widow too, just like you."

"What are they doing with the Sabastians?" Mary asked, suspiciously.

"Well, I heard that the Englishman is working for Dominic Sabastian now in that gambling place of his," Tillie reported distastefully.

Jamie had also noticed the new arrivals and overheard Tillie's remarks.

"Ladies," he smiled as he passed them.

"Good evening, Mr. Devereax," they said in unison, with lowered lashes and fluttering fans. What a charming young man," Mary sighed, looking after him.

Laura wondered if she had been too bold in her choice of this gown. She knew this shade of pink was flattering, but perhaps the neckline was too low she thought self-consciously when she saw the way Jamie Devereax was devouring her.

As he approached she nervously opened her fan and adjusted the white gardenia she had tucked in her up-swept hair.

"Good evening," he said to the group in general, then turned his attention back to Laura. "I'm so glad you could come," he said making her blush from the heat of his steady gaze, and jolting her heartbeat when he kissed the back of her hand holding it much too long.

Seeing her discomfort, he let it go and acknowledged her brother with a nod. He politely pretended to be glad to see Dominic Sabastian.

"Angela, you're looking lovely as always." Then wasting no more time, he asked Laura to dance, he couldn't wait to get her in his arms.

Richard had been searching the crowd in spite of himself. His eyes finally found what they were searching for, and his heart broke all over again. She was like a flame in apricot silk, with yellow ribbons in her hair to match the trim on the gown. She was radiant as she danced in Shane Coulter's arms. Richard grabbed a drink from a tray a servant held out to him, and gulped it down quickly.

"Easy, Fontaine, these are dangerous times and there's war on. Many men will die before it's over," Dominic Sabastian looked knowingly at him and Richard wondered if he knew that he had taken a shot at Shane.

"Having me followed?" Richard chuckled, trying to make light of it. He had been drinking heavily a few days ago and he knew if Shane were out of the way Christa would turn to him.

He had decided to take a ride, and was in a grove of trees on La Fleur land. He was about to turn back when he saw them and couldn't help taking a shot at Shane, but he was a good marksman and had only grazed him. If he wanted to kill him it would have been easy to do, but he wasn't a murderer.

A duel had come to mind, but Shane Coulter had the reputation of being a very dangerous opponent and not much of a gentleman when it came to a fight.

Richard thought from their fight on the island that they were pretty evenly matched. Shane had a more muscular physique but Richard was quicker and he had learned to defend himself as a schoolboy.

His thoughts were interrupted when Charles Devereax joined them. Charles was enjoying his role as host and suggested that there were card tables in another room if they were interested.

"Richard if you'll be good enough to dance with my wife, I'll see if I can make some easy money from our host," Dominic smiled smoothly.

"Of course, shall we, Mrs. Sabastian?"

Giving her husband a cold glare, Angela took Richard's arm and let him lead her out onto the dance floor.

Richard couldn't help comparing Angela to Christa. In some ways she was more beautiful than Christa, but she was distant and reserved, like a statue, perfect but made of stone.

Where Christa showed interest in almost everything and got excited over a pretty flower, or a good horse, Angela seemed not to care about anything but herself.

The music ended suddenly, and they found themselves face to face with Shane and Christa as they left the center of the floor. Christa spoke first trying to fill the akward silence. "Richard, I'm so glad you could come tonight, and Angela, what a lovely gown."

Not taking his eyes off Christa, Richard said, "Congratulations Shane," then remembering his manners he reluctantly offered his hand.

Christa let out the breath she hadn't realized she was holding.

Maybe she was wrong to suspect Richard of taking a shot at Shane. Perhaps it was just someone hunting where he shouldn't after all.

"May I dance with your lovely bride?" Without waiting for an answer he took Christa by her gloved hand and led her to the edge of the floor as the music started again. She looked helplessly at Shane, who shrugged his shoulders and turned back to Angela.

"Shall we?"

She smiled and moved into his open arms. Richard Fontaine would have been surprised at the lively interest in her eyes now, if he could have noticed any one but Christa. That interest was noted however by her husband.

Dominic and Charles hadn't yet left the salon for their card game.

They had stopped to talk to a group of men and as Dominic watched the dancers he wondered why he wanted the interest that she held in her cold heart only for Shane Coulter.

He knew she was in love with Shane Coulter when he married her, but he mistakenly thought he could make her forget Shane. Especially since Coulter had been more interested in the war than in her. He had been prepared to challenge Shane to a duel over her that night two years ago, but she had consented to his proposal and then Shane left town.

Angela was cold like a painting or a statue, but the Devereax girl was animated flesh. Lively and warm, he could feel her magnetic pull from here. He checked his lustful thoughts, for he had other things to think of tonight.

Angela finally spoke, as if just waking from a long sleep. "You're looking well Shane," she smiled, then chided herself for such a mundane greeting. Shane gave her a quick glance, tearing his eyes reluctantly away from Christa and Richard.

"You too, Angela." Then he smiled at the memory of his meeting with Christa in England, it seemed so long ago. She had believed that he was married to Angela.

"What's so amusing," Angela inquired resentfully, and felt the pain of losing him all over again.

"Oh nothing, I'm just in a good mood tonight, I guess," he answered, turning his full attention to her at last.

Angela was tall for a woman and much slimmer than his new bride Shane noticed as his hand circled her waist, but he wouldn't trade one of Christa's lush curves for all of Angela's charms.

Once again the music ended and Shane led Angela back to her husband. Her eyes followed Richard when he in turn gave Christa back to Shane. Then she searched out a servant with a tray and quickly gulped a glass of champagne.

It was torture to hold Christa and know that she was forever out of his reach, Richard thought. Maybe he would try to seduce her now that she was married, after a while, if he could see any sign that her marriage had grown stale. If she thought Shane had been unfaithful first, she might turn to him. It would take patience but just maybe... He would rather have her for a mistress than not have her at all. He smiled, feeling better than he had since she turned him down, as a spark of hope ignited in his heart.

When she found a chair against the wall and sat down gracefully, Angela was thinking along the same lines as Richard. She could tell that Shane was jealous of Richard Fontaine and perhaps it could be used as a wedge to pry the newlyweds apart.

For some reason Dominic didn't seem to be jealous of Richard like he was most men. Was he finally losing interest in her? She had quickly learned that money was her husbands strength as while as his weakness. He was addicted to the power and influence that money could buy.

He was nothing without it. He had bought her and he had bought Richard Fontaine, but she didn't think that Richard was aware of that fact yet.

The music played on as Christa danced with Governor Claiborne and Shane danced with his wife. Soon Jamie claimed her and Shane danced with Laura. It was then that Dominic Sabastian cut in and Christa had to admit that she was impressed with the man. He was of medium height and his dark wavy hair was graying at the temples. She guessed him to be about forty-five years old. Although he was slim, she could feel the power in his arms as he held her lightly. He was an accomplished dancer and she wondered why he hadn't danced with his wife.

She was about to speak when the dance ended. A hush fell over the crowd and every head turned towards the door. There Shane, Charles and Jamie were gathered around another man who apparently had just arrived. Shane drew Christa to his side and made introductions.

She was surprised to learn the new arrival was none other than the famous Jean Lafitte. Ever the gentleman he flashed her a charming smile and teased as he took her hand, "I only regret that I didn't meet you first, Ma cher." He kissed her hand then turned to Shane, still holding it loosely. "Since you have claimed the lady's heart, I will claim only a dance."

They joined the other dancers in a lively quadrille. "Madam Coulter, I find you the most beautiful woman I have ever seen. If Shane was not such a good friend of mine I would steal you away from him," Lafitte said with a wink.

"And if I weren't so in love with him I would let you," she laughed. She knew he was only teasing and she was drawn to him. The man exuded charm.

He had a way of looking directly at you, giving you his full attention, as if he really wanted to hear what you had to say. When the music ended he took her back to Shane, who was with a small group of friends.

"Have you eaten yet?" Laura asked Christa, after chatting for a while. "I'm starved. Come join me at the table and keep me company." Before she could protest, Laura lead her away. As they picked up plates and began picking out tasty morsels, Christa observed, "So you've been elected to keep me out of the way while they have a meeting. Is that it?" Laura just laughed.

They found a place to sit away from the crowd, and finished eating. "Did you know the governor left in a huff when Lafitte was so warmly welcomed."

"Oh well, everyone knows they don't get along. The governor thinks Lafitte is no better than a common thief, but I noticed he drank his share of the champagne," Christa said.

She sighed in relief as Shane and some of the other men came out of the library and rejoined them.

As soon as Shane had whisk her into his arms for another dance, Christa asked, "What was the meeting all about?"

"What meeting? We were just playing cards," he said, then added, "when are some of them going to leave? I want to have you all to myself."

He danced her over to the French doors and pulled her quickly out onto the veranda. Christa smiled, she was hoping to be alone with him for a least a few minutes.

Looking around they found there were still too many people. It was a warm night and many of the dancers had collected a drink and headed for the relatively cool veranda.

Shane lead her down the steps and took her around the corner, then stopped near some red hibiscus, where they were out of sight.

He gently pulled her into his arms and found her lips with his own. They pressed each other closer as their passions flared and were breathless when Shane drew back his head, but before he could speak they heard footsteps coming towards them.

A man's resonate voice spoke out of the darkness. "Alright, this is far enough away from the others. What did you hear?"

"Well, nothing we can use I'm afraid," another man answered in a higher tone.

"Tell me anyway and I'll pass it on and let them decide if it is important or not," the first man said.

"They talked mostly about whether or not there will be an attack on New Orleans. Lafitte is giving them his full support and they were talking about stock-piling guns and ammunition. Of course they thought it was foolish of the President to keep sending troops to Canada, when they think they need reinforcements here."

"All right, you've done well and you'll be amply rewarded for your trouble," the first man said.

Christa started to speak, but Shane silenced her with a finger to her lips. They waited a few minutes and after a quick kiss, they went back inside.

"Don't tell anyone about this, we'll talk later, but right now I want to talk to Adam. After all the guest had gone home or to bed, Shane and Adam got together with Charles and Jamie for another meeting.

Later, Angela Sabastian sat at her dressing table and brushed out her long silver blond hair. She smiled at her reflection and remembered the way it felt to see Shane Coulter again.

She knew she had made a mistake letting her mother talk her into marrying Dominic when the only man who could make her feel this way was Shane.

He had once been very interested in her and if she had waited a little longer he might have proposed. After all, his interest in the war hadn't stopped him from marrying Christa Devereax.

Her musings were suddenly halted when Dominic entered her room from his connecting door. He wore only a robe and she knew why he had come. She could see the hunger in his eyes. He would try again to make her respond to his desires. Sometimes she almost wished she could feel something.

Dominic stepped up behind her and stroked her soft hair. This beautiful women was his. He had bought her, and she would give him her body but not her heart. Did she even have a heart, he wondered. He slid his hand under the silk of her robe, and caressed her bare shoulder. Even her smooth white skin felt cold, he thought, but every time he saw her he wanted her and there was some satisfaction in touching her even if she never returned his hot embraces.

"Please Dom, leave me. I'm very tired tonight, I don't feel like...

He moved around and stood in front of her, then pulled her to her feet. He searched her face, but found no emotion. God, how he hated that cold indifference.

"No, you never feel like it, do you. But I'll bet Christa Devereax..., oh, excuse me, I meant to say, Christa Coulter, feels like it. Why I bet at this very moment she's, he paused as she pulled free and walked quickly away from him. She fought to control her anger because she knew he was baiting her. He waited hoping she would be angry, it would be better than nothing. She turned to face him.

"Must you be so crude, you know I don't like that kind of talk," she said as if she were reprimanding a child. Even as she spoke she knew she had no choice. She lowered her eyes and with a sigh of resignation she untied the belt that held her robe together and with a shrug of her shoulder, let it slide slowly to the floor.

At that moment his desire died and he hated her. "Cover yourself, Angela, I don't want you now," he said reaching for the door knob.

Shane and Christa began to receive invitations from everyone after the dinner party they attended at the Livingston's fashionable house. Louise Livingston was acknowledged to be the social leader of the city, and if you were accepted by her you were accepted by all the other hostesses. During the next few weeks the war was all but forgotten as people danced and entertained as if there were no blockade.

After returning from an early morning ride Mr. and Mrs. Shane Coulter were suddenly jolted back to reality from the dream that they had shared.

They were at La Fleur plantation having small cakes and coffee that September morning when Adam Michaels came riding up the tree lined drive. He swung down from his horse even before the animal came to a full stop. Running up the steps he rushed over to them. "Shane the British have raided Washington."

Shane jumped to his feet. "My God, when?"

"The twenty-forth of August. It's alright. They've already left and the President and Dolly are safe. All they did was burn some of the public buildings. As you can guess our side made a poor showing. Apparently Albert Gallatin, who was in England, had sent the President information that the British intended to sail into the Chesapeake Bay and attack the city, but the President did nothing," Adam explained.

"Here, read these newspaper accounts. I wonder if Lafitte knows yet?"

"I imagine so, he has his own spies you know, my friend."

"Yes, of course, you're right."

Christa had grabbed one of the papers and was scanning through one of the accounts of the incident. Adam sat down and helped himself to some of the coffee and then picked out a fruit filled tart. He waited silently for Shane to finish reading.

He was just finishing his third tart and second cup of coffee when Shane put the papers down, got up and walked to the edge of the veranda. Leaning against the railing, he drew a small cigar from an inside pocket. After lighting it, he blew the smoke slowly and massaged his chin in a thoughtful gesture.

"Well, what do we do now," Adam asked, as if Shane had all the answers.

"There's not much we can do without some military help. If we're lucky, maybe something will come from the peace talks in Ghent before it's too late." They sat, each lost in their own thoughts.

Finally, Shane spoke again. "I've been thinking about Sabastian, perhaps we can turn the tables on him. I'm sure it was him that night at the reception. If I'm right then maybe we could do a little spying on him. Christa and I have been invited to a dinner party at his house next Friday evening. But I think we can start even sooner. Adam are you in the mood for some gambling tonight?"

"Why, yes I was thinking of trying that new place, Domino's," Adam said innocently. They smiled at each other knowingly.

Dominic Sabastian drew deeply on his fine cigar and sipped his French brandy slowly savoring the sweet taste. He was satisfied.

Everything was going very smoothly. Except for that thorn in his side, Shane Coulter. Dominic had been making friends with Shane to get to Christa, but he wondered why Shane had changed his attitude from cold indifference to warm friendship.

In the past they had almost come to dueling and now it was as if he were no longer interested in the war or suspicious of Dominic. Was he tired of his lovely bride already? Was he still interested in Angela? Well, if that was the case, then Shane was welcome to her. He was tired of fighting with her for her favors and no longer desired her as he once had.

Yes, Dominic decided he would rather have Christa Coulter and soon he would. The more he saw of her the more he wanted her. She was lively and laughed easily and she was so beautiful, like a flame lighting up the night.

Besides the women he had another reason to get rid of Shane Coulter. It was getting harder to make contact with his English agent with Shane and his friend Adam Michaels close by.

He lay his head back in his comfortable chair by the cold fireplace and closed his eyes, then pictured Christa's lovely face smiling up at him from a bed with her flame struck hair spread out on the pillows and her luscious body bare and ready for him. He would use some other woman tonight to ease this ache in his loins, but soon he would have the real thing.

    Angela smiled as she heard the closing of the big front door. At this hour it meant only one thing. His mistress. He was too discreet to use a brothel. She had seen the way he looked at Christa and he had a way of getting what he wanted. If he went after Christa, that would leave her way clear to go after Shane.

Chapter 15

The next Sunday morning after their dinner at the Sabastians, the newlyweds woke at La Fleur because it was a very important day for Charles and Jamie Devereax. It was the day of the biggest horse race in the area.

The best horses from as far as Natchez and Mobile were entered. The Devereax's had entered Magic and had high hopes of winning a large purse. Charles had already invested a large amount of money in the war effort and if it was over soon there would be no problems, still it was always nice to have some ready cash on hand. He took a sip from his cup of coffee and then breathed deeply of the clean flower scented air.

He was proud of his children and he was pleased that Christa had married Shane Coulter. He had always liked Shane and now it was like having another son. Deep in thought, he was seated at the round wrought iron table on the white railed gallery that ran across the front of the second story of the house.

"Good Morning father," Jamie said breaking into his musings. After helping himself to some of the hot coffee from the large silver pot, he leaned a hip on the railing and looked out over the lush green lawns. "Great day for a race don't you think?" he asked cheerfully.

Charles smiled proudly at his son. "Yes it certainly is, and I'm looking forward to winning." He chuckled. "I suppose everyone will be there," he said, mischievously watching Jamie for a reaction. "The Livingstons, the governor and the Sabastians. Oh, and of course, Richard Fontaine and that pretty little sister of his."

Jamie knew Charles was teasing him and he smiled at his father, showing even white teeth. "Oh yes, you mean Laura."

"Yes, Laura," Charles chuckled. He knew the two were attracted to each other and wondered how far things had gone. He wanted to ask but thought better of it, if Jamie had honorable intentions he would surely declare himself soon and if not then it was none of his father's business any way.

Jamie poured himself another cup and took one of the still warm croissants he discovered on a plate under a napkin. "Mmm…, Hanah's done it again, this one's filled with apple's and it taste wonderful," he said after swallowing a large bite.

"Yes, I know," Charles smiled. "Although Hanah is a slave, she's part of the family and a real treasure. I've always treated my people well and they pay me back with their loyalty and good work."

"I know father, but I still don't think it's right to own other people. Sometimes I'm torn between this life that I was born to and the urge to go away and make a life of my own."

"I envy men like Shane and his friend Adam. They've fought Indians and lived with them and gone exploring in the west and sailed away to Europe, and I've only been as far as New York on that business trip with you that time." Jamie smiled uneasily, and wished he hadn't said what he thought, when he saw the concern in his father's eyes.

"Good morning," Shane said as he joined them. He poured some coffee and took a croissant then seated himself at the table with them, and added, "great day for a horse race, don't you think."

Charles and Jamie glanced at each other and laughed. "So we were just saying," Jamie chuckled.

They were soon joined by Christa, who was beaming as she gave each man a kiss on the cheek.

She sat down between Charles and Shane and let Hanah, who had come out to check on things, serve her. After a few bites she exclaimed, "Oh, this is so good. I think my favorite food in the world is Hanah's croissants. Shane, now do you see why I hated staying in England for so long, and why I missed being home."

"It ought to be a great day for a horse race," she said, gazing out at the bright sunshine. "What's so funny?" She asked puzzled as the men burst out laughing.

At the race track, a good size crowd was gathered around a carriage.

"Well gentlemen, as much as it hurts me to say it, unless something comes out of the peace talks in Ghent, I see very little help for us. The British have already burned our capital and got away with it, and they've also succeeded in blockading our coast line."

These words were spoken by a dapper elegantly dressed Dominic Sabastian and calculated to sway the group of men who stood around his carriage while his servant passed out whiskey. His orders were simple, just keep the people of New Orleans as disorganized and demoralized as they were now.

"General Jackson and others, myself included, think they will strike Mobile before New Orleans," Charles Devereax observed.

"Of course and so do I," Dominic said easily, "but gentlemen, I fail to see how so many put their faith in a man like Jackson, who has no military training at all, with the exception of a few skirmishes with the Indians. How long do you think his rag tag volunteers will last against the well-trained and experienced British troops?"

Any reply that might have been made was lost as a horn trumpeted the start of the second race of the day.

The talk naturally turned to the race and the horses and jockeys and how much to bet.

The ladies in their fine silks and muslins, mostly stayed in their carriages and made good use of their parasols and fans, as most of the men folk made their way to the rail surrounding the track.

While everyone else was watching the race with great enthusiasm, Christa was sitting patiently, admiring her handsome new husband. Shane looked especially handsome today in his newly tailored coat of blue superfine.

She liked the way the white shirt contrasted against his deeply tanned skin. As her eyes dropped lower she remembered the feel of that strong virile body crushing her to the bed last night and she wished they could be alone so she could at least get a kiss. "Nice day for a race," a familiar voice said breaking into her thoughts. She turned in the direction of the voice to see Richard Fontaine standing close beside the carriage.

Feeling uneasy and awkward she said the first thing that came to mind. "How are you Richard?"

He smiled weakly. "I'm doing fine. I'm even beginning to adjust to your marriage. I hope we can still be friends," he said watching her closely.

"Of course we can still be friends, I'm really very fond of you." She was acutely aware of the way he seemed to be trying to memorize her. She knew she looked her best in this white muslin trimmed in mint green lace. The silence hung like a cloud over them. She was relieved when Richard finally spoke.

"You're so beautiful, Christa. Shane must be treating you well, you're positively glowing."

Christa's creamy skin flushed at his reference to Shane treating her well. To change the subject she asked, " Have you placed any bets?"

"Yes, as a matter of fact I bet on your father's horse, Magic. I hope to make a killing."

They were interrupted as the already noisy crowd went wild with excited cheering and when Christa turned back to speak to him, Richard was gone.

A few minutes later Shane, Charles and Jamie joined Christa. They decided to take the picnic basket that Hanah had prepared for them down near the river to eat their lunch in the shade.

Shane winked at Christa as he helped her from the carriage, and gave her hand a little squeeze.

"If you don't stop looking at me that way, I won't be responsible for my actions, Mrs. Coulter," he whispered.

"Why Mr. Coulter is that a threat?" she smiled, behind her fan.

"No, that's a promise," he grinned, wickedly.

As they approached the shade of the big moss draped live oaks they saw a crowd gathered near the spot they had intended to use. "I wonder what's happened?" Christa asked curiously.

"Just someone making a speech probably," Shane replied. "Wait here. I'll go see."

"I'll go with you," volunteered Adam Micheals, who had just joined them.

Pushing their way to the front of the crowd they discovered Richard Fontaine standing over a man on the ground who was obviously dead. "What happened?" Shane asked.

"I don't know I just got here myself," Richard answered defensively.

"I was over there, the other side of those bushes and I heard a cry for help but there was so much noise I couldn't be sure. Anyway I decided to have a look. I came round the bushes and here he was," Richard ended with a shrug.

While Richard was talking, Dr. Raymond Lewis had taken a look and, turning to the crowd he confirmed what the knife and the blood oosing from the victim's back had already told them. "He was stabbed." Then he asked, "does anyone know this man?"

A murmur went through the throng as people looked at each other questioningly and shook their heads.

Shane decided it would be better if no one connected him to this man, whom he recognized as Peter du Buc, a frequently used informant. A knowing look passed between Shane and Adam, who was standing on the opposite side of the dead man.

Much later when they were alone in their room at last, Shane held Christa in his arms and like a bee gathering honey he fed on the sweet nectar of her kiss. Her excitement grew in sweet anticipation of what was to come when his seeking tongue sent ripples of pleasure through her.

His strong hands slid down her narrow back and the indentation of her waist, to cup her round buttocks and press her softness against his own hardness. He could feel her nakedness through the thin silk of her robe and he marveled again that he could never seem to get enough of her. He forced himself to let her go for a moment and began pulling off his own clothing.

Christa shrugged out of her wrapper and let it slip to the floor, a pile of turquoise silk and black lace. She lay back on the bed, her heart pounding excitedly as she watched him.

He was everything a man should be she thought, from his thick black hair and strong muscular shoulders down to his flat stomach and narrow hips. Her eyes boldly watched him taking off his buff colored pants.

As if he wanted her to see him, he walked slowly towards her and sat on the edge of the bed, amusement in his dark eyes. "Do you like the way I look, Mrs. Coulter?" he asked as his hands reached for her breast.

"Yes, very much, Mr. Coulter," she sighed huskily.

He had planned to take his time with her, but once again when he touched her and heard that husky tone in her voice, a dam of fierce desire broke and washed over him. He couldn't wait to touch and caress her.

He took her head in his hands and with a low moan he stole her breath away with the unleashed passsion of his kiss. When his hand moved lower she smiled in anticipation.

Joy swept over her like a benediction as she pressed him to her.

At first he just lay there, momentarily content, but she spoke his name again in that same husky voice. Her wild ecstasy took them soaring up into that paradise that lovers know. They shuttered together as wave after wave of rapture shook them. Their desire sated they slept exhausted in each others arms.

Christa was glad to see that not only had her father and Jamie accepted their marriage, but apparently so had everyone else. Every day there were invitations to some party or the theater or a concert. Always some social function or other.

It surprised her because she had always thought this was exactly the kind of life style that Shane didn't want. Was he only pretending to enjoy this social whirl to please her she wondered as they sat in the sun-drenched courtyard the next morning.

She liked to remember the simple things they had done when he took her to Paradise. One day they had taken a long walk down by the river and Shane had shown her how to fish. At first she had been squeamish about baiting the hook, but before the day was over she had caught almost as many fish as Shane and they took them back to the cabin where Maude had taught her how to clean and cook them.

She smiled as she recalled how proud she felt as she sat down at the table and saw the look of approval on Shane's face. She decided to ask him if they could stay home more often.

"We're invited to attend a play at the Theatre d' Orleans with the Sabastians tomorrow night," Shane said, after sorting through the calling cards and invitations that Harry had brought out on a silver tray with the morning coffee. That statement effectively, if reluctantly, brought her back to the present.

"Oh Shane must we?" Before he could answer, she explained, "I think Dominic likes me too much and I think Angela has her eye on you."

"Has he made advances? If he's said anything, I'll..., Shane started.

"No, he hasn't said anything, at least not yet. It's just the way he looks at me,"

"My darling wife," Shane said, "may I remind you of your many charms, you're a very beautiful young women. A man would have to be dead or blind not to take notice of you."

"Well, if you put it that way, I suppose we can use the same reasoning to explain why Angela can't keep her eyes off you."

"Touche, Mrs. Coulter," Shane chuckled at her and raised his coffee in a mock salute.

The next evening after the performance at the theater, Dominic insisted that Shane and Christa return with them to their elegant home for drinks. He had invited a few others including Richard and Laura.

As servants circulated among the guest offering champagne Christa took a glass and wasn't surprised when Dominic Sabastian joined her.

"May I say that you are ravishing tonight. The lights have set your hair to flame and I am drawn to you like a moth. I wonder if your touch would leave only ashes where a man had been?"

As he spoke he grasp her free hand and bent to kiss it. His warm mosist lips made his meaning quite clear. At Christa's look of discomfort he let her hand go. "I hope we can become very warm friends," he continued, as his eyes fondled her as if she were naked.

She stood at a loss as to what to do. She wanted to slap his leering face, but fought to control her temper. Shane had told her of his wish to socialize with the Sabastians so as to keep an eye on Dominic.

He had also told her of his suspicions that Sabastian had something to do with Peter du Buc's death. She was saved by, of all people, Richard Fontaine with Laura in tow.

"Oh, there you are," Richard said as he approached them.

"Laura has been telling me how much she missed you."

"Yes," Laura said, as the two women embraced. "You must come for tea soon."

Dominic wondered if Richard had appointed himself Christa's guardian.

After slanting him a look of annoyance, he excused himself saying he really should talk to his other guest.

While Dominic had Christa's attention, Angela had taken the opportunity to use her wiles on Shane and deliberately standing so that he couldn't see Christa she boldly told him, "After all this time, I still think you are the most attractive man I've ever met.

I think I was a bit hasty in my choice for a husband, don't you? But after all, just because we're both married doesn't mean we can't be friends does it?" she asked, laying a hand in his chest.

"Angela, my dear," Shane smiled, "If you can forgive my ancestry, I guess I can forgive yours." She knew he was referring to her aristocratic mother's objection to his Indian ancestry.

"Of course," she smiled, and realized that her beauty was no longer enough to win Shane. By now he was used to beautiful women. She decided to play the card she had been holding back. Her ace in the hole. Shane's suspicion of Dominic.

"You know Shane, friends talk to each other. They tell each other secrets. I bet I have secrets that you would like to know." She glanced knowingly up at him, opened her fan and walked away.

Adam Micheals had been frequenting the gambling room in Sabastian's hotel, hoping to pick up any information he could about Dominic's activities, so he was waiting for them when they returned home later that night.

"You go on up to bed, darling, I'll just be a minute," Shane told Christa, kissing her forehead.

Christa pretented to leave them, but hid behind the curtains by the French doors the way she had done before.

"So that's why you didn't let Christa join us," Adam was saying. "I was hoping it was because you were jealous of me. I guess I'm losing my touch." She knew that Adam was only teasing Shane, but was frustrated that she had missed the first part of the converstaion.

"Frist it was Richard Fontaine and then Dominic Sabastian and now you." Shane shook his head in disbelief.

"You better be careful or someone will try to steal her away from you," Adam laughed. He was enjoying his friends discomfort.

"I intend to make her forget every other man she's ever met," Shane winked.

Adam pretended to be offended. "What even me?"

"Especially you," Shane smiled.

The next day Christa was to have a fitting at Elaine's at two, after which she was to meet Laura for tea. As she joined Shane and Adam in the courtyard where they usually met for eleven O'clock coffee and croissants, she had the feeling that they had stopped their conversation at her approach. She poured herself some of the coffee and sat down.

"What's going on?" she asked setting down her cup.

"Going on?" Shane repeated, innocently glancing across the table at Adam.

Adam, looking equally innocent, lifted his golden eyebrows in a questioning gesture, and shrugged his shoulders. "Nothing's going on that I know of."

"You two are up to something, and I want to know what it is," Christa insisted.

Shane decided now was as good a time as any to tell her at least part of their plans.

"Well, if you must know, we're planning to go see Lafitte. I was going to tell you later today."

"When do we leave?" Christa asked cheerfully.

Shane glanced at Adam and nodded towards the door. "Well if you'll excuse me," Adam said, "I have some arrangements to make." He picked up his hat and left them quickly.

"How long will we be gone? Should I wear pants?"

"You're not going, Christa. You're going to stay here like a good little wife and wait for me."

"But why?" she demanded with her hands on her hips, an angry flame flashing in her eyes.

"It's no place for a lady."

"But Lafitte likes me."

"Every man that sees you likes you, that's why you're not going."

"But, Shane you'll be there to protect me. I want to go with you. I don't want to be left behind."

Shane knew she wouldn't like it but he hadn't expected an argument. "I said you're not going with us," he growled, giving her that intense look that he used when he meant to be obeyed. He stood up and threw his napkin on the table. "I have to meet someone before I leave. With any luck I won't be gone long. I'll see you later," he said, with a frown.

A feeling of déjà vu came over him as something shattered near his ear when he reached the front door. He turned back just in time to see Christa draw back her arm, prepared to hurl the second flower pot at him. And like another time he grabed her arm twisting it behind her. He pulled her up close and buried his face in her hair.

"It's too dangerous, you'll be safer here," he said and kissed her passionately.

She stood there speechless with her eyes closed in pleasure as he left quickly.

Dam, she thought, if there was going to be trouble she would feel safer with Shane and Adam.

When Harry came out to clear the table a few menutes later she tried to reason with him. "Please, Harry won't you at least say a few words in my behalf," she pleaded.

"Now, Miss Christa, if Shane says he wants you to stay home, then that's good enough for me," Harry said, as he stacked the small plates and cups on a tray he had brought with him.

"I suppose he's already given you orders to keep an eye on me," Christa probed.

"No. No, he ain't. I'm going with them," Harry told her over his shoulder as he left the room with the tray.

What could she do to make Shane see that she was more than a helpless female? She could ride and shoot, but apparently that wasn't enough. She smiled as the idea came to her. If she could snoop around and find out some important bit of information, then maybe Shane would see her in a new light.

Shane was suspicious of Dominic Sabastian, and Dominic liked her. She decided she would find a way to see him after her fitting this afternoon.

She dressed carefully in the room that was now her home. Shane had told her she was free to redecorate, but she liked the way it was, with his and her things mixed together.

She chose a new long sleeved violet gown for it was the end of September now and the days were much cooler. She wanted Dominic to be attracted, but not too attracted. She tied back her thick hair into a queue with a black velvet ribbon that matched the trim of her gown.

She gathered up her matching spencer jacket and reticule, and last but not least, she dabbed her favorite perfume behind her ears.

After taking a hack to the center of town, she decided to walk the short distance to Elaine's. It was such a lovely day and she was early.

"Here, this goes with it," Elaine said, handing Christa a turban of the same material as the new gown she was trying on. "I knew you'd look lovely in that shade of pale blue. Of course, it's a shame to cover that beautiful hair of yours, but turbans are the latest thing now, and... there," she beamed at Christa, "I just knew it. With a face like that, you'd look good in a flour sack."

"Oh Elaine, stop before my head gets to big to wear it," Christa laughed, and admired herself in the mirror. Was that really her? That mature, sophisticated woman. She had never been so happy, and it felt so good, so right.

A while later as she left Elaine's she thought that not only was she happy but luck was with her today, because she walked almost into Dominic Sabastian's arms and dropped her packages as a result.

"Oh! I'm so sorry," she gasped as he bent to retrieve them. She had planned to go have tea at the hotel and hoped to bump into him there, but this was even better.

"My dear Christa, what luck bumping into you so soon. After last night I was hoping to see you alone. Won't you join me for coffee or tea or something?" Before she could answer he stopped her by putting up a hand.

"I won't take no for an answer. I've had a bad day and I need the distraction of your company." Then hailing his waiting carriage, he gave her a hand in and sat opposite her.

"You know of course, that this will probably cause a scandal," Christa told him. "I would prefer that my husband doesn't know about it, let alone your wife."

"I shouldn't let it bother you, my dear. You see your husband and my wife are together right now. Surely you know that they were once lovers." Dominic lied, but he was glad to see the stricken look on Christa'a face.

He knew Angela had been a virgin when he married her, but did Christa? If she thought Shane was having an affair she just might figure, that what's sauce for the gander... He was tired of Angela and if she took Shane as her lover it would be an excuse to call him out and get rid of two birds, with one shot.

Shane was with Angela. The thought cut like a knife, and in her minds eye, Christa saw Angela running her fingers through his soft dark hair as he kissed her. She closed her eyes and tried not to cry.

"I'm sorry to be the one to tell you my dear," Dominic said sympathetically. "It's common knowledge that she only married me for my money, and of course he only married you because you're from a good family and it's the only way he could get you."

If she thought it hurt to think of Shane with Angela, it hurt even more to think that Shane had only married her for her body. Was she so naïve? Had she misjudged Shane so completely?

Was Dominic lying to her? Yes. Yes. He must be lying to make her betray Shane. She decided to pretend to believe him to see how far he would go.

She opened her reticule and found her lace trimmed hankerchief and dabbed at her eyes.

"I fear you may be right Dominic," she sniffled. "Shane and I had a terrible argument earlier today. He stormed out of the house saying he didn't know when he'd be back."

By now they had arrived at their destination, Dominic's hotel. He escorted her through the lobby and up a short flight of wide red carpeted stairs, then stopped at a door marked private. After fumbling with a key he ushered her into what was obviously his office. He motioned her to a chair and poured wine from a crystal decanter on the desk.

Feeling better now that she realized what he was capable of, Christa gave him a wistful little smile.

He could restrain himself no longer. Taking the drink from her, he quickly set it aside and pulled her to her feet. Before she knew what he intended he took the ribbon from her hair.

She had expected him to make some move, to say something about an affair, but now that the time had come she was afraid and fought the urge to rebuke him in some way. He took her in his arms and she turned her face so that his kiss missed her mouth and landed on her cheek instead.

"Why are you holding back Christa? Are you so innocent that you think only one man can give you pleasure? You're wrong, my dear. Let me show you how wrong you are," he said, as his hand covered her breast.

Just as Christa was looking around for something to hit him with, like a vase or a statue, she was saved by a knock at the door. "Go away," Sabastian shouted. "I don't want to be disturbed."

But the knocking persisted and Christa recognized Richard Fontaine's voice. "This is about tomorrow. It's important."

Scowling, Dominic released her. He straightened his coat and neck cloth and went to the door.

Christa found her ribbon and was tying back her hair when Richard stopped in his tracks as he saw her there. His eyes widened in disbelief and then turned cold with disgust.

"Christa," he said with a stiff little nod of his handsome head.

"Richard," she answered in the same way. Then she quickly gathered her things. "Dominic, thank you so much for the wine, but I most go home now," she said.

Dominic wasn't willing to let her go so easily and followed her to the door, sending Richard an angry frown as he passed him.

"Perhaps another time we shall meet under more favorable circumstances my dear," Dominic said, kissing her hand. A gesture that didn't go unnoticed by Richard Fontaine.

The little bitch, Richard thought, if she stoops to cheat on her husband so soon it should at least be with him. He could understand her falling in love with a man like Shane Coulter, but what did she see in Dominic Satastian?

Somehow the pieces of this puzzle just didn't fit. If she had realized that she had made a mistake in her hasty marriage than surely she would have turned to him before Sabastian.

Christa wondered what was so important about tomorrow that Dominic would let it interfere with his plans for her. She stopped in the hallway and glanced around. No one was about, so she walked quickly back to the door she had just exited and leaned in close to listen.

"I still don't see why you want me to go with them," Richard was saying.

"Because I still don't trust you," Dominic answered. "If you go with them and it goes well, then I'll know you're still a loyal Englishman, but if things go wrong I'll know that you betrayed me.

"Another thing. If Shane Coulter shows up, kill him. He's been a thorn in my side too long."

"What about Lafitte's men? I hear he has that warehouse very well guarded." Richard said.

"That's Blackie's job. You have to leave before dawn, so just drive the wagon and see that those guns get to their destination."

Excitement made Christa's heart pound. This was just the kind of information that she had hoped for. Now maybe Shane would let her in on things. After meeting Laura for tea, she hailed a hack to take her home.

When she arrived the house was empty. Even Harry was gone. What am I going to do now she wondered as she climbed the stairs to the bedroom.

It was so quiet. Then she saw the note. A folded piece of paper with her name scrawled across it in Shane's handwriting. It simply said they were going to meet Lafitte in the bayous and asked her not to try to follow. She crumpled the note and sat on the edge of the bed, then let out a sigh of disappointment. If they were meeting in the bayous then she knew she wouldn't find them, at least not alone when they had a head start.

She smiled as the idea came to her. She could follow Richard and Blackie. They would have a wagon load of guns and they would have to travel slowly. She started to write Shane a note but she didn't know the destination, so she just wrote, "I am following the guns."

She figured that by the time he found the note he would know about the guns.

She striped off her gown after struggling with the hooks at her back and searched till she found the boy's clothes that she had worn aboard the *Falcon*. Only this time she wore her soft leather riding boots.

A further search brought her a pistol and an old hunting knife of Shane's. Charles had taught her how to use a pistol years ago.

She didn't know much about using a knife, but if all went well she wouldn't have too. She would stay well behind them and just follow until she had an idea of where they were headed.

Chapter 16

"What you doing here boy? Snoopin' round?" A voice from somewhere behind her asked. Before she could answer, the voice ordered, "You just march right on in there so you can get a better look, if you're so interested." Then something poked her hard in the back. She was half shoved and pushed forward into the dimly lit building.

"Hey, Blackie," the voice called out to one of two men, who had just finished hitching a team to the wagon.

"Yeh, what do ya want? Blackie growled, then glanced up and saw what appeared to be a young boy with his men. "Who's that?" he snapped.

" Found him snooping around outside," the voice with the gun in her back explained to the man by the wagon. So this is Sabastian's henchman Blackie, she thought.

Christa wasn't surprised to see Richard was the other man. She glanced around silently counting the men in the huge room with her. There were five altogether.

"Well why didn't you just shoot him?" Blackie asked, impatiently.

The three men just looked at each other. One shrugged. Another scratched, and the third one, who was dressed in buckskins, like an Indian, just looked puzzled.

"Don't you want to ask him who he's working for or something?" the tall man with the pistol asked.

"What difference does that make? Get rid of him and do it now," Blackie ordered.

The tall man raised his pistol once more and Christa felt faint and then she saw Richard and got an idea. She yanked off her hat and pulled out the black ribbon. Then shook her hair loose.

"My God, it's a women! I ain't goin' ta kill no woman," the man with the pistol said, lowering the weapon.

In the calmest voice she could muster at the moment, Christa said, "Richard darling, tell these men who I am. Then she flipped her hair back over her shoulder and walked slowly to him, swaying her hips suggestively.

He smiled at her boldness. After all she had put him through, she expected him to save her pretty neck again. He laughed out loud.

"Well, if it isn't my pretty little Christa? I told you I can't take you with me," he said, going along with her. He pulled her up close to his chest and whispered, "You fool, you'll get us killed."

It felt so good to hold her. "Now give me a kiss good-by and go home sweetheart." Overwhelmed by her nearness he kissed her the way he always wanted to, long and wet and hard, and Christa had no choice but to let him. Lack of sleep and fear combined with the force of his kiss made her knees buckle and Richard lifted her in his arms as she went limp against him.

The next thing she knew she was waking up in the back of the wagon, with a rough blanket covering her and the bright sun shinning in her eyes.

She wondered if Shane or anyone else had discovered her note yet. Did anyone even know where she was? She sat up slowly. When she saw that it was Richard Fontaine on the wagon seat, she climbed up beside him.

He took a deep breath and said, "Christa, do you know what you've done?"

"I overheard you talking to Dominic Sabastian about the guns. I was going to tell Shane, but he wasn't home, so I decided to follow for a little ways so I could tell him which direction you were going."

"I left him a note and I know he'll come," Christa said bravely.

"Shane is smart enough to find out where the guns were going without any help, Christa. We'll probably all get killed," he answered grimly. "I didn't want to take sides in this war, but now it's out of my hands."

"I let you go without a fight before, Christa, and I've regretted it ever since. I've got you now and I won't let you go again." You'd better pray that nothing happens to me because I'm all that stands between you and Blackie and his men."

"Thank you, for saving my life, but I'm in love with my husband and I want to live the rest of my life with him, if we live through this."

"If you're so in love with your husband, what were you doing in Sabastian's office the other day? It was obvious he had been pawing you. It was all I could do to keep from killing you both," Richard said, bitterly.

"Oh, Richard I never wanted to hurt you. If I had stayed in England like everyone told me to do, it would have saved all this trouble. When Blackie's men caught me I was just thinking of turning back, and if I get a chance I'll try to escape from you yet." And so they began the tormenting journey north.

When they stopped to eat and rest, Christa stayed close to Richard. Now that she had slept and eaten the imminent danger of the situation came home to her.

She was afraid of Richard too, but he was her only hope of staying alive until Shane came. She prayed silently that he was only a few miles behind. They must know she had been captured by now, and Shane was part Indian, he of all people, should be able to follow their trail.

When they finally stopped for the night, Richard put his arm around her back and led her some distance away from the others. Then tied her hands in front of her, and spread a blanket on the ground.

"Madam your bed awaits." he said, bowing politely. Maybe it was from tension and fear but Christa suddenly felt very tired. She lay down and tried to make herself comfortable.

Richard took off his hat and arranged his pistol so that Christa couldn't reach it without disturbing him. Blackie's men had surprised her and she didn't have time to pull her pistol from her coat pocket. They must have taken it along with her hunting knife.

She rolled on her side facing away from him and he pulled her back against his chest. "I want you Christa, but you're safe for now," he whispered. "When I take you it will be in a nice room where we can be alone without any riff-raff to watch us, and we'll have a nice bed with clean sheets and a bath first. I may have to endure their company for a time but after all, I'm still a gentleman. Good night."

When Christa woke the next morning she thought it had all been a nightmare. She felt a man's strong arm around her waist and thinking it was Shane she snuggled closer to the warm muscular body behind her.

"Oh! God Christa don't, just hold still, and then I'll untie you," Richard said, huskily. Her eyes flew open and she knew that her nightmare was the reality and Shane was the dream.

"I'm sorry, I was dreaming I was home with…"

"Yes, I know," he said, not wanting to hear the rest of her dream.

She had turned to face him as they spoke and when their eyes met, Christa was shocked by the pain that stared back at her. He took his hand from her waist and then holding her face with one hand he brushed back her hair with the other and then kissed her lightly on the cheek.

She knew he was fighting to keep a tight control on himself and she was grateful.

After a hasty breakfast of dry bread and coffee they moved on.

At first Richard was very quiet and Christa didn't know what to say, so she remained silent. The man she thought of as the Indian, seemed to be their guide and always rode a little ahead of them. She was glad to discover that her horse was tied at the back of the wagon next to Richard's.

Shane couldn't be far behind, she reminded herself. Maybe it would be better not to try to escape yet. If something happened to Richard she had no doubt what these other men would do to her. Already she could see a sullen resentment in Blackie's green eyes. If not for the perpetual frown and his unkempt appearance he wouldn't be a bad looking man, she decided.

She noticed he looked at her in a puzzled fashion as if he were trying to remember something and she wondered if he had seen her before. Maybe with Shane or when she went to Sabastian's office that time.

So another day passed. They never stopped for long but when they did, Christa tried to listen when they talked to find out their final destination. Richard said it was better if she didn't know too much.

Her mind was constantly on Shane. She knew he would come and she remembered the way he looked after the ship wreck, the way he had fought with Richard, and she knew a confrontation would come, and there would be nothing she could do to stop it.

Shane was thinking what he would do to Richard Fontaine when he got his hands on him. He knew they were close, so close.

The thought of Richard or any other man touching Christa infuriated him. He only hoped she was still alive when he found her.

He tossed another piece of wood on the small camp fire. It was his turn at watch. If he were alone he would have caught up with them by now. But Charles and Jamie had insisted on coming and so did Adam and Harry. And then Lafitte added two of his men.

He stretched out his legs and lay back with his head on his saddle, but he didn't want to get to comfortable. He took off his hat and ran his hand through his hair, then rubbed his eyes. Crossing his arms over his chest, he remembered how he had rushed home, after finding out about the guns. Two of Lafitte's men had been killed. He would have come after them even if Christa wasn't involved.

His heart sank once more as he recalled finding the note telling him that she was with the guns. He had sought out Laura, hoping Christa might have confided in her, and then found out Richard was gone too.

Shane figured somehow Christa must have found out about the robbery and got caught but did she go willingly with Richard or was Richard just an innocent bystander? Did she talk him into going with her to the warehouse because she couldn't find her husband? Richard Fontaine worked for Dominic Sabastian and no one who was involved with Sabastian was innocent.

Some time later, the fire had burned down and everyone was sleeping.

Even Shane was dozing lightly, when some imperceptible sound alerted him. What was that? He froze and listened. A horse nickered. Someone was out there in the darkness. The others were still sleeping soundly. Should he wake them?

Shane got up slowly and stretched, then walked casually towards a nearby tree where he had left his rifle, but before he got any further a hail of bullets shattered the silence of the night. He dived for the cover of darkness outside the circle of the campfire.

The moon ducked behind a dark cloud as if it was trying to get out of the way. The sleeping men had been jarred awake and came up with pistols in hand. Someone had kicked dirt into the fire and total darkness embraced the night. Then they heard the thunder of hoofs and nicker and whinnying of horses and Shane stepped back into the camp and put down his riffle.

"It's alright, they're gone and they took our horses with them," Shane explained as he worked at rekindling the fire. Adam and the others came back to where he had uncovered some red hot coals and was adding some small pieces of wood.

"Well, we can buy some more horses can't we? Jamie asked.

"Yes, but it will slow us down considerably just when we were so close. Dam it, now this will give them a longer lead. I was hoping to catch up with them in the morning. Well, I blame myself for underestimating them. I never considered they might double back on us like that. The next time I won't be so careless," Shane said adamantly.

Christa wondered where Blackie and the other three men were going as she spread her blanket on the hard ground. They left the Indian to guard her and Richard. It was obvious that Blackie didn't trust Richard any more than he did her. She thought she heard some shooting sometime during the night, but had dozed off and didn't know if it was part of her dream of being rescued or not.

She noticed the next morning that Blackie didn't seem to be in as much of a hurry as before. Perhaps they were getting close to their rendezvous. She had no idea how far they had come or how far it was to Natchez, but she knew she would sell her soul for a hot bath and a clean bed and clean clothes. Except for the use of Richards comb she had no way of grooming herself.

Later that day, after they had eaten some hard cheese and washed it down with water, she asked if she could ride her horse for a while. The hard wooden seat of the wagon was making her backside ache. Of course the leather saddle wasn't much of an improvement, but at least it was a change.

Blackie gave his consent and told Richard to ride beside her and watch her, then after telling one of his men to drive the wagon for a while he even smiled.

Christa began to worry again. Had she heard gun shots last night? Shane should have caught up to them by now. Was that why Blackie was so pleased with himself? If Shane had been killed then all her hopes had died with him. No. No, she wouldn't think about that.

He'll come. Shane, and her father and Jamie. They'll all come she told herself.

One man they called Slim, she guest it was because he was, had been doing the cooking, that is when they cooked anything. They had some loaves of bread and some cheese, and apples, when they started and coffee, of course, which was supplemented by fish or small game, occasionally. But now Slim was complaining that cooking was women's work and he didn't see why he had to do it when they had a women with them.

"Well, I'm not a very good cook," Christa admitted, nervously. When the men all looked at her, she moved closer to Richard.

"Well, what kind of woman are you? Blackie asked with a knowing smile. "You one of them fancy kept women we always hear about. Mr. Fontaine's kept women?" Blackie crossed his arms and leaned against a tree, leering at her as he continued.

"Well, if you don't cook, what do you do, Honey?" He smiled and glanced around at the other men amused at Christa's discomfort.

The others, looked at each other and chuckled.

"Get behind me, Christa," Richard whispered softly. She could feel the tension in his touch, when he tugged her arm.

"I'm a fast learner Slim, why don't you just show me how you cook and then I'll take over," she challenged, hoping to defuse the situation.

"Oh. Ok. I'll just show you once though," Slim agreed, spitting out tobacco juice.

"I think your quick thinking saved both our hides today. I was ready to kill Blackie," Richard told her later.

"Yes, I know," Christa sighed.

They were sitting on the rough wooden seat of the wagon, and every time they hit a bump or a hole, Christa was thrown against Richard. He would glance at her and then look quickly away as she scooted back to her side of the wagon.

"Christa, I'm beginning to think Shane's not coming. He would have been here by now, if he was able. If we're still alive after we deliver the guns, I'm taking you with me to Canada. You know I was there when I was in the army."

"I won't go with you Richard," she said, shocked at his boldness.

"Not even if Shane is dead?" he asked, searching her eyes for a reaction. "I don't want to be cruel, but I think it's time you faced the possibility."

As the days wore on, Christa began to despair of ever seeing Shane or any of the people or places she had known and loved before. She became withdrawn, and simply sleep-walked through the day and did as she was told.

At the start of the trip, she had been embarrassed to tell Richard of her need for privacy.

When she finally did he was very polite and understanding. He would lead her into the woods away from the others, and then walk back about half way giving her time to herself.

The first time she had thought of running away, but what good would it do with her on foot and them on horse back.

A few times she had tried to be cheerful, and they had even talked of better times when they were in England, and later at La Fleur. They would laugh about something someone had said that was very amusing at the time, but seemed so out of place now.

Towards the end of… How long had it been? At least a week. As they camped one night by a little stream, she overheard enough of the conversation, after super, to know they were very near Natchez.

She knew Richard had some soap, and she thought about how good it would feel to take off her clothes and wash all over, but she was reluctant to ask him for it. He had a small mirror too. He was using it now, trying to shave the best he could with a dull razor. It seemed there was never enough time for that in the morning, so about every other night after super he did his best.

It was a moonlit night and warmer than it had been all week. Richard had been watching her in the mirror as she watched him shave. Turning to her after he finished, he said, "Christa, come with me."

Thinking he wanted to tell her something without the others knowing, she followed him, and so did Blackie's suspicious eyes.

Richard led her down stream a little from the camp, then stopped near some rocks by the water's edge. "Come on over here," he urged, spreading his arms open when she hesitated. He had done similar things before to show the other men that she was his woman, and so she went to him.

He produced the bar of soap. "Like to have a bath?" he asked, with a twinkle of amusement in his eyes.

"Oh Richard", she beamed, then grabbed the soap and smelled it. It had a clean woodsy scent. "I want a bath more than you know, but I'm afraid that little scrap you've been using to shave won't make much of a bath towel."

"That's why I brought this," he said, then he produced a large clean bath towel from somewhere behind him.

"Where did you get that?"

"From my saddle bags. I was told to travel light, and I couldn't bring much with me. I also have a change of clothing."

"And being a good little Englishman you did as you were told," Christa finished for him, a bitter note in her voice.

"This is English soap Christa, do you want a bath or not. Make up your mind, they might send someone down here."

"I'm sorry, I didn't mean to hurt your feelings, and I do want a bath."

"Alright, but you'll have to hurry, I'll turn my back, although I'd rather watch."

"Oh Richard, how can I ever thank you," she blurted out, taking the soap. She put her hand to her mouth, and flushed when she realized what she had said.

"I'm sure we'll think of something," he laughed, amused by her slip of the tongue.

It was funny how people took things for granted when they were used to having them, like soap and water and clean clothes she thought.

She striped quickly, then waded out into the shallow water and forced herself to hurry.

It felt so good she didn't want to leave, but she was afraid Blackie might send one of the men to check on them if they stayed too long.

Richard was frantic with desire for her. Just the thought of her naked a few feet away was maddening.

"Richard, will you hand me the towel?" He turned towards the water, and almost stopped breathing. He looked at her innocently waiting for him to hand it to her. She was a goddess, with moonlight glistening on her face and shoulders. Then the sound of the other men laughing drifted down the bank to them and the knowledge that they might be intruded upon at an inopportune time cooled his desire somewhat. "Richard?" Christa asked, puzzled by his inaction.

"Oh, right," he answered, handing her the towel and then turning his back again.

She dressed as fast as she could, and tapped him on the shoulder minutes later. He jumped.

"Richard, what's wrong?"

"Nothing, I guess I was thinking of something else and I didn't hear you coming, that's all."

"Oh. Well it's your turn now and the waters warm. Thanks again," she smiled. He could be so charming, Christa mused. Why did he have to love her, when she was in love with Shane. He deserved someone who would love him back.

"You know how to use this," he said, holding up his pistol.

"Yes, of course," she replied, as he handed it to her.

"All right, be alert, my life is in your hands, and remember I'm all that stands between you and them." He shed his buckskin jacket and pealed off his shirt while Christa stood as if in a trance.

When he started to unbuckle the wide lather belt at his waist he hesitated, a questioning look in his eyes.

Only then did Christa realize she had been staring at him. This rugged male that exuded charm, and at the same time a real threat, was a far cry from the dandy she had known in London. Had he always been like this and had she been blind to it or had he changed so much since he came to this country?

He smiled, and continued with the belt, his eyes holding hers. Suddenly she turned away embarrassed again.

Seconds later, she heard him splash his way out to the deepest part of the stream which only came up to his waist.

After awhile she heard splashing again and knew Richard was behind her. Suddenly she felt his arm circle her waist. He took the gun from her, then he turned her in his arms and pulled her against his bare chest.

To her great relief she discovered he did have his pants and boots on. It was all she could do to fight the response that he evoked when he kissed her. She closed her eyes and saw Shane's face in her mind.

As if he sensed it, he drew his head back and managed a sad little grin. "I almost had you, didn't I?" he said slowly releasing her.

That night Richard didn't come to lay beside her as he usually did and she noted that he was drinking freely from the jug that the men passed around the circle of the campfire. She wasn't surprised, but she was afraid.

Chapter 17

The next evening Blackie took three men and rode off with them to the west, and she knew they must be very close to Natchez.

"Richard, we must be near a town or city, why didn't they take us with them?" Christa asked, anxiously.

"Well, with your looks, I guess they were afraid people would remember you if anyone should ask about us. You see, they don't trust me where you're concerned. Can you imagine, Blackie actually thinks I might let you go," he replied, sarcastically.

Like Christa, Richard was wondering what had happened to Shane. He had expected to see him come charging to the rescue long ago. He knew about the horses, but he didn't think that would slow them down this long. Perhaps they were out there in the darkness even now, ready to attack the camp.

Christa had just finished putting the supper things away and she noticed that Richard seemed a little more friendly. Maybe he had decided to forgive her for rejecting him the other night.

She walked to the edge of the clearing and listened. What did she expect to hear? Riders? Shane and her father and Jamie? Maybe they were all dead. Oh no. Her heart sank. No, she wouldn't let herself believe that. But why hadn't they come? What was keeping them she wondered.

"Don't look so sad Christa, he'll come soon," Richard said, and there was a hard edge in his voice as he came up behind her.

"Oh, Richard, why don't you just let me go? I don't want you to kill each other. Why do men always have to kill each other?"

Christa turned to face him. The tears she had been holding back finally spilled over and she covered her face with her hands.

Richard took her in his arms and stroked her soft hair gently. "Oh Christa, I don't want you to cry. I only want you to be happy." Lifting her chin he continued. "Do you know what purgatory is Christa? It's a place between haven and hell where a person waits to find out which place he's going. Christa, it's like a taste of haven to hold you in my arms, so close, and at night to lay beside you and wake up in the morning with your hair in my face."

She sniffed, and felt his arms tighten possessively as he went on.

"And it's like a taste of hell to know that you're married to someone else and that he's coming to try to take you away from me."

Christa pushed hard against him, and he loosened his hold on her. "I don't love you Richard. I love Shane, he's my husband and if you kill him, I'll hate you." Fear had made her voice a fierce, hoarse whisper.

Anger flared in his clear blue eyes and he grabbed her roughly by the upper arms and pulled her close again, then searched her face. "No, Christa, I'll make you love me," he stated firmly. His questing mouth found hers and he kissed her with a desperate passion.

She couldn't deny her body's shocking response as he moved his lips sensuously on hers. She was surprised and afraid at the way her arms of their own accord circled his neck and her hands sought his silky gold hair. But when he tried to deepen the kiss with his probing tongue, she ended it with her only weapon, her teeth.

With a yelp he released her and put his hand over his mouth.

Before he recovered she slapped his face as hard as she could. The loud smacking noise drew the attention of the Indian, but she didn't care. "How dare you?" she hissed.

The anger Richard felt at first, was quickly dissipated by the elation he felt at finally getting a physical response from her.

Tension hovered in the air around them and the Indian watched in amusement. They stood glaring at each other for a moment. Richard rubbed his burning face gently where she had slapped him and grinned knowingly. "Are you angry with me or yourself Christa?"

She couldn't stand to have him know she did feel even a little attracted to him and drew back her arm to slap away that smug look on his face.

He was ready for it this time and caught her wrist and held her arm down. He caught a handful of her hair pulling her head back so she was forced to look up at him, bent his head and kissed her neck where he saw her pulse throbbing and left little hot kisses at each corner of her mouth.

"Can you honestly say that you wouldn't care if he kills me?" he whispered.

He had intended to let her go after he taunted her with those words, but holding her so close he couldn't resist one last kiss. Christa closed her eyes in preparation for another furious onslaught. He let go of her wrist and put his hand on her cheek. This time his lips were gentle when he moved them sweetly on hers.

Tears gathered in her eyes and she went limp against him. Oh Shane, come soon, she prayed. She could fight almost anything, but how could she fight love? And how long would Richard protect her if she continued to resist him?

Shane had awakened her sexual appetite and now she realized what Dominic Sabastian had meant when he said she was naive to think only one man could satisfy her. She knew she had to escape somehow. The pounding of the horse's hoofs on the hard ground announced Blackie's return and Richard reluctantly let her go and joined the men who had gotten pretty drunk in town.

Sitting around the campfire he found out they would soon reach their destination. They were to rendezvous with a man named Smith at a place called Bent's Creek, not far from here.

What then? After they delivered the guns? He could hire the Indian to guide them east. Christa would like that better than Canada. Perhaps Boston or New York. She was a lady and used to the best.

He didn't have much money now, but he was a gambler and he mused, if his luck would hold, he could establish a casino like Dominic Sabastian.

As far as the war was concerned the outcome didn't really matter to him. He was born an English gentleman but that way of life was useless, unless you inherited an estate and the money to go with it.

On the other hand he liked America and the idea of making his own way. He smiled to himself, he even liked the land and the trees, the bigness of it all.

One by one the men sought their blankets and bedrolls. Blackie watched sullenly as Richard joined Christa away from the rest of the group. Why should he let Mr. High and Mighty Fontaine have all the fun he wondered, just before he passed out.

The next morning, Christa was the first one up. She had made a few plans of her own last night. She had decided to try to escape today. She cursed herself for not trying before. If she could make her way to Natchez, then maybe she could find a way to get home.

She made a fire the way Slim had shown her and set the large coffee pot over the flames. She would have to wait until they were ready to leave and she could say she wanted to ride for a while.

Then she would make a break for the woods. She hoped Blackie and the others wouldn't care enough about her to follow. That left only Richard. She hid the knife she used for cutting the bacon in the pocket of her coat, but hoped she wouldn't have to use it on him.

Blackie woke up feeling mean and the more he watched Christa the more he wanted her. The sunlight danced in her auburn hair and a light breeze lifted it gently away from her pretty face.

He wondered why men like Sabastian and Fontaine always seemed to get the prettiest women, and the most money, when it was men like him who did all the dirty work for them.

As they were getting the horses ready he saw Richard helping Christa saddle her horse, and in a flash it came to him, where he had seen her before. He knew he had seen her before, but not with Richard Fontaine.

He had seen her with Shane Coulter, and she had been dressed like a queen at some party at Sabastian's fancy town house in New Orleans. And now, he remembered seeing her with Dominic Sabastian, going into his office.

While Richard finished saddling the horse for her, Christa picked up their blankets and was shaking them out and folding them, when she felt a hand stroking her hair. She dropped the blanket, put her hand in her pocket and was comforted by the feel of the knife.

She turned and froze.

It was Blackie not Richard. He smiled mockingly. "Well Christa," as he spoke he put his hand on her cheek and rubbed gently. "You been with Coulter and Sabastian and Fontaine, you must be about ready for a real man by now, and I'm the realest man you ever met Honey."

Her eyes widened in fear and she tried to scream but no sound came out of her mouth.

"Get away from her Blackie," Richard ordered with his pistol drawn and ready.

The others just stood there watching, not caring about the outcome. Blackie Harris was nothing to them but a man who hired them to do a job and Richard Fontaine was even less.

Suddenly Blackie whirled and faced Richard with his own pistol drawn.

"Get away from her," Richard said contemptuously. "She's mine."

"Yah, yours and Coulter's and Sabastian's and now she's gonna' be mine."

At last, Christa came to life. She pulled the knife from her pocket and held the sharp blade to Blackie's neck, then nervously ordered, "Drop it. Now." She hoped no one saw her shaking. She had never been so afraid and desperate.

"I'm sick of this whole situation," she said in a hoarse voice, "and I intend to ride away or die in the attempt."

Blackie dropped the pistol when he realized none of the others were about to back him up. He doubted if Mr. Fontaine could hit the side of a barn, but an angry female with a knife at his throat was another matter.

"I'm going home," Christa said to everyone in general and ran to her horse.

"Christa wait I'm going with you." Richard held his pistol pointed at Blackie while she mounted and then moved cautiously over to his own horse.

The horse was skittish and moved just out of his reach, so Richard had to take his eyes off Blackie for a few seconds.

Blackie dropped to the ground and retrieved his pistol.

He shot without taking aim and hit Richard just as he was throwing his leg over the saddle.

Christa heard the shot but didn't stop to see what had happened. She heard another shot and a rider behind her but kept going anyway. Tears of joy or fear, she didn't know which, almost blinded her at times, but she kept going.

At first, she thought Richard was behind her. After awhile when she didn't hear the other horse she feared he was dead or he would have caught up with her.

She kept riding, not knowing where she was going. Hoping to find help soon. She wanted to get as far away as she could before dark.

The terrain turned rough and rocky. She remembered coming by here when they were going the other way. She had been riding in the wagon with Richard and they had to slow down so the wagon wouldn't tip over.

She kept going. Suddenly she was flying through the air, as her horse fell from under her. She felt a sharp pain in her head and then nothing.

Shane Coulter was riding hard because he knew they were getting close now. He had to know if Christa was dead or alive and if she had gone willingly with Richard Fontaine. They were approaching some rough terrain now, so he slowed down a little. They couldn't afford to lose any more horses. What was that up ahead? A horse with no rider.

"It's Christa's horse," Shane shouted to the others, turning in his saddle. He reined in his own horse and jumped down. When he checked Christa's horse, he discovered one of it's front legs was broken.

By now Charles and Jamie had joined him on the ground. Harry and Adam and Lafitte's men stayed mounted.

"What's that over there," Charles asked. Shane and Jamie looked in the direction he was pointing. Shane ran to what at first appeared to be a pile of old rags. Just as he bent to investigate, the sun came out from a cloud and revealed her hair.

"Christa!" he shouted. Dropping to one knee he turned her over carefully. She was dressed in the clothes she had worn when she first came aboard the *Falcon*.

He slipped his arm under her back then brushed her hair back from her face and gasped when he spotted the bloody gash just above her temple near the hair line.

He hugged her to him and felt her steady breathing against his chest. "Thank God, she's alive," he whispered as the others gathered around smiling.

"She must have been riding too fast. Maybe someone was after her.

The horse stumbled and broke it's leg and threw her. There's blood on that rock. Let's take her to Natchez and have a doctor check her over.

When I'm mounted, hand her up to me," Shane said, handing her over to her father.

"Thank God she's alive," Charles said aloud and wondered to himself if it was possible that she went willingly with Richard.

She had always been impulsive and stubborn. If she had quarreled with Shane she might have done it on an impulse. But he was sure she loved Shane.

There was no use speculating about it now. When they got her to Natchez she would be properly taken care of and she could tell them what had happened.

Richard Fontaine examined the wound in his left leg. He took another drink from his canteen and wished he had something stronger to drink. Well, perhaps when they found him they would take pity on him and share what they had.

When he had come to his senses after passing out and falling from his horse, his first thought was to go after Christa. But he discovered he was to weak to stand for more then the time it took to get his canteen from his saddle.

He couldn't even pull himself up enough to climb back on his horse. He guessed, correctly, that when Christa found Shane and the others, they would come back his way. If not for him, then for the guns.

He would have to give Christa up now, and take his chances with Shane. He was too weak to fight Shane now anyway. If it weren't for Christa he and Shane would probably have become great friends.

So. What now, Mr. Fontaine? He asked himself. Could he go back to New Orleans and pretend nothing happened. He laughed. Nothing did happen. Nothing had changed. Or had it? He could have helped Christa escape. Too late to think of that now, old boy.

He'd tell them about the rendezvous. Maybe that would smooth things over a little, but if Shane demanded satisfaction he would have to wait awhile.

He called himself every kind of fool. Why did he want her anyway. She had repeatedly rejected him. He deserved better, and he resolved, he deserved a women who loved him the way she loved Shane.

As if the effort of these decisions had drained what little strength he had left, he lay his weary head back against the huge old oak tree and shut his eyes.

The next thing he knew he was surrounded by horses. He glanced up and saw the horses each had a rider. Struggling to rise he winced painfully as a mantle of darkness fell over him.

Shane and the Devereax's took the wounded to Natchez, while Adam and Harry and Lafitte's men went after the guns. Blackie and the Indian had gotten away and Slim and the other two had surrendered quickly saying they didn't get paid enough to risk their lives.

In Natchez they were welcomed into the home of an old friend of Shane and Adam's, a prosperous gambler and business man, Jack Trent.

The doctor had come and gone. Christa would be fine, but would have a headache when she woke. Richard too, would be good as new, but had lost a lot of blood and would need a longer time to recover fully.

Sitting on the terrace in the bright autumn sunshine the next day, Shane thought how much better things looked after a good night's sleep, a bath and a good meal.

He had just finished explaining to Jack about the guns and how Christa had gotten involved when they were interrupted by jack's wife Cora, who told them, " That man you brought in is awake now, if you want to speak to him, but he's pretty weak and might pass out again."

Cora led Shane through the drawing room, across the hall and up the wide lushly carpeted stair case. It appeared Jack was doing well, Shane thought, as he looked around at the elegant furniture and the crystal chandelier that hung from the high ceiling.

Jack Trent was an entrepreneur. He gambled and from his winnings he loaned money to others for half interest in what ever business they had in mind to start. He must own half of Natchez, Shane mused.

They paused to check on Christa, who was now dressed in a high necked white gown and tucked safely in a large bed in one of the many guest rooms in the mansion. She went on sleeping peacefully as Shane bent to kiss her on the cheek and brush back a stray curl from her forehead.

He joined Cora once more and she pushed open the half closed door across the hall before Shane had a chance to think what to say.

The sunlight spilled over the bed where Richard Fontaine lay looking steadily back into Shane's questioning face. He grinned, then said casually, "So, you finally caught up with us. What took you so long?"

Someone ran off our horses and we had a pretty far walk before we could buy more. I don't suppose you'd know anything about it would you?"

"I just came along for the ride. You know, mend a broken heart and all that. Have you caught Blackie Harris and the others yet?"

"No. Blackie got away but we got the guns back and my wife and you."

Shane was torn between a grudging admiration for this Englishman and a very strong desire to strangle him.

Cora took the tray a servant had just brought and set it beside the bed.

"I'll leave you gentlemen to talk," she said, pointedly.

Shane grabbed a wooden chair, turned it toward him straddled the seat and braced his arms on the back. He took a deep breath and poured some whiskey from the bottle on the tray into the two small glasses then silently offered one to Richard.

"Thanks," Richard said, draining it quickly. After making a face and some coughing, he held the glass out for more.

Shane refilled the glasses and they drank, silently watching each other.

"All right, now why don't you tell me what my wife was doing with you and your friends?"

At the words, "my wife," Richard closed is eyes for a moment. A picture of Christa, her auburn hair flying out behind her as she rode away from him, flashed into his mind.

"Where is the lady in question?" He was beginning to feel sleepy again. "What did she tell you or didn't you believe her? Oh, I understand now, you want to see if our stories match, is that it?"

Christa was thrown from her horse and hit her head. She's been unconscious since we found her."

A frown creased Richard's handsome brow and he struggled to sit up. "Where is she? Is she going to be alright? Where are we by the way?" He glanced around the unfamiliar room, his gaze finally stopping to rest on the lovely brown eyed girl standing in the doorway. If anyone could make him forget Christa, it was this dark haired angel. He smiled weakly, and reluctantly returned his gaze to Shane.

"We're near Natchez, at the home of a friend of mine. This is his daughter," Shane said, then made the proper introductions.

Richard's smile charmed the girl.

"May I say it was worth getting shot, just to have this pleasure."

Judith Trent fell in love that instant with the handsome blue eyed Englishman. She had always dreamed that she would one day meet and marry a handsome fair-haired stranger, and now her dream was coming true.

Suddenly realizing that she was standing there smiling like an idiot, she tried to compose herself.

"I don't think you should have any more whiskey right now. I'm going to get you something to eat. I'll be back soon. With a last smiling glance at Richard as she left, she bumped the door frame on her way out.

Shane sighed. He just wanted to go lay down beside Christa and hold her close while she slept, but it was still early and Richard hadn't given him any answers yet.

He ran his hands over his face and through his dark hair. He would have to try again. Pushing back his chair, he grabbed Richard by the front of the shirt and growled in exasperation, "What was my wife doing with you?"

"Take your hands off me," Richard gasped defiantly. " You know how she is, she wants to be in on everything. She was snooping around Sabastian's office and she overheard him talking about stealing the guns."

"I guess you had gone off somewhere, so she decided to follow us just long enough to find out where the guns were going, but Blackie's man caught her."

"She pretended to be my lady friend. I suppose she knew I'd go along with her and I did.

Blackie was going to have his men shoot her, then she fainted, so I told Blackie I would take responsibly for her. He didn't really care one way or the other. He just wanted to get the job done."

Angry now, Shane shouted. "So, you just took my wife?"

"Well, I couldn't let them shoot her could I?" Richard made an effort to be angry but he was too weak.

Deciding to let it go for now, Shane asked, "How did you get shot?"

"Blackie made a play for her and she decided she'd had enough. He wasn't afraid of me when I drew my pistol but you should have seen him when Christa put a knife to his throat."

Richard paused as he remembered. "She was magnificent. 'I'm going home,' she announced and just stomped over to her horse, climbed on and didn't look back," he chuckled, to see what was happening to me.

Shane wondered why she hadn't tried to escape sooner. Well, she was only a women, he reasoned, she was probably scared to death. Perhaps it was better if Richard was there with her, to protect her from the others.

"Blackie was in charge not me. Sabastian didn't trust me enough for that. I think he sent me along to get me out of the way." Richard chuckled again. "He wants her too you know. He must have been furious when he found out she had followed us."

"I guess it doesn't matter now, but we were supposed to meet a man named Mr. Smith, a British agent, who's been stirring up some renegade's." Richard's voice began to fade and his eye lids fluttered shut.

Christa was dreaming she was in a nice bed with clean sheets and Shane was lying next to her with his arm across her waist and his face close to hers. She turned and felt his warm breath on her cheek. Her eyes flew open. "Shane, is that you or am I still dreaming?"

He gathered her into his arms and laughed. "If this is a dream, we're both having the same one." When he kissed her they knew it was real.

Chapter 18

Finally Shane drew back a little and asked, "How do you feel? Are you alright?"

"I'm fine now that you're here," Christa sighed, slipping her arms around his neck. "Oh Shane why didn't you come? Every day I prayed you'd catch up with us, but still you didn't come."

"I'm sorry, someone drove our horses away one night."

"Did they hurt you or anything Christa? Did they rape you? You can tell me. You're safe now. Shane was almost afraid of her answer but the question had to be asked, it had been in the back of his mind from the beginning of this fiasco.

She sat up bringing him with her. "Oh, no darling. Thanks to Richard. I guess they must have killed him after I left. I heard shots but I just kept on riding. My head aches a little," she said, feeling the bandage.

"No, he's not dead. He's in a room down the hall. He's been shot in the leg and he lost a lot of blood," Shane told her, "but he'll be alright."

"I don't want to talk about Richard, but I'd hate to think what would have happened to you if not for him."

"I'm glad he got away," Christa said, relieved.

"Christa, tell me what you were doing with them," Shane urged softly.

"I know Richard Fontaine is in love with you and we quarreled before this, this, "he said, waving a hand in the air, " before this all started."

"I thought maybe you went to see him and he might have persuaded you to leave me."

Christa pulled away from him. "Shane Coulter, how could you think such a thing?"

"Well, there are some women who might find him attractive," Shane answered, remembering the way Judith had walked into the door and couldn't seem to get enough of him.

"I overheard Sabastian talking to someone and he mentioned taking the guns from Lafitte's warehouse. I was going to tell you, but you weren't home, so I left you a note. I was sure you'd come as soon as you found it. I never planned on getting caught, you know."

"If I had planned on leaving you for someone else I would have taken some decent clothes with me. Oh darling, please don't be angry with me," she coaxed, sliding her arms around his chest and snuggling against him.

He stroked her coppery curls and sighted, overjoyed to have her back in his arms again, but at least she needed a good scolding. "Don't you know how dangerous Sabastian is, you could have been killed. And are you saying you were with Richard Fontaine all this time and nothing happened. That he didn't try to..."

"I didn't say he didn't try, but nothing happened."

She took his face in her hands and kissed him hungrily, moving her lips sensuously on his mouth. Only then did she become aware that she was wearing a long flannel night gown.

She quickly discarded the garment and threw it to the foot of the bed. "Let me show you you're the only man I want." Dropping back onto the pillows, she watched Shane peel off his own clothing.

A tender yearning swelled up in her heart as she savored the sight of that broad chest and taunt stomach. Her gaze roamed appreciably lower then snapped back to his face, with a smile of anticipation. She reached her arms up to him in sweet invitation.

Shane drank in the sight of her. A flaming Aphrodite, her hair spread out on the pillow like a shinning halo, as her perfect breast beckoned his touch. His eyes traveled lower and he noted she was thinner. He wanted her and he forgot about Richard Fontaine and the guns and Blackie Harris.

He forgot everything except Christa. When he lay half on top of her, she turned her face to receive his kisses. His hands caressed her soft creamy skin and his own body hardened, straining with the memory of her warm moist flesh.

He bent his head and sucked gently at her breast as he massaged and probed her with his hand.

A sigh escaped her, when he moved his attention to the other breast and then kissed her mouth again, taking her breathe away.

She was on fire and he kept feeding the flames with every kiss, every touch. They were together again and he wanted to make her forget every other man in the world but him.

"I can't wait any longer, I want you so," he whispered, and slid gently into her. He was still for a moment, wondering why this women had the power to bring him to this state of blissful frenzy. She wreathed under him and moaned his name softly, shattering the last of his weak control. He couldn't get enough of her.

Christa reveled in his loss of control. She enjoyed the feeling of knowing she could evoke this wild passion in him. Straining together, wave after wave of ecstasy washed over them. Sated, they slept in each others arms.

As dawn stretched it's faint light over the low hills to announce the coming of another day, Blackie Harris reined his horse into the yard of the Wayside Inn, and although it was just getting daylight the chubby French proprietor was up and about.

He looked up from his chore of feeding some clucking and cackling chickens. When he recognized the surly man who had paid for a room in advance, he simply nodded, and continued his work.

When he reached his room, Blackie threw his saddle bags and bedroll on the small table near the window and then threw himself on the bed.

He would have to face Dominic Sabastian later, but now he was tried. He should have just kept on going instead of returning to New Orleans, but then he had the message from Mr. Smith to deliver, and he wasn't afraid of Sabastian.

Richard Fontaine had been awake for some time and had been wondering what he was going to do now. What if Shane and the Devereax's wanted revenge? Would they try to have him arrested or punished in some way? No, probably not, but he didn't want to go back to New Orleans with them.

At least not yet. There was nothing there for him now. Well, no that was wrong. Laura was there, probably going crazy with worry. She had no way of knowing what was going on.

Perhaps he should go back, temporarily. He had come to terms with the fact that Christa wanted to be with Shane and she would never love him that way, and he didn't want to settle for less. He wondered if it was an omen when the door opened a moment later and Judith Trent came tentatively into the room carrying a tray.

"Are you hungry?"

"Starving. What have you got there? It smells like ambrosia. I must have died and gone to haven and you are a beautiful angel sent to take care of me."

She blushed when Richard smiled at her, then sat the tray down, and asked, "How is your leg this morning? You're lucky the shot went clear through. The worst part was losing all that blood, but with a little rest and some good food you'll be on your feet in no time."

"How is Christa? Is she alright?"

"Yes, she's fine. She's conscious and her husband is with her."

Her words hit him like a physical blow and he closed his eyes momentarily.

"Are you alright?" she inquired unaware of the pain her words had caused.

It was at that moment that Richard really let go of Christa. She was married to Shane Coulter and they were together again. She had made her choice. So be it.

Even though his hunger was gone now, he grinned, "What's under that napkin."

Judith lifted the cover and the aroma of coffee and bacon tantalized his nostrils and revived his appetite once more. "Mmm… bacon and eggs," he exclaimed and took up his fork.

Richard finished and lay back on his pillows. Judith could see the effort had tired him, so she picked up the tray and left him to doze for awhile.

Christa was finishing her bath, as Judith Trent entered the room. "Here's a towel for you," she said, handing one to Christa, and laying the clothes she carried on the bed.

"This was Mother's but she wants you to have it," Judith explained, holding up a dress of blue muslin. It had long sleeves, puffed at the shoulders and a round neckline."

She thinks the color will look good on you," she confided, with a grin. "Do you mind if I stay for a while? I'd like to talk to you. That is, if you're feeling alright. I don't want to tire you."

"Oh, please, I'd like you to stay." Christa picked up the clothes from the bed and slipped behind a screen in the corner. "Excuse me while I get dressed."

They were delighted to find the blue gown fit Christa perfectly. Now Christa sat on the edge of the bed brushing her hair while they talked, both carefully avoiding the subject each wanted to know about and that was, Richard Fontaine. Then they came to the same decision and started to speak at the same time.

"I'm sorry," Judith laughed, "You go first."

The smile left Christa's face and she hesitated. "Well, I was just wondering how Richard is doing."

"He is alright, isn't he?" she asked, and then wondered if Shane had told these people about her relationship with him.

"What is he to you?" Judith asked bluntly. "It looked as though you might have been running away with him. Is that true."

"No. I was abducted, and Richard saved my life, that's all. He asked me to marry him once, it seems so long ago now," Christa said, then continued, "but I fell in love with Shane. I think Richard is over me now," she added, and hoped she was right.

Richard Fontaine eased himself down onto the bed and lay back against the pillows. His leg was throbbing. He shouldn't have tried it yet, it was too soon to see if he could still walk.

It would soon be time for dinner, then maybe he could get some brandy or something for the pain. He closed his eyes for a few minutes. When he opened them again he thought he must be dreaming.

He rubbed them and looked again. There was Christa standing in the doorway. All clean and fresh and dressed in a pretty blue gown. He felt a tug at his heart but steeled himself. Her hair was loose about her shoulders and he remembered it's softness then noted the bandage near her hair line.

"Come in, come in, Mrs. Coulter," he beckoned, emphasizing the title. "Won't you sit down," he said politely, indicating the chair by his bed. He glanced behind her. "What, no chaperon? They let you see me alone?" He couldn't keep the bitterness out of his voice.

"I believe Judith is coming with your supper soon," she replied coolly, moving the chair, so it wasn't so close to him.

"I'm sorry Christa, that was uncalled for, my leg is throbbing and I'm a bit irritable. You don't have to be afraid of me. I'll keep my distance." He smiled. "Friends?"

"Of course," she grinned, then added, "I'm just glad we're safe and alive." She thought he was going to say something more but he paused and she followed his gaze to the doorway where Judith had appeared with a tray.

Christa left them then and went down the wide polished staircase to have dinner with the others.

The next day dawned clear and bright, as Shane opened his eyes he brushed a soft curl from his face, and laid it back on Christa's pillow.

He raised himself up on one elbow and watched her sleep, the memory of their lovemaking fresh in his mind. She stirred a little in her sleep and snuggled closer to his warmth.

He gently gathered her into his arms and his heart ached from the fullness of his feeling for her. When they were together like this, he felt stronger and yet weaker and more vulnerable too.

Christa woke in Shane's strong loving arms, and smiled contentedly.

"You awake, Mrs. Coulter?" he asked, kissing her smooth cheek.

"Yes. Are you, Mr. Coulter?" she inquired, kissing his stubbly cheek.

"I'm not sure, I think I'm still dreaming. You see last night, I dreamt I was with this beautiful, luscious, young women, and do you know the liberties she let me take? It was disgraceful," he confided. "Why she let me kiss her like this," he whispered, demonstrating," and she let me feel her like this," he whispered, demonstrating again.

Christa pretended to be shocked. "Why the brazen hussy," she replied soberly, then burst out giggling. Soon what had started as playful teasing turned into something much more serious, and they fed the hunger that desire had awakened.

After lunch Shane, Jack and Charles rode the short couple of miles to Natchez, where arrangements were made to take them back to New Orleans by riverboat.

Christa found herself alone on the terrace with Jamie. "Well, brother dear, you don't seem as happy as the rest of us."

"Why don't you tell me about it?" she said, watching him closely. He still seemed troubled, but didn't answer right away. "I'm sure you'll be glad to get home and see Laura again," she prodded.

When he saw the concerned look on her face he decided to confide in her, maybe she was the one person who could advise him. " I don't know how to start," he said, pausing. "It is about Laura."

"I suppose you know we care for each other. I well, we..." He cleared his throat. "That last day before all this started, about the guns, I mean. I went to see Laura and she was alone and we,…" He rolled his eyes heavenwards.

"Oh, I see," Christa smiled, as she realized what he was trying to tell her. But that's not a problem, is it?"

Jamie smiled back at his sister. "No, I want to marry her."

"Jamie, I don't understand what is the problem?"

"It's Richard, I'm afraid after all that's happened he might not take kindly to letting his only sister marry the brother of the women who turned him down so hard."

"Now, that sounds more like a problem." She rubbed her jaw, then spoke again. "Well, there's only one thing to do, and that's to talk to him and tell him how you feel. He said he's forgiven me, so why should he hold anything against you. I'm sure he'll want Laura to be happy."

"I guess you're right. I think she'd marry me anyway but it would be better if he gave his consent.'

The doctor visited that afternoon and said Richard was well enough to walk with the aid of the crutch he had brought with him. Richard was happy to be able to get up and came down stairs feeling quite himself again with some fresh clothes, provided by their host.

Christa couldn't help notice the way Richard's eyes and attention followed Judith and not her this evening. He was letting her go, and she would have to let him go now too.

After supper, Shane and the Devereax's began talking of the return trip. "It'll be a lot quicker and easier than coming up the Trace," Shane said, using the name most people called the trail north of New Orleans.

Richard Fontaine looked around the elegantly furnished drawing room and wondered what he was doing here. He felt out of place with these people. He was running out of time. He had to make a decision and soon.

A few minutes later as Richard was about to return to his room, Jamie Devereax appeared, effectively blocking his way.

"Could we talk, Richard. Alone?" He asked.

"Of course, but I'm getting rather tired. Don't mind if I sit, do you, old boy?"

"Oh, no. Here let me help you."

When they were comfortable, Jamie confessed, "It's about Laura."

"Well, go on, what about Laura?" Richard asked sternly. He knew what Jamie wanted but he couldn't resist the urge to make him squirm a bit.

"As you know we have become very good friends, well what I mean is," Jamie paused. This was going to be harder than he thought.

Richard continued to stare at Jamie blankly as if he hadn't any idea what he wanted to say.

Jamie tried again, "Laura and I have become very close and…"

"Are you telling me that you've seduced my sister?" Richard exploded, his voice filled with outrage.

Jamie swallowed hard. "No, that is, you don't understand. I want, that is we want to…," Richard continued to stare at him, but the frown was dissolving fast.

"We want to be married," Jamie blurted out, on the defensive now.

Richard's stern face collapsed into a wide grin, and then a full smile as he patted Jamie on the shoulder. "Not easy is it?" he said, with a wink.

Relief washed over Jamie. "Then it's all right with you."

"Of course, Laura deserves some happiness. Her first marriage was a farce, you know. Help me up and we'll go tell the others and see if we can find something to drink to celebrate the occasion properly."

Chapter 19

It was a gray November morning when Edward Livingston made his way to Shane Coulter's home. Entering the library, he discovered Charles and Jamie Devereax were already there. When they all had refreshments and were comfortable, Edward spoke first.

"I tell you Shane something's got to be done. It's a good thing you got Lafitte's guns back, because we're dam well going to need them if the British attack here."

"We've just received word that General Jackson is on his way to New Orleans at last. He's driven the English garrison out of Spanish Florida and reinforced Mobil as much as possible," Shane informed them.

"As far as we can tell Dominic Sabastian is above reproach, but he's been cultivating his relationship with Governor Claiborne. I imagine Claiborne is unwittingly telling him every thing he needs to know. Keeping the feud going between Claiborne and Lafitte and encouraging apathy among the people of the city will go a long way in helping the English cause. At least, that's the way I see it gentlemen," Shane said, as he pushed back in his favorite chair and blew a smoke ring towards the ceiling. "What do you say, Charles?"

"Surely Jackson won't listen to Claiborne. He's always been against Lafitte, but turning down his offer of men and arms borders on insanity."

"He gave the order to mobilize the militia, but those who do not wish to serve are simply ignoring it."

"Well, we have the volunteers from Mississippi, Tennessee and Kentucky. Why they're pouring into the area.

"Ready for a good fight too, from what I hear," Jamie observed, taking a sip of his coffee.

They agreed nothing more could be done until Jackson arrived.

Edward Livingston had to meet a client, but he would keep in touch, he told them as he left.

When he was gone Shane and the others joined Christa in the drawing room.

Soon Jamie excused himself, he wanted to see Laura, he said.

Shane patiently made small talk with Charles, but he wanted to be alone with his wife. He caught her eye and smiled. It felt good to be part of a family again. He had never felt lonely before he met her. He had good friends and there had been women, but when he had been without Christa on the Trace, not knowing what was happening, he felt alone and lonely. Now he knew what people meant when they referred to their spouse as the other half.

Charles Devereax was pleased with his daughter's marriage, and now Jamie would soon be wed. He saw the look that passed between Shane and Christa and decided it was time for him to take his leave.

They went with him to the door and he shook hands with Shane and kissed Christa, and told her, "I only regret that your dear sweet mother couldn't be here to see you and Jamie wed."

"Oh, Daddy," Christa said, putting her hand to his cheek. "I do too, but somehow I think she knows and she's with us always in our hearts. I just hope that Shane and I can be as happy as the two of you.

She's been gone a long time Daddy, don't you get lonely. I know," she said, her face lighting up with an idea. "Daddy, you should get married again."

"Not a bad idea," Shane told her as he put his arm around her.

They looked questioningly at Charles, as if they expected him to give them the name of some prospective bride.

"I promise to think about it, if I can find someone who will have me," Charles chuckled and was gone.

Christa ran her fingers through Shane's thick black hair as they lay snuggled together after their fierce lovemaking. His hand was again massaging her breast and he kissed her yearning lips once more.

"Why can't I get enough of you, woman?" he whispered, huskily, kissing her earlobe and then her neck. Do you know how shocked decent people would be if they knew that these two old married people were in bed together in the middle of the day, let alone for the purpose of making love to each other?"

He went on without waiting for her answer. "I love you, Mrs. Coulter," he said, gazing into her eyes, and joy filled her heart.

"And I love you, Mr. Coulter," she answered breathlessly, as his hand worked it's way down her belly seeking that triangle of pleasure between her thighs.

Later, when they became aware of the world again, Christa asked, "Shane darling, would you mind if I gave an engagement party for Jamie and Laura?"

"No, of course not, but I don't think the house is large enough, do you?" he wondered, as he watched her slip her gown over her head.

"Will you fasten me please?" she asked turning her back to him.

"All right, but I'm much better at unfastening," he teased with a twinkle in his soft brown eyes. When he finished he drew her back against his muscular chest and kissed each side of her neck.

"Yes, I know," she smiled, looking up at him from under her long lashes. She turned and put her arms around him.

"You are the most distracting man I've ever met, Shane Coulter. Now about the engagement party?" she questioned with arched brows.

"Well, I suppose we could rent a hall or something, I'll leave the details to you, my love. I'm surprised, you haven't mentioned having it at La Fleur."

"It did cross my mind but I feel this is my home now. You were right when you said home is where the heart is. I want this party to be a celebration for us too, because I've left La Fleur behind me, and now my home is with you. I know La Fleur is just a house and I clung to it because I was happy and loved and safe there. It was my father and Jamie and the memories of my childhood and the good times that I wanted and missed and memories are in my mind and I can have them with me anywhere I go. I discovered that on the Trace."

Kissing her lightly on the nose, he said, "You're the most distracting women I've ever met. I almost forgot I have an appointment.

If I leave now I won't be too late."

"What do you want?" Dominic Sabastian growled, his eyes cold as his manner when his wife Angela glided smoothly into his office that same afternoon.

"Why Dom, darling," she admonished, "is that any way to talk to your wife?" She smiled charmingly at him while she pulled off her gloves and her bonnet.

He watched her suspiciously, she never came to his office unless she wanted something.

"A wife? Is that what you are Angela? I bought you the same way I'd buy a mistress and we both know it, only with you the price was higher. You held out for marriage. Well, you got what you wanted and at first I thought I did too."

"You used to at least pretend you wanted me, but we know who you want, don't we? Whenever Shane Coulter walks into a room you light up and act like a simpering school girl." He turned from her trying to control his anger.

"Well! You should talk," Angela exploded, "the powerful, great Dominic Sabastian. Every time you see his wife Christa, you start drooling like an idiot."

He turned. They glared at each other and he wondered why he had married her. Oh yes, it was because he enjoyed taking things away from other men, and especially handsome young rakes like Shane Coulter.

In his youth he had loved a lovely young women. Her father had given her in marriage to an older man, who was rich and had vast estates. That was when he learned the power of money. He would never have a title, but he had more than enough money and if all went well in the next month or so, he would have even more. Then he could go anywhere, even back to England and become one of the ton.

Angela would have to be gotten rid of somehow, he thought, although she was beautiful, he conceded as she waited for him to speak. Her silver blond hair was up in the back and she wore a gown of deep blue velvet trimmed in black. Her ivory skin was so clear it was almost transparent. She reminded him of a statue he had seen once, of some love goddess, was it Venus or Aphrodite.

"Well," Angela said, "I take it you've decided not to talk to me now. Then just listen. I have a suggestion. It's obvious our marriage is a mockery. I say why don't we go after what we really want. I can keep Shane busy and you can have his wife."

There was a loud crack as Dominic slapped her face, almost knocking her down. Before she recovered, he grabbed her with both hands on her throat.

His eyes showed his rage and her eyes grew large with fear.

"You bitch, don't you understand. I don't want you anymore, but I'll see you dead before I'll see you with another man, especially Shane Coulter."

"Dom, please," she gasped hoarsely, "I can't breath." He looked at her coldly. He liked making her beg. He thought of killing her right now, but then this wasn't the right time or place. If she died, it would have to be an accident. He loosened his grip and shoved her away from him and ran his hands through his hair and straightened his neck cloth in the mirror behind his desk.

Angela had slumped into the nearest chair. Tears formed in her eyes, but she willed them not to fall. She was still shaking and drew a white lace trimmed handkerchief from her reticule. She wished he was dead. If he was dead, she would be free and she could have any man she wanted even Shane Coulter.

Dominic turned from the mirror and told her coldly, "Get out, I have business to take care of, and I'm expecting someone very important. I don't want you here when he comes."

Without a word she got shakily to her feet, gathered up her things and left him.

In the hallway she passed a tall, slim man, who tipped his hat and smiled politely at her. She had never seen him before and knew he must be the someone very important that Dominic was expecting. She wondered what was so important.

Turning around she walked back the way she had come and stopped in front of a door that she knew was a bedroom with a connecting door to Dom's office. Glancing around to make sure no one saw her, she tried the knob, turned it slowly and peeked into the room.

Good, it was empty. She stepped cautiously in and closed the door carefully behind her, then crossed the room to the other door. Kneeling, she looked into the keyhole. The two men were facing the fireplace with their backs to her. Her heart pounded as she slowly turned the knob so she could hear what they were saying.

"Don't worry, I'm not known in this area," the stranger was saying, as Angela opened the door just a crack. "Marvelous brandy, may I have another?" he asked, holding out his empty glass. Angela noticed that he spoke with a British accent. They moved over to Dominic's desk, and while Dom poured the brandy the stranger continued to talk.

"They've given you a very important assignment. You must be a very good marksman."

"I'm the best," Dominic said and smiled his amusement, then sipped his brandy. "That's why they're going to pay me so much."

"Just who is this Joker I've been hearing about?"

"Why, Curtis, I'm surprised they didn't tell you?"

"Come on Sabastian, you know you can trust me."

"Well, alright. It's Jackson."

"You mean, Andrew Jackson? They want you to kill Andrew Jackson? That's incredible." Curtis swallowed some brandy, a puzzled look on his face. "I've got just one more question.

"Yes. What is it?" Now they were seated. Dominic, in his big leather chair behind his huge desk, was very satisfied with himself and Angela was satisfied with herself too, now.

Curtis got up and leaned over the desk. "If you're so good, why not just challenge him to a duel. I've heard he's famous for his temper."

"It's been tried. The man's like a cat. He has nine lives. This way it's a sure thing."

"But he has so many friends and sympathizers around him all the time, how are you going to get close enough?" Curtis asked, dropping back into his chair.

"You don't need to know everything. I have my ways."

The next day dawned gray and cloudy, and cold as well. Christa Coulter drew her cloak closer around her shoulders as she stepped out of the carriage and ran quickly up the steps of the Sabastian Hotel.

She hadn't seen Dominic Sabastian since her return to the city and she wondered how much he knew about what had happened to her. Maybe he thought Richard Fontaine had been killed. Shane told her that Blackie Harris had gotten away. He must have told Sabastian everything.

She took a deep breath and when she entered the lobby, she pulled back the hood of her velvet cloak. She glanced around and decided to ask the clerk about reserving the ballroom for Jamie's engagement party.

Just as she was about to speak to the thin young man behind the counter, she was stopped by a familiar voice. She turned and hoped her bright smile would hide her nervousness.

"My dear Mrs. Coulter, I heard you were back from your trip, and looking as lovely as usual, I might add."

"Mr. Sabastian. How nice to see you again." As he took her gloved right hand in both of his, the memory of their last meeting flashed into her mind. What would she have done if Richard hadn't intruded?

"Please, call me Dom my dear," he said. He was surprised to see her here like the fly landing on the spider's web, or did her husband send her to spy on him he wondered.

"My, word does get around doesn't it? However did you know about our little trip?" Christa asked, innocently.

"Oh, I don't remember who it was, but someone mentioned it."

He released her hand quickly, although reluctantly, when some ladies passed by on the way into the restaurant, and gave them a knowing look. Christa felt uncomfortable but continued as if nothing had happened.

"I've come on business today. I'm interested in renting your ballroom. You see, my brother Jamie got engaged recently, and I'd like to have a party for them."

She paused, knowing she would have to reveal his fiancee's name soon. Well, she thought, you've come this far, then she felt in her pocket for the pistol she had put there just in case she got into trouble. She hoped she wouldn't have to use it.

"What is the young ladies name?" he ask, adjusting the sleeve of his new coat. Dominic Sabastian was a vain man, so he was glad he looked his best on the chance meeting with Christa.

At forty-five he was still in good health and he had been assured last night in the arms of his latest mistress he was still very virile.

"It's Richard Fontaine's sister, Laura Sims," Christa said, watching him closely for a reaction, but he didn't show any sign of surprise or concern.

"Richard seems to be a man of mystery now. He quit his job and left the city about the same time that you went on your trip," he chuckled, "perhaps you saw him on the road."

"No. I'm afraid not." Christa laughed, although she didn't think it was a bit funny.

"I suppose his sister knows what's become of him," he ventured.

"Laura told me he often talked of going back to Canada," Christa suggested.

"Well, no matter," Dominic shrugged. "Come, I'll have my clerk check the records and you can consult with him on a suitable date for your party."

After he left her in the lobby with his clerk, Dominic went to his office. He took off his hat and threw it in a chair, then poured himself a drink and sat behind his desk. He wished he knew just what had happened. All he did know was that Christa Coulter was acting as if nothing had happened, but he knew Shane had gone up the Trace after them and had come back without Richard Fontaine and with the guns. Blackie seemed to think she was running away with Richard.

Did Shane kill him? She must have used Fontaine good to get information from him.

She was the only one who could have told Coulter. No one else knew. Shane Coulter always seemed to be in his way. Perhaps he should get rid of him before he got in his way again.

He finished his drink, picked up his hat and went back down to the lobby. Christa was just being helped back into her carriage by Harry Patch. Dominic walked back over to the desk and asked his clerk what day she had settled on.

The fire crackled and the flames leapt up to meet and warm the hands that were held out in welcome. The gray skies of the past week were gone today and the bright sunshine brought a promise of a warmer afternoon, but Angela felt a chill in her bones.

She poured herself another glass of wine and set down in the big overstuffed chair near-by, then picked up the invitation from the side table and read it again.

She had been wondering how she could stop Dominic without incriminating herself, then she found this invitation to Jamie Devereax's engagement party on the silver tray this morning with all the other invitations the Sabastians always received.

Yes, she mused, now she had a weapon she could use to get even with Dom and get rid of him at the same time. She was an American after all. It was her duty to report what she knew. She would have to be very discrete and repentant so that Dom wouldn't be suspicious and she would have to be submissive if he came to her room.

Ever since that awful day in his office she had been afraid of him. That first night she had tossed and turned thinking of ways to kill him.

Yes, she had married him for his money on the advice of her mother. Unfortunately, her mother had taken a fever and died a year after the marriage. She thought about the men she could have had and it almost made her cry.

Shane Coulter had some money and a lot of people liked him, but he was a half breed and a privateer after all, and not accepted into the higher social order, until he married Christa Devereax. The Devereax name gave him that now. Angela laughed at the irony of it all.

Tillie Farnsworth sat across from her sister having coffee and cake at eleven o'clock that same morning in another part of town.

"Have you received your invitation, my dear?" she inquired slyly.

"Well, I have several invitations right here," her sister Mary Fields said, picking up a handful from the tray on the side table and holding them up for inspection.

"Oh, Mary don't' be so obtuse. I'm referring to the party that Coulter women is throwing for her brother and that what's her name."

At Mary's blank look, she continued. "You know, that English widow. Her lover's sister."

"Now Tillie, you don't know that they were lovers for sure. You shouldn't say something like that unless you know for sure," Mary scolded.

"Well, it was common knowledge that he was crazy for her, and that he left the city after she got married," Tillie said emphatically.

"Yes but she did marry that handsome young Mr. Coulter, didn't she?"

"Probably had to," Tillie answered, haughtily.

"Then I take it you're not going to their party?" Mary inquired with a knowing smile but she already knew the answer, as she innocently sipped her coffee and put down her cup.

"Not going," Tillie repeated, a note of surprise in her voice, her brows raised in question. "My dear, I wouldn't miss it for the world."

The carriages came one after another, dropping off the well dressed occupants at the front steps of the hotel. Everyone and anyone of New Orleans society was here tonight. Governor Claiborne and other high ranking city officials and the Livingstons and of course most of the plantation owners of the area. The Creoles, the English and Americans.

All here from curiosity, and some just to get another look at the beautiful woman who not long ago had married the notorious ex-privateer, Shane Coulter.

Three large chandeliers hung from the high ceiling giving light as well as warmth.

Below, Charles Devereax beamed proudly as he stood with his grown children and he couldn't help but wish their mother, his lovely Marie could be here tonight.

Christa, always beautiful, was positively radiant in a gown of gold satin trimmed in black lace.

Jamie smiled happily as he accepted congratulations from admirers, who shook his hand and patted him on the back while their ladies pecked Laura on the cheek and everyone said they were a perfect match.

After most of the guest arrived the dancing began. Jamie and Laura started first and then other couples joined in the waltz.

Shane held Christa as close as was proper even if they were married.

"Just think, soon Jamie and Laura will be as happy as we are," Christa sighed, smiling at the engaged couple.

"No one could be as happy as we are darling," Shane corrected.

Jamie couldn't take his eyes off Laura. She seemed to have blossomed before him. He always thought she was a beauty, with her golden hair curling about her heart shaped face. Maybe clothes make the women as well as the man. When they first met she wore black and although she was friendly enough, she seemed to hold herself back.

Tonight she wore a pretty gown of blue silk with little pink rosebuds embroidered around the neck and hem. Little pink rosebuds adorned her hair. She was perfect and she was his.

When Shane left Christa in search of something to drink a while later, Dominic swept her out onto the floor. Shane returned with two glasses and set them on a near-by table. He didn't like the way Dominic Sabastian was smiling at Christa, but what could he do.

"It seems our spouses have abandoned us, Shane," Angela Sabastian, smiled sweetly up at him. This was the moment she had been waiting for.

Sensing she wanted him to, Shane gallantly asked her to dance. Angela had been drinking all evening to fortify herself for what she had to do. If Dominic ever found out he would kill her, but if all went well, he would never know what happened. She took a deep breath and closed her eyes wishing she could be in Shane's arms forever.

"Mrs. Sabastian? Isn't that a bit formal? After all we were very close friends once. Perhaps we could be again. I'm willing if you are."

When he didn't answer she glanced around casually, then continued, "Friends share secrets and I know a secret that I'd tell you if you say yes."

He hated to lead her on, but he wanted to know her secret. "Of course I'll be your friend," he said, with as much intimacy as he could. A smile of delight crossed her face. "It's about my husband. You know, of course, he's an English agent?" She glanced around the room, as if she was bored and saw her husband dancing with Christa.

"Why are you telling me this now?" Shane asked, curiously.

"I've just recently found out something that he's going to do or have done and after all, I am an American. I thought you might be able to stop him."

"And just what is this awful thing?"

She scanned the room again, to make sure no one was paying attention. "He's going to kill Andrew Jackson," she stated, simply and quickly just before the music ended.

Chapter 20

At first Shane was stunned by what Angela had told him but the more he thought about it, the more it made sense. Jackson was their only real hope because the common people liked him.

If Jackson were eliminated the American forces would be no better than a bunch of disorganized rabble. At least long enough for a British invasion. But Angela hadn't given him the time or place. Everyone knew Jackson was on his way to New Orleans. Would they try to stop him from entering the city?

Deciding there was nothing they could do until tomorrow, Shane once again sought out his wife. Finally when the guest had dwindled down to just a few drunks and die-hard card players they took their leave but not before Shane asked Charles and Jamie to come to his house the next day.

At home Shane shared his information with Harry. "Tomorrow we'll send someone to warn Jackson and keep a closer watch on Sabastian." He was tired as he climbed the stairs to join Christa, who was already in bed and half asleep.

" Is something wrong darling?" she asked groggily.

"Nothing that can't wait until tomorrow," he said, sliding under the covers and pulling her into his arms.

Christa turned her face to eagerly receive his kisses. She thought she would be too tired to make love tonight, but now she realized she was wrong.

In Shane's strong arms she felt renewed and refreshed. It always surprised her how much she wanted to be with him. Day after day and night after night.

"I love you so much," he whispered. His hands worked their magic and they were soon lost in their loving.

The next day Angela Sabastian was the talk of the town. Harry Patch brought in the papers with their coffee and cakes. Shane was just taking a sip of his coffee and almost choked on the hot liquid when he saw the headline that announced her death. He stared at it in disbelief.

"Darling, what is it," Christa asked, when she saw the incredulous look on his face. "What's wrong?"

"It's Angela Sabastian," he paused, then added, "she's dead."

"Dead? I don't understand. We just saw her last night. How could she be dead?"

"It seems that upon her arrival home last night she caught her foot in the hem of her gown, fell down the stairs and broke her neck."

Shane read aloud while Christa listened attentively.

"Her husband Mr. Dominic Sabastian, a prominent businessman of this city was grief stricken. Funeral arrangements will be announced later.' "The rest is just about her background," he said in conclusion.

"Shane, you don't believe it was an accident do you?"

"To be honest, no, I don't. I think he killed her."

"But why?"

"You remember when I danced with her last night," he asked.

"Of course, I was very jealous."

"She told me something about him. Something very damaging."

"I think he found out she talked and killed her so she couldn't talk anymore."

"What did she tell you that was so incriminating?"

"First, that he is indeed a British agent and that he intends to assassinate Andrew Jackson."

"Oh, my God." Christa put a hand to her breast and collapsed back into her chair. "Shane we have to stop him. But how?"

Shortly after their marriage, Shane had brought home two servants, Joe and Jessie. A young married couple, who were grateful not to be separated. He had bought them and then given them papers setting them free. They were to work for him in exchange for a room of their own and wages.

When he finished writing some letters, one to Adam Michaels, telling him what was happening, Shane went in search of Harry Patch.

"Harry, I want you to send Joe to Adam with this letter. I know he's a good man and loyal to me. If there's any trouble he knows how to take care of it and himself."

"I'm going to see Lafitte and tell him what I learned yesterday.

Oh, and Harry," he said, from the doorway, "please keep an eye on Christa. I don't want her following me or especially snooping around Dominic Sabastian. You know how she is, always wants to be in on everything."

"Well, Jessie's with her right now, and I'll be sure to pick her up later and bring her home when her and Laura get their shopping done."

Since the military had burned Barataria and confiscated his main warehouse in September, Lafitte had supposedly been in hiding, but never to those who knew him best.

His real friends always knew where he could be found or word could be left for him. Shane was soon admitted into the home of a beautiful young widow. Her husband had been one of Lafitte's captains. He died at the hands of the British.

Lafitte was glad to see him and hugged him, kissing him lightly on each cheek. "Mon ami, it's so good to see you again. I thank you again for the return of my weapons, they are safely stored at my secret warehouse, but I fear it may have been in vain."

"Have you heard what has happened to me of late? The Governor is against me and therefore takes every opportunity to harass me and my brother and I might add my friends as well."

"Jean, I've come because I have some very important information for all of us who care about keeping Louisiana free of the British."

Shane spoke with so much passion that Lafitte knew it was something very important indeed.

"Mon ami, sit down and have some wine with me and tell me all about it, and then we will think of a way to stop it." Jean listened quietly as Shane related his information and his suspicions about Angela's death.

Lafitte rubbed his chin thoughtfully. "You think Dominic Sabastian pushed his wife down the stairs?"

"That's exactly what I think," Shane said, emptying his glass. "But I'll probably never be able to prove it."

"Well, Shane my friend, as for the other thing. The killing of General Jackson. I think you have done all you can, for now. He will be on his guard and so will his men, yes?"

"I hope you're right, Jean."

The Frenchman's big brown eyes turned serious. "Have you thought about what you're going to do after the war is over Shane?"

"Not too much. You mentioned once you would like to go to Texas and it's been in the back of my mind ever since, but I have a wife now and I don't know if she'd be agreeable."

"You should talk to her about it soon, my friend. One way or the other the war will soon be over, and now they have steamboats plying the waters. You can't stop progress, eh. I know that you're new father-in-law is a large plantation owner, but that too, I think is a dying way of life. Already there are those who would out-law slavery and with out the slaves there would be no profit in the large plantations. The days of the privateers are numbered.

"Yes, I know you're right about this too, on the way back from Natchez, we were on a flatboat, but we saw steamboats. I wanted to ride on one, but we would have had to wait another week to leave and we wanted to get back as soon as possible. A short time later, Shane bid his friend a good day. He had others to see today.

Christa smiled at Laura as they sipped their tea. They had stopped for lunch at a fashionable little café not far from the business district.

"Christa, you've hardly touched your food. Don't you feel well?"

Christa reached across the table and put her hand over Laura's.

"I'm fine Laura." She was sure now that she was with child. She wanted to tell Laura, but she thought Shane should be the first to know.

She thought he might have guessed when she had gotten sick to her stomach a few times lately but it seems he believed her when she said it was something she had eaten that didn't agree with her.

As Laura chatted casually Christa nodded in agreement once in a while but her mind was making plans as to how to tell Shane. Tonight she could tell him. She would carefully feel out how children fit into his plans for their future.

She knew most men wanted a son to carry on their name. What if they had all girls? No. That wasn't likely. They could just as easily have all boys. She smiled dreamily.

"Christa?" Laura broke into her thoughts, "Are you all right?"

I swear you were a million miles away just now."

"Oh, Laura, I'm sorry. I was just thinking about tonight. We haven't excepted any invitations and I'm looking forward to just staying home with my husband. I love the social life of the city, but it does get so hectic at times. Don't you think?"

Shane turned quickly and looked behind him. He had the strange feeling he was being followed, but when he looked no one was there.

He continued at a leisurely pace down the tree lined street to the Devereax's house where Charles and Jamie were expecting him. They had been trying to find out all they could about Dominic Sabastian, by whatever means they could, including the use of bribery.

After they were seated with a brandy in one hand and a cigar in the other, Charles began. "I had lunch with my banker today. You know Farnsworth, don't you Shane?" He went on, without waiting for Shane's answer. "Well, anyway, it will come as no surprise that Sabastian has already sold his town house and the hotel. He could have gotten a better price, if he had waited, but he took less, insisting on cash."

Charles took a sip of his brandy and went on, "Then Farnsworth said he withdrew all his funds, saying he was going North to New York where he had friends. He said he couldn't stay here any longer without Angela."

"And if that's not enough," Jamie added confidentially, "I was at my tailors today and he told me Sabastian has paid off his bills."

"Well, he's let it be known he's leaving the city. My guess is that will be right after the assassination attempt," Shane told them. "By the way, I saw Lafitte earlier, and filled him in on everything."

"Shane, you know I don't like his methods, but I guess his heart is in the right place, and that's what counts," Charles Devereax conceded. "I wonder where Sabastian is right now?"

"He seems to have dropped out of sight, but I've got some men looking for him, if he's still in the city, we'll soon know about it," Shane said. He didn't tell them about his feeling that something bad was going to happen.

The man they spoke of lay on a bed fondling the large breast of a women who resembled Christa. He ran his hand along the indentation of her waist and over her full hips. Dominic Sabastian smiled, everything was going according to plan.

He was hold up in a cozy hotel room, and was staying out of sight.

He had even changed his appearance a little. Wearing glasses and a phony mustache when he went out.

He hated using a prostitute, but when he saw her hair it made him think of Christa Coulter and he couldn't resist. He moved his hand again and she moved suggestively. As he felt the warmth between her shapely thighs, he thought how pleasant it was with a willing woman.

Angela had always managed to make him feel as if he had raped her. Well that part of his life was over now.

Harry Patch opened the door and stood aside to let Christa and Jessie enter the house first. "I'll take these packages up to your room," he said to Christa as he passed behind them and took the stairs two at a time.

"I'll get started on dinner, Miss Christa, you just go sit down and warm your self by the fire, and don't worry about a thing. I know you want this meal to be special," Jessie said, taking Christa's cloak and gloves. "I'll bring you some tea. It might settle your stomach," she added with a knowing smile, and was gone before Christa could think of a suitable denial.

She took off her bonnet and laid it on the small table in the hall, then looked at her reflection in the mirror above it. She smoothed a stray curl back into place and thought she looked the same. Yes, the same blue-green eyes and the straight nose, the full lips. Looking down, she crossed her arms over her belly and smiled.

It was near the end of November and there was a chill in the air. She shivered and hugged herself, rubbing her arms as she walked into the small salon and checked the fireplace.

Harry came in just as she lifted the poker. "Here, I'll take care of that," he said. He smiled and laid a piece of wood on the fire. "You sure look happy, Miss Christa, and I think I know why too. "It's cause you're going to be stayin' home tonight. Just the two of you. Well, am I right?" he asked with childlike excitement.

"Yes, I want tonight to be special Harry." She sighed and wondered if Harry had guessed her secret, like Jessie obviously had.

"Any time a man gets to spend time alone with a beautiful women like you is special, little lady," Harry informed her.

"What a sweet thing to say. Thank you, Harry," she said, stretching up to lay a kiss on his leathery cheek, affection tugging at her heart.

Jessie came into the bedroom a while later, as Christa was admiring some of her new finery. "Do you want me to put these things away for you," she asked. Christa knew Jessie loved to touch her lovely clothes, and secretly envied her.

"Yes, thank you. I think I'll have time for a nap, if you help me out of this gown. I don't know if I can sleep, but at least I'd like to lie down for a while."

"Jessie," Christa asked, as the maid was hanging her discarded blue velvet day dress in the armoire.

"Yes," Jessie turned a questioning face to her, and handed her a yellow silk wrapper.

"Will you teach me to cook? I know a woman of my position doesn't need to know, but it's something I want to do. When Shane took me to meet his grandmother, I helped her with some baking and I loved it. She showed me how to make an apple pie and I was so proud when Shane said it was the best he ever had." She crinkled her face. "I don't think he'll mind, do you?"

"Miss Christa, I'll be glad to teach you what I know, but I'm just a plain cook you know. I'm not a French chef or anything like that. Just meat and potatoes and bread and…"

"But Jessie that's what I want. That's what Shane likes. I think you're a very good cook."

"I'm glad you like it," Jessie said, bowing her head shyly, "but I don't understand why you want to learn. You're a lady and nobody expects you to do nothing'."

"My husband is very adventurous and he may decide to go out west again or someplace where we may not have servants on hand and I want to be prepared. I want to be able to take care of my family."

"I better get back to the kitchen or there won't be any thing to eat," Jessie chuckled. "That's the most important part of cooking. Plannin' ahead and gettin' the things you need together."

When Jessie was gone, Christa lay down on the big comfortable bed.

As if waiting for her to close her eyes, the image of Shane appeared before her. Smiling that amused smile of his, a twinkle in his brown eyes.

She wondered where he had gone today and she wished he was here now to hold her close. She missed him beside her in the big bed, but he would be home soon, and she would tell him her news.

It was late afternoon as Shane Coulter entered Morgan's Exchange, but he hadn't come to this famous auction house to buy slaves today. He was hoping to find a certain man who might give him information for a price.

He moved slowly towards the back of the room, then paused to watch as the auctioneer pointed out the strength of a couple young slaves. Scanning the crowd, he didn't see his man.

"Shane, my friend," someone called above the noise, "over here." He swiveled his head in the direction of the voice. "Come sit down and have a drink with me. We don't see you around here often," Andre Beaushard said, as he shook Shane's outstretched hand.

"Andre, it's good to see you," Shane smiled and sat down.

Andre ordered more drinks from a passing waiter, who served them quickly. "I heard you got married. Some gorgeous blond, no doubt," Andre winked.

"Not a blond, but gorgeous," Shane replied.

"Well at any rate, I'm glad you're out of circulation. Now maybe the rest of us bachelors will have a chance with the fair ladies of New Orleans," Andre grinned.

Shane laughed at his old friend, he knew Andre was teasing him about his first days in the city.

The ladies loved his dark good looks and he had been young and foolish enough to pursue as many as he could, gaining for himself a reputation as a heartbreaker.

Breaking hearts had never been his intention. Each time he thought was the real thing, each flirtation he thought would be the last, but then he would discover another lovely lady smiling sweetly from under lowered lashes and it would start all over again.

After courting a couple of young ladies, having dropped one in favor of the other, he found himself called out by the father of one and the brother of the other, and learned to confine himself to mistresses, but that was long ago and no women before or since seemed to hold a candle to his auburn-haired wife.

"Surely you had your fill while I was gone. Tell me about your life and I'll tell you about my wife," Shane said, lifting his glass.

Andre Beaushard was a Creole and the son of one of Louisiana's oldest families. They talked of old times and the present but when Shane began to discuss the war, Andre seemed to lose interest and grew impatient.

"Shane, I don't see what difference it makes who wins. New Orleans has had many flags. What does it matter, French, Spanish or British? Life will go on as before."

Shane was appalled at the apathy of his old friend. "I'm sorry you feel that way, Andre," he said stiffly.

Chapter 21

"Many feel the way I do Shane but you were never one to turn away from a good fight were you? Well I must be going," he said, finishing his wine. "I'm courting a young lady and having dinner with her family tonight. Wish me luck and perhaps I will join you soon in the state of wedded bliss. It really was good to see you again."

After they parted, Shane realized it was getting late. He wanted to go home to Christa, to just talk to her about Texas and see how she felt about it.

Would she be willing to give up her life of leisure, to follow him, and if not could he go without her? No. She was part of him now. He would have to persuade her to with him.

It was dusk as he walked into the street. The sun was slowly sinking, after making a late afternoon appearance. Drawing his collar about him, Shane decided to walk home even though it was some distance to his house.

He was anxious to see Christa, but he had been drinking more than usual what with wine with Jean and then brandy with Charles and Jamie, not to mention more wine with Andre. He thought the fresh air would clear his head.

After they shared a very nice meal, Shane and Christa found themselves alone in the cozy living room. Shane told her about his meeting with Lafitte.

He was relieved when she said she would follow him anywhere.

Shane lifted her into his arms and carried her up to their room. Kicking the door shut, he sat her on her feet. His kiss took her breath away while his hands unfastened the back of her gown. As it slid to a pile at their feet, anticipation made him drunk with desire.

He ran his fingers through her silky hair and with his hands at the back of her neck he kissed her again but this time the gentleness was gone and in it's place was a savage passion that was answered by her own.

His hands slid down her back pushing her body into his, kneading and massaging her through the thin material of her underskirt.

She pushed the garment off her shoulders and pulled it down over her hips exposing her full firm breast. Arching her back in invitation, she was rewarded when his hands and mouth tasted her offering.

Her own desire was burning hot and she wanted to see his naked body, to touch him, to feel him. She tried to unfasten the buttons of his shirt and was all thumbs.

He laughed at her impatience and pushed her slowly away, then drew back the covers of the bed. Kissing her lightly on the lips and on each shoulder, he pushed her back so she was forced to lay down.

His eyes never left her as he stepped back and quickly discarded his own clothing.

Christa watched in fascination as his magnificent body was revealed to her. Then he was beside her on the bed and she was crushed happily against his hardness.

After kissing the pulse beating wildly in her throat he left a trail of burning flesh where hot kisses seared her stomach and the tops of her thighs.

She gasped with delight as his hands probed and caressed her hot moist flesh. Unable to hold back any longer they strained and struggled together until the world exploded and they lay exhausted. Shane gathered just enough strength to roll off her, so she could breathe, then pulled her back into his arms. Just before he fell asleep, Christa said hoarsely, "Darling, we're going to have a baby"

Dawn crept in the bedroom window and spread itself thinly over the sleepers, insinuating itself relentlessly into the man's consciousness, making him aware of the new day.

Shane slowly opened his eyes, and chuckled to find Christa nestled in his arms. He watched her sleeping peacefully and brushed a stray curl back from her forehead.

Did he dream that she said, they were going to have a baby or was that real? He had noticed that her breast seemed a little fuller and she had complained of feeling nauseous lately. He would talk to her about it later, but first things first.

Right now, he had to find Dominic Sabastian and stop him. He reluctantly got out of bed, slowly and carefully sliding his arms from around Christa's warmth.

By the time he came down stairs Jessie had made coffee and Harry and Adam were waiting for him. They were soon joined by Charles and Jamie in the dining room.

"Sabastian seems to have disappeared from the city. No one has seen him in at least two days," Adam reported, then waited for their reaction.

"Well gentlemen," Shane said, "since we don't know where Sabastian is, I suggest we go and watch General Jackson make his appearance. We'll keep a watch out for Sabastian. If he intends to assassinate Jackson, it will have to be soon, before he can get things organized."

The people of the city of New Orleans took heart as they watched the tall, thin, hawk eyed man in the uniform of the American army, riding towards them. Then a cheer went up from the crowd and some of the militiamen fired their rifles into the air.

After the morning meeting, Adam Michaels rode out to warn Jackson and now rode with his entourage. Adam and several of the General's most trusted men scanned the crowd.

Shane was on his way to station himself on a balcony down the street. He couldn't believe his luck. He stopped abruptly and pretended to examine the display in a shop window. It was Dominic Sabastian.

When he saw Sabastian go into the Plaza Hotel, he followed again but found the lobby empty.

The aging clerk looked up at him over the rim of his glasses and asked, "May I help you sir?"

"Yes. Well, you see I was just outside, watching General Jackson, when I thought I saw an old friend from school. He came in here. I called to him, but I guess he didn't hear or perhaps I'm mistaken." Then Shane gave the clerk a short description of Sabastian and waited hopefully.

"Why of course you must mean Mr. Jones," the man beamed, pleased with himself. "He's in room ten."

"Yes, Jones, that's him. Room ten? Thank you very much," Shane smiled as he walked casually to the stairs.

At the landing he drew his pistol and paused to listen, as another cheer when up from the crowd outside. He glanced around. To his right were more stairs, going up to another floor. To his left a long dimly lit hall. He checked the numbers on the doors until he found the one he wanted, then slowly opened the door and stepped inside.

No one was there. He scanned the room. On the balcony. Dominic Sabastian was on the balcony with a gun in one hand and a hat in the other.

A lot of people in the crowd had already shot guns into the air in celebration. One more shot wouldn't be noticed. At least not until Sabastian was long gone.

"Put it down, Sabastian," Shane ordered.

Dominic swung around and snarled, "You bastard Coulter. This is the last time you'll get in my way," but before Sabastian could pull the trigger, Shane shot the weapon out of his hand.

Sabastian grabbed his smarting hand, a startled look on his face. He had heard Shane was a crack shot, but he was one himself and of course he thought he was the better man.

"All right, Mr. Jones, come with me. We're going to the authorities," Shane said smoothly.

"Do you think I'll just go with you without a fight?" Sabastian asked sarcastically.

Shane smiled, "I hope you do put up a fight. I'd just love to beat you to a pulp."

Sabastian shrugged and put up his hands in a gesture of surrender, so Shane was surprised when he dived low for his ankles and brought him down to the floor.

Shane cursed himself for underestimating Sabastian again. They struggled. Dominic landed a vicious blow to Shane's jaw, but Shane clung to the front of Sabastian's shirt so he couldn't get away.

Sabastian quickly pulled the little dagger out of his coat pocket.

He always carried it for just this kind of circumstance. It was small, with a jeweled handle but it had a long sharp blade. He often used it for a letter opener, but now he skillfully plunged it into his nemesis.

Shane's arm felt numb and his grip on Sabastian's shirt weakened enough for Dominic to leap to his feet. Blood flowed heavily down Shane's arm as he staggered to his feet and started after Sabastian.

Adam had seen Shane go into the hotel and followed. Hampered by the crowd, he didn't see Dominic Sabastian walk casually out into the street and disappear in the throng.

Just as Adam entered the lobby, Shane came staggering down the stairs and collapsed. A doctor was summoned and then a carriage.

At home Christa and Jessie fussed over him like a mother hen with a chick or as Shane pointed out, a mother with a new born babe.

"He's got to be found, before he kills someone," Shane insisted when they wouldn't let him up, then discovered maybe they were right, when he tried to stand and got light headed and dizzy.

Putting her hands on her hips, Christa reasoned, "If you eat all your lunch and lie down for the rest of the day the doctor said you might be strong enough to go to the reception for General Jackson tonight at the Livingstons."

They had put him on the sofa in the library and there was a nice blaze in the fire place. "Oh, all right," he relented, "I am going to that reception. I'm certain Sabastian isn't through yet. Now come over here and take care of me little mother," he smiled, a tender light in his eyes.

"How can I resist when you smile at me like that. Shane darling, I'm so glad you're all right, but please promise me that if he is there tonight you'll just point him out and let the authorities arrest him."

"I should have shot him when I had the chance," Shane muttered, then took her hand and pulled her down to the floor beside the sofa, so that their faces were close. "Now kiss me and make me forget about Sabastian for a while."

Christa eagerly obeyed.

Their lips met in sweet contentment and Shane lay back against the pillows and yawned. The doctor had given him something to make him sleep and it was beginning to take effect.

"Is it really true about the baby?" he asked softly with his eyes closed.

"Yes darling. It's true," she whispered as he fell asleep smiling.

"There, how's that," Jessie asked standing back to inspect her handy work.

Christa smiled at her reflection in the mirror. "Oh Jessie, what did I ever do before you came into my life?"

"Mrs. Coulter you got such beautiful hair. I just love to see how I can fix it up for you."

"I really wanted to look my best tonight and thanks to you Jessie, I do." Looking in the mirror she smoothed the front of her new violet satin gown and adjusted the long puffed sleeves. Lace trimmed the neckline and the hem, along with gold embroidered flowers.

Jessie handed her her reticule and gloves and opened the door for her.

Shane was already dressed and waiting downstairs. After sleeping most of the day, he was feeling much better. Harry had helped him bathe and shave and get dressed.

He walked restlessly out into the hall and stopped at the foot of the stairs. Looking up, he saw Christa, a vision of loveliness coming towards him.

Christa smiled at the handsome man who was her husband.

It gave her a thrill of delight to know that the muscular physique under the fine evening clothes was hers to touch and admire at her leisure.

Shane was amused by her bold appraisal. She held out her hand to him and he kissed it gallantly.

"How do I look?" she asked, turning slowly around. She knew she looked her best, yet she wanted Shane's approval.

"Too good to share with the rest of the world Mrs. Coulter." They stood staring spellbound into each others eyes.

"I hate to break this up, you two, but I think we should get going," Harry said breaking the spell and handing Shane the velvet cloak that matched Christa's gown.

Once in the carriage and on their way, Shane put his good arm around Christa and drew her close. He was about to kiss her lightly on the cheek, when she turned her face to him and pulled his head down to meet her hungry lips.

A spark arched between them and Shane slowly pushed her away breathing hard. "We'll never get to the Livingston's if I allow you to have your way with me. I admit I'm addicted to your charms, however I must insist that you stop mauling me," he said, in a mocking tone, " but just until we get back home," he added, smiling.

A dozen carriages lined the street in front of Edward Livingston's home. Shane took Harry aside and instructed him to keep a sharp eye out for Dominic Sabastian. They were greeted by their host and his wife, the lovely Louise, a dark haired beauty in a rose velvet gown.

"Christa?" It was Laura Sims on Jamie Devereax's arm. It's so good to see you again," Laura said, giving Christa a hug.

The host and hostess left them to mingle and they were joined by Charles Devereax. A few minutes later there was a commotion at the door

General Andrew Jackson had arrived. The quest circled around him, and waited to be introduced. He charmed all the ladies with his compliments and when introduced to Christa he was lavish in his praise. Christa liked him immediately.

"My dear, if we were not already attached, I would surely come calling" he teased, with a merry twinkle in his eyes.

He was a compelling figure in his army uniform. Tall and painfully thin, it was rumored that he had recently been ill and was still not fully recovered.

He walked with great self assurance and laughed easily although he was said to have a fierce temper.

His secretary Major John Reid, a handsome man with piercing blue eyes and coal black hair stayed by his side and Christa saw him casually scan the crowd several times.

She stood back as the entourage moved into the main salon and heard someone behind her say, "What is it about him that inspires such confidence in people?"

"He has a way of getting the job done, that's what it is," another voice answered.

Christa was hungry and wandered over to one of the food laden tables, with Shane and the others trailing. It seems I have my own entourage, she thought, very amused.

"Christa, are you all right, for someone who was so hungry a few moments ago, you're not eating very much," Shane observed.

She swallowed, " I'm fine I... It's your fish. The smell." She put her hand over her mouth. "I'm sorry," she whimpered. "I'm just a little queasy again," she said, trying to keep her voice steady.

Louise Livingston always the perfect hostess noticed Christa's discomfort and asked, "My dear would you like to lie down for a while?"

"No, Louise, I'll be fine. I just need some fresh air. I've had a touchy stomach of late."

"I'll send someone for your cloak," Louise offered, " it's a bit chilly tonight.

"And I'll go with you," Laura volunteered.

"Thank you, just a few breaths of fresh air, I'm sure will revive me."

"Christa, I'm coming too. I can't allow you and Laura to go outside alone when Sabastian is still at large," Shane said, concern in his eyes.

On the flagstone terrace a sinister figure slid quickly into the shadows as the French doors opened and a man and two women stepped outside.

"I've had a letter from Richard," Laura confided.

"Oh, that's wonderful," Christa exclaimed. "Will he be coming home soon?"

Laura smiled, "I don't know. He said he was going to propose to that Trent girl you told me about."

"I'm not surprised," Christa said, remembering the way Judith had looked at Richard, with her heart in her eyes.

"I'm going to talk to Jamie and see if we can set a wedding date and then I'll write to Richard. Perhaps he'll come back to New Orleans for our wedding."

"Christa darling, feeling any better?" Shane interrupted.

"Yes, much better, thank you."

"Well let's get back inside and see if we've missed anything important. Shall we?"

A little while latter, in the library, the main topic of conversation was the war. Of course everyone wanted to get General Jackson's opinion of everything from the attack on Washington, to their chances of withstanding a British attack.

The evening was almost over and not a sign of trouble. Could it be that Sabastian had given up, knowing that they were on to him now Shane wondered as he stood with a small group that included Charles and Jamie Devereax and his Creole friend Andre.

"General, we made plans for you to review the troops tomorrow afternoon," they heard Governor Claiborne say.

"How many men do you have?" Jackson asked.

"Not enough, I'm afraid," Claiborne conceded.

"General, have you been informed that Jean Lafitte has offered his men and arms?" Edward Livingston asked, and received an offended look from Claiborne.

"Which I turned down. I see no need to do business with that pirate," the Governor exclaimed angrily.

"And I agree with the Governor," Jackson stated emphatically.

"I think once Jackson reviews the troops he may change his mind," Charles chuckled.

"Let's hope that Lafitte doesn't withdraw his offer," Shane remarked. Just then he glanced up and saw Adam Michaels motioning to him from the doorway.

Adam was looking around nervously as Shane approached him. He led Shane out into the hallway then told him, "He's here. A few minutes ago one of the guards was knocked unconscious and when he came to, his uniform was gone. What should we do now?"

"Well, the party should be breaking up soon. Just be alert and warn the other guards to be watching for a man in uniform that is not where he is supposed to be. I think I better tell Jackson now, I hoped it wouldn't be necessary but…"

Shane had a hard time trying to get Jackson alone, but when he finally did he told him everything about Dominic Sabastian.

Jackson thanked him for his concern then laughed, "I've been shot before and lived to tell about it and if the good Lord's willin' this spy will soon be apprehended and before he can do any damage. I truly believe the Lord sent me here to stop the British invasion, and by the Eternal I shall." There was fire in his eyes as he spoke and then he smiled weakly as if to reassure Shane. He put his hand on Shane's shoulder and turned him to the door.

"There's nothing to be done until he shows himself and if he does we'll get him. Now you go back to your lovely wife and enjoy her company while you can. I wish my Rachel were here tonight but I take comfort in the knowledge that she will be joining me soon."

"Yes sir, I suppose you're right. If you'll excuse me," with a bow he left Andrew Jackson standing among his many admirers and aids.

"Shane darling, father and Jamie and Laura are getting ready to leave, perhaps we should too, after all you've been wounded and you should get some more rest." She was worried about Shane because he had almost been killed earlier.

"Yes, I am getting a little tired but if I go home with you, I'm afraid I won't get much rest anyway," Shane grinned.

"You know you're right," she smiled and then the smile froze on her beautiful face as she gazed up the stairs across the hall.

"Christa what is it? What's the matter?" Shane said and then turned. There standing on the landing of the staircase was Dominic Sabastian, with a pistol in his hand. Shane saw the glint in his eyes and knew he was about to fire.

"Get down," Adam Michaels shouted, making a dive for Jackson, while Shane threw Christa to the floor and the four of them took cover under the hall table. The shot missed and lodged in the frame of the oak paneled door.

Shane and Adam raced up the stairs with their own pistols drawn, but Dominic Sabastian had disappeared down the hallway. Shane and Adam carefully checked each room.

There was a great commotion because most of the guest were unaware of the circumstances, and wondered what was going on. Jackson ordered his men to help in the search. A few of the guest that had already started to leave, returned after hearing the shot. Edward Livingston herded everyone back into the main salon, and hurriedly explained what had happened and what was being done about it.

Suddenly Shane opened a bedroom door and Dominic Sabastian stood cornered in the middle of the room. It was ironic that he was wearing an American Militia Uniform, but held his pistol pointed directly at Shane's heart.

"This is the last time you're ever going to get in my way Coulter," he snarled.

But Shane had learned his lesson and fired his own weapon quickly.

Sabastian's eyes widened in surprise as he realized he was fatally wounded. He stared at Shane in disbelief. "Dam you," he said, firing his own pistol into the floor as he fell.

"Shane," Christa cried and rushed up the stairs when she heard the shots, fear quickening her steps. When she arrived at the bedroom door she paused and took a deep breath before looking in. She sighed in relief when she saw Adam Michaels and Shane bending over the prone body on the floor. They stood and turned towards her.

She flew into Shane's open arms. "Is he…"

"Yes." He's dead."

Christa stood back a little and examined Shane. "Are you all right? I heard two shots. I was afraid he'd killed you and I think I would have died too if he had," she said softly with her heart in her eyes.

"I have too much to live for," Shane said smiling as he pressed her close, "to be killed by the likes of Dominic Sabastian."

By this time everyone who was down stairs had come up. Edward Livingston and Andrew Jackson rushed forward to thank Shane and Adam for their quick action.

Shane and Christa were surrounded by family and friends and even Tillie Farnsworth made an attempt at being civil to Christa and Laura. After a few more minutes, Christa and Shane took their leave and wearily made their way back home

The firelight flickered and threw dark shadows over the walls as Shane let himself into the bedroom. Seeing Christa taking the pins from her hair, he stopped to watch her. She shook her head until the auburn mass fell around her shoulders and half way down her back.

As he walked up behind her, she smiled at his reflection in the mirror. Bending from the waist, he lifted her hair and kissed the back of her neck. She put down the hairbrush and stood up facing him, then put her arms around him.

"Still haven't had enough of me, Mr. Coulter?" she teased, searching the depths of his loving eyes.

His mouth covered hers, fanning the flames of their passion and his tiredness fell away as his eager hands worked at the fastenings of her gown. He drew back his head and grinned, then said huskily, "No, Mrs. Coulter and I never will."

LaVergne, TN USA
09 March 2010
175317LV00003B/3/P